"Jonathan, Please . . ."

she sighed weakly as she tore her mouth from his. She was fast losing hold on what little control she still possessed. "You must desist."

What in the world had come over her? For the last two years she had been an active part of the patriots' cause. In truth, she was a vital part of Washington's immense spy ring, and this evening she had suddenly turned into a gawking, stuttering, fumbling fool. . . .

"Do you not realize your kisses are like a drug?" he murmured. "Only just sampled and I'm all but addicted."

His tongue darted into her ear with sharp quick thrusts that left her body shuddering and helpless, her mind swimming in a fog of pleasure. . . .

Dear Reader,

We, the editors of Tapestry Romances, are committed to bringing you two outstanding original romantic historical novels each and every month.

From Kentucky in the 1850s to the court of Louis XIII, from the deck of a pirate ship within sight of Gibraltar to a mining camp high in the Sierra Nevadas, our heroines experience life and love, romance and adventure.

Our aim is to give you the kind of historical romances that you want to read. We would enjoy hearing your thoughts about this book and all future Tapestry Romances. Please write to us at the address below.

The Editors
Tapestry Romances
POCKET BOOKS
1230 Avenue of the Americas
Box TAP
New York, N.Y. 10020

Whispers In The Wind

Patricia Pellicane

A TAPESTRY BOOK

PUBLISHED BY POCKET BOOKS NEW YORK

To Patty, Nancy, Jenny and Toni,
who bring sunshine to my life

Books by Patricia Pellicane

Charity's Pride
Whispers in the Wind

Published by TAPESTRY BOOKS

This novel is a work of historical fiction. Names, characters, places
and incidents relating to non-historical figures are either the product
of the author's imagination or are used fictitiously. Any resemblance
of such non-historical incidents, places or figures to actual events or
locales or persons, living or dead, is entirely coincidental.

An *Original* publication of TAPESTRY BOOKS

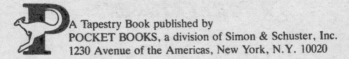

A Tapestry Book published by
POCKET BOOKS, a division of Simon & Schuster, Inc.
1230 Avenue of the Americas, New York, N.Y. 10020

ISBN: 0-671-53015-1

First Tapestry Books printing April, 1985

10 9 8 7 6 5 4 3 2 1

POCKET and colophon are registered trademarks
of Simon & Schuster, Inc.

TAPESTRY is a registered trademark of Simon & Schuster, Inc.

Printed in the U.S.A.

Chapter One

DARK, MENACING FORMS MOVED STEALTHILY, CAUSING eerie shadows amid the dappling shafts of silver light that filtered through the low, hanging branches in the dark night. The air was warm and damp; the scent of seawater giving evidence of the Long Island Sound rolling gently upon the island's rocky shore some hundred yards away.

In place now, each shape blended invisibly to the dark tree trunks upon which they pressed. All were masked and heavily armed. Their dark, rough clothing spoke of many nights of plying their trade and, as befit the seasoned veterans they were, not even their breathing could be detected were you to stand within touching distance. Patiently, they waited to spring their trap.

A thick rope had been strung tightly across the lonely dirt road and secured to heavy trees on each side.

1

Smiles formed beneath covered faces at the unmistakable sound of a lone approaching rider.

"No matter, mates," the smallest figure and apparently the leader of the group whispered. "One be better than none. Mayhaps this one will prove worth our while."

In the past, these nightly jaunts had proven to be most worthwhile, and many documents, accompanied by their bearers, had seemingly disappeared from the earth.

From between the trees a rider atop a chestnut horse could be clearly seen in the strong silvery moonlight. The horse stood nearly twenty hands high, his neck lifted proudly, as his tail swished in a cloud of dark brown silk behind his rider.

The leader of the group gave a silent sigh, as the rider coaxed his horse in a gentle, meandering pace along the roadway, knowing no one would meet his Maker this night. The thought of killing, even one of these hated redcoats, was repugnant to the rebel's senses. It was sabotage and intrigue that stirred the flames of an eager heart. More often than not, their work was accomplished in silent, swift accounting, while not a soul was lost and Rebel spirits flared high with pride.

Upon the horse, the English soldier's red coat glowed in the moonlight, while his white leggings fairly shouted against the dark horse and black leather boots shone a high polish from knee to stirrup.

Breathlessly, they waited. Closer and closer he came. He was taller than most men and the taut rope caught him at mid-chest, lifting him nimbly from his saddle and flinging him unceremoniously to the dirt road with a soft thud.

In an instant the five Rebels surrounded the dazed soldier. The leader, in size measuring no larger than a boy of twelve, barked out orders in a husky whisper. "Check his pockets, mate, and be quick about it. I'll have his papers. Someone see to the stallion and the bag he carries."

A moment later, the dazed man moaned softly and made to move. Instantly, the boot of the leader clamped itself on the man's arm. The weight of it brought a sharp curse to the prone man's mouth.

Suddenly, the small form was nearly toppled, as the man lifted his arm, irregardless of the weight, and brought the Rebel off the ground. His arm relaxed as a thin blade was drawn from the leader's belt and pressed threateningly to the redcoat's throat.

"A moment of your time, English, 'tis all I ask and all here will live to see another morn," warned the husky voice above him.

"The bloke's a doctor, me thinks. He carries a bag tied to his horse filled with such tools as one would use," one of the men spoke out.

"Be it truth, English?"

"Aye," the prone man reluctantly admitted, with the aid of the slightest pressure the Rebel administered to the blade. His anger grew rapidly at being held at knife point, while his arm ached with the full weight of his adversary.

"He boasts no weapons," another remarked after a thorough searching.

The leader scanned the papers taken from the redcoat's inside pocket. He was a doctor in truth. A Captain Jonathan Townsend, recently injured and ordered stationed with the King's Dragoons in Huntington, Long Island. Probably to regain his strength, the leader mused. Just what we be needin', the slight figure sighed, another hated Britisher in Huntington. This one would not be worth the effort to send to Washington. A doctor would have no information.

"Take what he has to offer and tie the beggar to a tree. On the morrow someone will pass to free you, English."

The leader lifted the weight imposed on the redcoat's arm and stepped back. The soldier rose to his feet. Feigning a weakness he did not feel, he stumbled, while giving a purposeful groan.

Involuntarily, the leader stepped forward, as if to forestall his fall, and was instantly ensnared by a steely arm. Forced to stand before him, the Rebel was helpless, as the redcoat dragged his prisoner backward.

"Keep your wits about you, English," the small figure warned, "and you'll suffer no more than a lightening of your pockets for our night's work."

Ignoring the warning, he continued to back away, until the definite pressure of a gun barrel pressed hard into the small of his back. Another curse slipped from his thinned lips, and he reluctantly relinquished his hold, as a deep voice behind him taunted, "Have a care redcoat, lest you find this night to be your last on earth."

Silently, he allowed them to guide him to a tree. He towered over most of them and almost laughed as the leader of the group sauntered in a supposedly mannish walk to stand before him. The boy came only to his chest in height and Jonathan was sure his voice would be high were it not disguised by a low whisper.

Quick fingers emptied his pockets. The leader remarked as the bills were quickly scanned, "How is it you carry only New York currency, English? Has George taken to paying his loyal officers in Clinton bank notes now? Or could it be the whole of these gutless swines are trying to spread those counterfeit notes again?"

The soldier only glared his hatred for an answer.

"'Tis of no importance," the leader remarked with a flippant shrug of a slender shoulder. "Should these prove real, they will, of course, be put to good use."

The captain's hand raised slightly, obviously wanting to strike the taunting figure before him. Thinking better of it, he clenched his fist to his side, but he was too late. The ring he wore caught the rays of the moon and the attention of the one before him. "I'll have that ring, English."

"'Tis naught but a family crest. It will bring you little."

"It will bring enough," the small one contradicted. "Hand it over."

The ring was flung at the Rebel's feet amid a roar of rage-filled curses.

Neither the Rebel's mask nor the dark cap that was pulled low over a pale forehead hid the laughing golden eyes that glowed with pure delight at the Britisher's rage and discomfort. A muffled, low laugh came from beneath the mask; and suddenly, and quite unbelievably, something vibrant and with a silent breathless force moved between the two combatants. A soft gasp came from the Rebel, while Doctor Townsend muttered a low curse at the astounding feelings that shook his being.

Good God, man, he groaned in silent disgust, have

you suddenly taken an interest in young boys? Looking closer, his dark gaze bore into the tawny almond-shaped eyes, and a flicker of a thought threatened to overtake the rationality of his mind before he brushed it aside as ridiculous. Fool, t'was your imagination combined with the moonlight, nothing more.

Suddenly, the eyes lowered and a step back was taken, leaving in its wake a haunting scent of lemon. "Tie the bloody bastard and be quick about it," the Rebel growled out in a low voice that was suddenly shaking; and the Rebel could not have sworn to the cause of it.

Why should a dark look bring such a trembling? This was not the first outing, nor the first sign of hatred evoked from the English beast. Why was it suddenly impossible to stare him down. What had he seen? A shiver of apprehension crept over the small form and the Rebel knew instinctively to keep away from this one.

As the leader mounted his horse and reined it to a stop before the struggling captain, the Rebel spat, "Gag the English dog, before he calls the whole regiment down on us."

An instant later, the black figure was gone, soon followed by the others, leaving the lone soldier tied, with only the sound of galloping hooves to give evidence to the night's happenings.

Chapter Two

IN THE SHADOWS OF THE DARKENED BEDROOM, DEFT fingers moved briskly through the official-looking packet. She gave a short sigh of relief and a quick prayer of thanks that the seal had been previously broken. Suddenly, her gaze fell upon her objective and her quick mind registered the number of troops, their departure date and final destination. The sound of footsteps on the first landing sent a prickle of fear down her back, and she instantly replaced the packet beneath a pair of trousers at the bottom of the carpetbag. A moment later, she had pushed it into its original position beneath the low-slung bed.

A muttered low curse escaped her when she tried to slide out from under the bed and realized she was stuck. The fichu that she had pinned inside the slightly too-low bodice of her dress was snagged on something.

7

Leaning on her elbow, she tried to free the cloth from the ensnaring wood above her.

"Damn," she muttered. "What the hell is holding this?"

"If you would permit me, Mistress, I will see to it," a deeply amused voice suggested from above and behind her.

Merry almost shrieked with surprise and, as his voice startled her into banging her head against the frame, she unconsciously allowed another epithet to escape her. A moment later, she moaned with mortification as she realized her position when she felt his weight against her rump. The bed was quite low to the floor and, as she was on her knees, her derriere was lifted high in the air; unbelievably, his hand rested upon it, as he nonchalantly used her for leverage.

Strong fingers tore the fichu free of the rough wood and assisted a red-faced Miss Merry Gates to her feet. Merry had to force herself to control the rage she felt toward the tall man who stood chuckling before her, for she wanted more than anything to slap his handsome face.

"Were you a gentleman, sir, you'd not laugh at a lady's mishap," she snapped, as her topaz eyes glared murderously.

Indeed, he was a gentleman, for he did not refer to her unladylike language and, although it was obvious he was struggling to regain a more somber mood, he managed to reply in a voice that showed only the merest touch of the humor he felt. "Excuse me, Mistress. I'd not offend you."

Suddenly and quite unexpectantly, he felt again a stirring in his loins and the same unnameable force he had felt the night before. The temptation to take this golden piece of fluff into his arms was so intense, he found himself suddenly breathless with the need.

What had come over him of late? His reaction to the young Rebel last night had left him confused and disgusted; and now, gazing into this little maiden's huge tawny eyes, he felt the same intense yearning. Was he so in need of a good toss that he felt desire for anyone who happened his way?

Merry's rage knew no bounds, as she suddenly realized the condition of her fichu and recognized the English bastard her group had waylaid last night as having caused its destruction. With a quick, angry yank, she pulled the tattered material free of her bodice, tearing her dress as she did so and crying out in fury, "Look what you've done. You've ruined it!"

Doctor Jonathan Townsend stood calmly before the vaguely familiar and decidedly angry young woman. His gaze moved slowly from her fabulous golden eyes, over her creamy skin, to her full lips thinned now in rage, to the ripped exceedingly low neckline of her dress. For a long moment, his gaze rested on the heaving, soft mounds of flesh that peeked tantalizingly from beneath the thin material.

His humor long gone, he took in the beauty before him. Long tendrils of golden hair had escaped her ribboned mobcap and fell fetchingly over her shoulder to lay temptingly against the creamy swell of her breast. A haunting scent of lemon assailed his senses. Where had he breathed that scent before?

A slow smile formed and showed straight, even teeth that flashed white against his tanned skin, and Merry felt an unexpected and frightening leap in her stomach.

"I beg your pardon, Mistress," he ventured in a deep voice that caused her pulse to throb noticeably at the hollow of her throat. "I had no wish to ruin your scarf, but I fear it proved necessary."

Merry felt mesmerized, as she watched him take a short step toward her. His eyes glowed the darkest blue she had ever seen, and she wondered, were the room not so dark, would they appear as vivid.

He moved again and Merry stiffened and took a step back. Was she imagining it? Was he truly about to kiss her?

He grinned at her obvious nervousness. The silence was total. She could hear her heart pounding in her ears. The bed pressed against her legs. Again he moved. The top of her body leaned away. Suddenly, she gave a soft gasp, as she found herself falling and landing with a hard bounce upon the bed.

This time she heard more than a soft chuckle, as he burst into deep laughter.

"Stop laughing and move aside, you big oaf," she snapped, as she tried to come to her feet.

"Truly, I'm sorry," he choked, as he tried to control his laughter. "There was no need to fear me. I'd not bring you harm."

"Fear you!" she snapped, angrier yet that he should think she might cower before a Britisher. "Why in the world should I fear you? Move aside!" she roared.

He laughed again.

My God, the man was the most obnoxious of all the arrogant bastards they had been forced to accept beneath their roof. Here he stood, laughing like a buffoon, while she struggled to get to her feet. Unless she crawled to the opposite side of the bed, she was forced to sit and wait for this rude beggar to move aside, which he appeared to have no intention of doing.

"Have you a problem with your hearing, sir? I've asked you to move aside," she asked coldly, her voice trembling, despite her attempt to hide her fury.

"So you have, my lovely," he grinned down at her with a decidedly lecherous gleam in his eyes, "but it occurs to me your present position is most appropriate."

Merry fairly sputtered with rage, as she was forced to crawl in the most ungraceful manner and position to the opposite side of the bed.

The tall, dark man stood grinning at her, as she calmly walked around him and the bed to the door of the room, stopping only a moment at the threshold to shoot him a withering glance and utter, "Lout!" Her chin raised with cool distain, she heard his mellow laughter float after her, as she escaped the room.

Jonathan sighed with appreciation as his gaze followed the tiny, beautiful young woman up the stairs, pleased that he managed to glimpse a bit of ankle and calf as she angrily swished her skirts. God, she was a lovely little thing. He could almost swear he had seen her before, but he knew it was not so. He'd never have forgotten her. Never!

Grabbing his bags, he walked down the tiny corridor to the corner room the innkeeper had told him was to be his. As he waited for the promised tub and water to arrive, he gave a weary sigh of exhaustion and stretched out upon the small but comfortable bed. Having no sleep during this past night had left his still recuperating body weaker than ever. He sighed again, already drifting off to sleep. He was in dire need of a bath and hoped the management would hurry.

Until a few hours ago, he had been tied to a tree. About to give up hope, it was long past the noon hour, before a rider happened by close enough to hear his strangled sounds and stopped to free him. If he ever got his hands on that bunch of Rebels . . . He left the thought unfinished, too tired at present to delve into his potential actions.

It had taken him another hour of riding before he reached the town of Huntington and he felt a weariness he had not previously known. Turning on his side, he was asleep in a matter of seconds.

He had imagined himself healed, but, obviously, that was not totally true. The fragment of cannon shell had struck him in his shoulder, while in the midst of an operation. Although the pain had been intense, it was unthinkable that he leave his patient with a gaping hole in his middle. He had to finish; there was no alternative.

By the time the last of the stitches were in place and the orderly asked to see to the bandaging, he had lost an enormous amount of blood. The back of his shirt was saturated with it, and he could feel the warm wetness seeping into his pants, as well.

It took another two hours before a doctor was free to see to his wounds. It wasn't long before fever set in and kept him in bed for weeks. So it was he had drawn light duty. He gave a wry smile, hoping his first experience was not to be the norm.

A knock at his door brought him awake and his thoughts back to the girl he had just teased so miserably. For a moment, he couldn't imagine what had come over him. He had never treated anyone like that before. Unexplainably, her anger made him want to continue his teasing and he knew not why. Then, too, he realized he had never felt such instant longing to reach out and touch. He shook his head as if to deny his thoughts. He had for too long been without a good toss, 'tis all. She was a pretty lass, no doubt, but no more special than a hundred others, he insisted, even though the silent statement did not quite ring true. Still, when he called out, he was more than a little sorry to see it was a young boy dragging in a brass hip bath, rather than the little mistress of his thoughts.

Merry's topaz eyes flashed pure liquid gold, her small, delicate lips pressed together with barely controlled rage. "Truly, Father, I cannot abide the beasts a moment longer."

"Hush, Merry, I know you've no liking for it, but 'tis necessary if we are to accomplish our ends. Keep that temper of yours under control and bring these two pails of water up to the corner room."

"Where is Seth? 'Tis usual for him to carry them."

He carried some, but the Britisher's horse was ridden hard and needs tending. Be a good lass now and listen to your father."

"Aye, Father," Merry sighed, having no wish to face the wretch again, but knowing she had little choice. Their paths were sure to cross many times during his stay (however long that might be, she shuddered); t'would be best if she let him know from the beginning, he was less than nothing and his teasing had no effect on her whatsoever.

From the pump in the kitchen she took two pailfuls of icy water. A small smile played about her lips as she imagined his discomfort when he tried to sit in cold water. British swine, she mused silently, he deserved no better.

Gasping for breath, she put the pails down outside his door. Rubbing the ache from her arms, she silently cursed him at being forced to do his bidding. She knocked sharply and grunted with disgust when she heard his call to enter.

Opening the door, she was hit with a blast of heat and relaxed some. At least Seth had started a fire. One less chore for her to do. Even though this month of July had proved to be unusually warm, the room had been unused for some weeks. As the inn's property boardered against the Sound, a fire was needed to dispel the everlasting dampness from all such rooms.

She never looked into the room, but bent over and picked up the two pails. She was well into the room before her eyes lifted from the dark cotton rag rug. With a gasp, she saw he was already sitting in the bath. A broad grin split his mouth, while his eyes glowed with humor.

Merry, probably for the first time in her life, was dumbfounded and stood gaping at him like a moron.

His grin widened further when he asked, "Have you come to assist? If so, perhaps you might retrieve my shaving gear from my bags." A long-fingered hand moved over his jaw, his fingernail scraping the dark shadow found there, as he casually remarked, "I've a need of a shave."

Merry finally came out of her stupor, her face flushed crimson, as the level of the water left nothing to the imagination, and the vile beast didn't bother to reach for a covering, but blatantly showed her his male form.

Lowering her eyes, she nearly bit her lip in two, trying to control her rage. "Nay, sir," she barely managed, "I've brought you more water, 'tis all."

"Well, let's have it then, Mistress," he grinned, as he watched her struggle to bring the heavy pails closer. "Shall I help you?"

"Nay!" she nearly bellowed at seeing him begin to rise; and then, upon seeing the teasing gleam in his eyes, she raged all the more, while adding in a softer voice, "Nay, sir, I can manage." And, as she finished with the words, "just fine," she took one of the pails and poured its icy contents over his head.

Merry had no time to stay and enjoy the sight of him gasping and leaping from the tub. Barely did she hear his cry of shock as she dashed for the door, her heart pounding with fright that she could do something so stupid, no matter the satisfaction gained.

But as fast as she was, she wasn't fast enough, and he caught her just before her hand touched the doorjamb. She gave a short shriek as he scooped her up and held her against his wet chest. Cold water ran off his dark hair and dripped on her face. His dark blue eyes crinkled at the corners with humor.

"Did you think I'd be angered?" he asked softly, while watching her wary expression.

She was very aware of his nakedness and was suddenly terrified of what he might do next; yet, she managed to snap bravely, "Put me down this instant!"

"Oh," he grinned dangerously, "are we finished playing now?"

"I hear someone coming," she groaned out, while trying to twist herself free of his arms.

"In that case, we'll close the door," he smiled, as his bare foot reached out and kicked it shut.

"My father owns this establishment, and if you do not release me this instant, I'll scream."

"Oh, lovely," he breathed above her, "I'll put you down, never fear."

Merry looked up, unsure of the meaning of his words, and couldn't help but notice his eyes were studying her mouth. Nervously, her small tongue peeked out and licked at her full lips, not yet sure what it was she read in his eyes. The glinting humor was gone, replaced by an expression she had never seen before.

She never knew if it was anger, frustration or simple inquisitiveness that kept her still, for she realized later she never lifted a hand, and it would have been so easy and satisfying to strike his handsome face.

Jonathan, his blood racing and his stomach tightening with the need to taste her sweetness, felt no compunction to ignore this delicious temptation.

Merry heard a sharp gasp, just as his mouth covered her own, but wasn't sure from which of them it came. His lips rested firmly, but gently, against her mouth in a tender kiss that caused her heart to flutter madly. She tensed and his arms tightened, refusing to relinquish his hold.

Slowly, his mouth continued its tender assault as he moved to her cheek, only to return once again to her lips. This time a bit more pressure was applied, as he tried to gain entrance to the sweetness of her mouth.

Merry twisted her face away. "Stop!" she breathed,

her voice trembling and sounding husky and raw to her ears.

"Nay," he groaned into her neck. Involuntarily, her whole body jerked, and she nearly cried out at the exquisiteness of his warm breath and burning mouth on her skin. It was worse than when he kissed her, this tingling. She had to stop him.

"Please," she cried softly, pushing against his wet shoulder with the palm of her hands, until she realized her hand was touching naked flesh. She pulled her hand away, suddenly trembling with the shock of having touched him. He felt warm and hard and she longed to touch him again, but she wouldn't . . . not ever. His mouth rode smoothly up the golden column of her throat to cover her lips once more. He nibbled gently on her lower lip, and she whimpered a soft sigh. "English, please," she sighed weakly, as she tore her mouth from his. She was fast losing hold on what little control she still possessed. "You must desist. Have you not extorted revenge in full."

"Would that I were seeking revenge, little one, I'd likely agree," he rasped breathlessly against her lips; and then close to her ear, sending chills down her back, he murmured, "Do you not realize your kisses are like a drug? Only just sampled and I'm all but addicted."

His tongue darted into her ear with sharp, quick thrusts that left her body shuddering and helpless, her mind swimming in a fog of pleasure.

Against her will her hand had returned to touch him. Her fingers spread and allowed the springy black hairs of his chest to rub seductively between them. Sliding over his chest to his broad shoulders, they entwined around his neck.

Oh, God, she wanted to cry out with the joy of touching him, but his mouth barred any sound. She could scarcely breathe, while the drumming in her ears grew all but deafening, as his mouth moved like velvet over her. In contrast, his chin scratched the delicate flesh of her cheek and the slightly painful friction left her alive with a burning need she could not name. His tongue, intent on parting her lips, teased the sensitive flesh just inside them.

"Open your mouth, Merry, I hunger to taste the sweetness I know lies within," he breathed raggedly against her lips.

His words brought from her a moan of delight, which was lost against his growl of greediness to savor her honeyed essence, and Merry felt as if she were falling, swirling helplessly into a vortex of liquid sensation.

Jonathan gave a low groan as he felt her soften to liquid fire in his arms. God, she possessed a passion that easily matched his own, and his mind swam dizzily with the thought of her response should he take her to his bed.

His tongue licked a burning path to her small jaw, teasing at the flesh around her mouth, until his lips once again covered her own.

Her mouth opened to the insistent probing of his tongue, and she felt a rush of heat spread deliciously through the length of her. A soft moan was torn from deep within her, as his tongue slipped into the sweet, warm hollow of her mouth.

Merry stiffened at the new sensation of his rough tongue rubbing over and under her own. She had never realized a tongue could be smooth and still rough, warm while sending chills down her back and tasting of the tantalizing scent of this man.

She was drowning in sensation, as he moved to seek out every dark crevice, drinking in her delicious essence. Rational thoughts long gone, her hands roamed freely over his shoulders and chest, running up his neck to his thick, wet hair. Her fingers twisted through it, grasping at him, pulling his face to her own.

Dizzy with a need she didn't understand, she clung to him, her soft cries giving clear proof of her longing for more of this sweet, lovely torture.

Suddenly, she choked out a startled cry at finding herself plopped in the tub. The cold water drenched her cotton dress and seeped through the many layers of petticoats to hit with shocking force against her flaming skin. In a reflex action, Merry swung a small, fisted hand at him; but Jonathan had already stepped away and walked with a definite swagger to the bed. Humor lurked just beneath the surface, as he taunted her with a daring stance, and his eyes challenged her to deny the pleasure they had just shared. Nonchalantly, he took a linen cloth from the bed and wrapped it around his hips.

It was no more than a split second before she was on her feet, her hands clutching at the tub now nearly empty, since her clothing had done a marvelous job of absorbing the bath water.

"Why you wretched beast," she snarled. "I could kill you with my bare hands."

He chuckled softly and taunted as his eyes moved over her, "Could you, Mistress? Personally, I think those hands should only be used to give pleasure."

Merry gave a gasp at his words, her rage so great, she found she could not speak. He stood with his feet slightly apart, his hands resting confidently on his hips, as if he were displaying himself for her benefit. The light from the fire played an erotic, flickering dance over his glistening dark skin, and she couldn't prevent her traitorous gaze from sweeping over him.

She had never seen a naked man before, and now, only partly covered, she couldn't seem to drag her eyes from his still bare chest. Her gaze lowered to his stomach and then his hips, remembering what lay hidden beneath the draping towel. A rush of heat suffused her cheeks, as she realized an insane need to reach out and touch him, no matter his loathsome behavior.

Hate such as she had never known surged through her, as she forced her gaze to meet his taunting eyes and heard his challenge, "I see our thoughts are running in the same direction."

Merry knew her face was crimson, as her cheeks burned furiously. He had read her thoughts! To deny it would only prolong this confrontation, and she could bear no more of the barbarian. Livid with rage and dangerously close to violence, she lifted her chin and moved silently past him. She knew full well the back of her dress clung to her like skin, and she had no doubt his eyes were upon her, but she was helpless to do more than slam the door viciously behind her departing figure.

Jonathan imagined her speeding to her room and pulling the wet dress from herself. His loins tightened as he thought of her cool, wet flesh turning hot beneath his caress, should he follow her in reality, rather than merely with his mind. Thinking better of the temptation, he gave a shrug, discarded the towel and slid his clean, bronzed form between warm sheets.

Amazingly, the scent of lemon assaulted him once again. Thrice in two days' time he had breathed that scent, and this time it brought back delicious memories of sweet, tender kisses. His tongue touched the smooth surface of his lips, remembering the taste and texture of her warm mouth. God, she stirred a man's senses like no other. Forcing his mind away from the lushness of her answering kisses, he murmured sleepily, "'Tis wise, I think, to forgo the evening meal," and then added with a soft chuckle, "I'd not put it past Mistress Gates to season with a bit of rat poison for my benefit."

Merry stood amid a pile of soaking wet clothes, as she toweled her back dry. This was the second time today she had been forced to go to her room and change. Only this time she had to change everything.

"Arrogant bastard!" she muttered. How she wished she could scream it from the rooftops. Her head ached with suppressed fury. When would this wretched lot be gone from her country? How much more was she to bear before it was over?

Her face flamed again, as she remembered the scene that had taken place only moments before. Even though he had behaved abominably, she had wanted to touch him and he had known it. The shame of it all! How was she to face him again after their kisses and her scandalous response to his near naked state?

Quickly, she pulled a dry chemise over her head and stepped into clean petticoats. Her homespun dress of gray cotton, the third for the day, was buttoned quickly to her throat and another crisp white apron tied around her tiny waist.

"If the beast be half as smart as he appears, he'll stay clear of me on this night," she sneered, as she bundled up her wet clothes and left the room.

What in the world had come over her in these last few hours? For the last two years she had been an active part of the patriots' cause. In truth, she was a vital part of Washington's immense spy ring, and this evening she had suddenly turned into a gawking, stuttering, fumbling fool.

Tomorrow, she vowed, she'd start again. She'd put aside all that had happened between them and use all her energies and concentrations on ignoring the wretched Englisher.

Chapter Three

MERRY GRUNTED WITH EFFORT, AS SHE AND NETTIE Loring finally managed to push the heavy crate to the rim of the wagon. With heaving bosom and a sigh of relief, she leaned against the wagon as the box fell in. As usual, she mused silently, when there was work to be done that lazy Seth was nowhere in sight. Filled, these crates would be impossible for her to move. Luckily, all she was expected to do was to get the wagon to the Hewlett farm. Once there, one of Mr. Hewlett's many farmhands would load the wagon with farm produce. Upon her return, her father would have that layabout Seth see to the unloading and she would have spent an enjoyable day with her best friend, away from the ever watchful eye of these cursed Britishers.

In truth, Merry and her father had much to be thankful for. Mr. Gates, as the owner of the town's only inn, was forced to secure food for the hated English officers who were quartered there, and so, neither he nor his daughter had to go hungry.

Such was not the case with many others in the town. Frequently, Merry could secure an abundance of food and she secretly gave what she could spare to those whom she knew to be suffering under the harshness of their occupants.

Unbeknownst to the two laughing young women, against the back of the building stood one very handsome and well-rested British doctor, whose appreciative gaze raked the slender, yet voluptuous, form of the petite blonde who had taken such an instant dislike to his person. Jonathan wondered why she felt such aversion to him. He had never been one to brag of his conquests, but this was the first time in his recollection that he had had such an effect upon the gentle sex. He gave a lopsided grin, as he pushed away from the building and began to walk toward the object of his thoughts.

Perhaps her snarl of hatred more than anything else proved to be the most enticing thing about her. Certainly, she was a pleasure to look at. If truth were told, she was lovelier than any he had seen before; yet it was her attitude he found most appealing. He only knew that he wanted to get to know this little spitfire and, no matter her objections, to know her in every way possible.

Merry lifted her skirts into her left hand, unknowingly offering a tantalizing display of trim ankle to the man who had suddenly come from behind and lifted her into his strong arms.

With a choking gasp, she found herself sitting atop

the roughly hewn wagon, her worst fears confirmed, as a grinning Jonathan Townsend climbed aboard and pulled an obviously surprised Nettie after him.

"You have no objection, do you, ladies, if I join you on your outing?" his dark blue eyes glittered with amusement, daring Merry to object.

"Nay," Merry snarled through clenched teeth, her rage threatening to choke her. How could she object? These blasted British were allowed to do anything they pleased, and he knew it. To whom did he think she could go to complain of his boorish behavior?

Damn, she groaned silently. She had been looking forward to a pleasant day of amicable chitchat and easy comradery. Now she could forsee nothing but several hours of silent seething.

Shooting him a murderous glance, she noticed for the first time how his dark hair was tied back with a piece of rawhide, while tendrils of shorter hair fell boyishly over his forehead and glistened with health in the strong sunlight. Neither last night nor today had he powdered it, as did many of his fellow officers. Today he wore a full-sleeved white shirt left open to mid-chest and revealing the dark, crisp hairs her fingers had touched the night before.

Merry, with flaming cheeks, pulled her gaze away, lest the beast read something more than simple inquisitiveness in her face. His dark brown pants bordered on being indecent, so tightly did they conform to his body. She raised her chin and swore silently. He had absolutely no effect on her, and he could grin from now until doomsday, for she cared not a whit.

Forcing her wandering gaze to return to his grinning face, she ignored the flutter she felt in her chest.

Stubbornly silent, she sat at his side, staring straight ahead as he spoke a cheery good day to Nettie, and pushed aside the ridiculous feelings of annoyance that she was being ignored. She wanted nothing more than that. If this man and the rest of the hateful English were to ignore her from now to forever, she would be the happiest woman in these colonies, nay on this very earth.

The wagon jerked to a start as he snapped the reins, and Merry almost growled while shooting him another raging glance when his arm came familiarly around her back and held her to prevent her falling. But her look of fury at his temerity was lost on him, since he had turned to Nettie and was conversing politely as to the heat this month of July brought.

Merry nearly groaned out loud. The big oaf was taking up most of the seat and left her to balance herself precariously close to the edge. Her hands clutched at the rough wood, as she fought to keep her seating. It was obvious she was not only uncomfortable, but dangerously close to a serious accident, as she tried to prevent their bodies from touching. Should the wagon encounter one of the many ruts in the dirt road ahead, she could be thrown. Merry realized she was only making it apparent that his presence caused her some discomfort, and decided she cared not what he thought and would not risk her well-being for an Englisher.

Ignoring his look of surprise and the unnamed fluttering in her chest at what she supposed was to most a charming smile, she moved away from the edge of the wagon and distastefully, but necessarily, leaned with no little force into the large, dark man at her side.

In truth, she mused, as they proceeded down the country road, this brute was a sight more appealing than those overstuffed, wigged and powdered fools she was forced to wait upon. No matter the disgust he invoked in her, she could not deny his handsomeness. Were he not English, he might have been deserving of a smile in return.

Over these last eight years, her hatred had known no bounds, as these English barbarians had purposely made her and her fellow citizens' lives a living hell. Because the town of Huntington was suspected, and rightly so, to sympathize with the patriots' cause, they were openly treated as the enemy. Therefore, the taxes levied were almost unbearable and left little, if anything, for the populace. It was not unusual to find whole families starving, perhaps existing solely on wild onions and fish caught in the Long Island Sound.

One by one, the personal properties of the townspeople had been confiscated, particularly those of the widows and children of the brave men who had fought against these barbarians. Their church was used as a stable for their officers' fine horses, while the rectory became the headquarters for the English Colonel Thompson. In the meantime, the parson was forced to take handouts for the survival of his family. Worse yet, the cemetery was being desecrated, as a new fort was erected on that exact spot. Unbelievably, these English swine were using gravestones for the bakery's ovens. A shudder ran through her, as her morbid thoughts lingered on those disturbed souls.

As her thoughts wandered, Merry barely noticed the warmth of the sun against her, nor did she feel the soothing summer breeze ruffling the tendrils of golden hair that had escaped her frilly cap. The lush green countryside passed by unnoticed, as did the blue swells of the Sound visible where the woodland thinned.

Pressed to this man, she became slowly aware of his leg moving against hers and was suddenly swept back to the previous night, remembering the scent of his skin, his smooth, nonchalant gait as he had reached for his towel, the long length of his naked body, his easy smile as he leaned against the bedpost and, most horribly, her wild urge to reach out and touch him.

She stifled a soft gasp and moved back, as his arm brushed against her breast, and tried to remember this man is English, the most despicable of creatures. She hated him, she hated all of them, and yet, at the same time, he had the most startling effect on her. She shook her head and refused to acknowledge the truth of that thought. Nay, t'was not so. He affected her neither more nor less than any of the abominable breed.

They had been traveling for nearly an hour and, although her companions had tried, Merry had contributed nothing toward the conversation and had answered direct questions in the shortest terms possible.

They were nearly at the Hewlett farm. The scent of animals in the July heat was unmistakable and grew in strength as they closed the distance. Soon a clearing came into view in which dozens of people could be seen loading their wagons with supplies.

Jonathan pulled the wagon alongside the last in the clearing and brought it to a stop. Jumping ahead of Nettie, he helped her down and then grinned up at Merry. Noticing her hesitation, he raised his dark brow, his look taunting, as he silently dared her to move toward him.

Bristling under his arrogant gaze, she moved quickly, but not quickly enough, for strong brown hands reached for her waist and lifted her to the ground. For just a moment they were alone, as Nettie had instantly disappeared, having seen the blond head of her betrothed, Jeremiah, amid the farmhands.

"There be no need for you to handle me, English!" she spat out. Her voice lowered with rage to a husky whisper, one which Jonathan would not long forget.

Both brows rose in surprise as he gazed down at her, while the scent of lemon hit him again. As comprehension dawned, so did a definite gleam of respect enter his eyes. A taunting smile spread slowly over his firm mouth, as he remarked smoothly, "You are indeed welcome, Mistress Gates. Worry of it no longer."

Merry lifted one brow and curled her lip with disgust, refusing to answer the gentle rebuff. With a flash of skirt and a toss of an arrogant chin, she left the handsome doctor and went off to find an able back to do her bidding.

The audacity of this man was not to be borne and Merry would be damned if she'd give the rogue a moment's thought. A short time later she caught up with Nettie and her handsome fiancé.

Nettie and Jeremiah had been her friends since childhood. Slowly over the years, their amiable affection for each other had grown to love, and Merry could easily understand why. The girl possessed a sunny, even disposition and an ever-ready smile. She saw good in everyone, even those monsters who occupied their town.

If Merry complained of their barbaric behavior, Nettie would only soothe, "'Tis not their fault, Merry.

The men must follow their orders. I'm sure they have no liking for it any more than you."

Merry realized the girl simply did not see the evil in them and soon kept her own counsel.

Jeremiah was just as easy going and likeable. Friends for as long as she could remember, she knew there'd not be a better nor sweeter couple were she to search the entire colony.

The three of them were laughing, as a young boy ran in one direction and then another, trying to convince a dozen or so squealing chickens they would be happier upon someone's table. In the process he had fallen enumerable times, and was so thoroughly covered with mud, that not a single feature of his face was recognizable.

Merry's laughter was short-lived, as she sensed Jonathan's presence at her side. She knew she was being unbelievably rude, but she refused to introduce him to Jeremiah. In her opinion, his English citizenship classified him as lower than all other humanity and, therefore, not worthy to speak to these good people.

Finally, and with a jovial smile, Jonathan extended his hand in a good-natured offer. "I fear Mistress Gates is a bit annoyed with me and will not introduce us. May I present myself?"

Merry heard no more as she flashed him an angry glare and walked away. She hated him even more as she heard the two men's voices ring out with laughter.

Merry, forgetting the annoying Britisher for the moment, checked the quality of the farm products, as she had her wagon filled with potatoes, lettuce, corn, two sides of beef, three dozen chickens, and several bushels of freshly picked apples and peaches.

It was quite a while before the wagon was finally filled and longer still before accounts could be settled. Finally they were to leave, and Nettie calmly stated she would be accompanying Jeremiah back to town in his wagon.

Merry, in the midst of eating a juicy apple, choked with surprise, as she sent her friend a desperately pleading look. She couldn't mean it! Surely Nettie wouldn't leave her alone with this wretched Englishman! But, of course she would, for Nettie hadn't the slightest notion about the events of the previous night. So upset was Merry that it was some time before she felt the heavy pounding of Jonathan's slaps against her back.

Already forgetting that she had just been choking, she turned to fearlessly face her attacker, and fairly bellowed, "Have you lost what little mind you possess? What the hell do you think you are doing?"

An instant later, her small teeth gripped her lower lip and her cheeks burned scarlet at Nettie's gasp at her flagrant use of profanity. The sound of the two men's stifled chuckles did nothing to relieve her distress and she shot them both a glare.

A few moments passed before Jonathan managed to gain some control of his silent laughter, and he finally answered, "My apologies, Mistress." Again, he nearly burst out laughing, as he gazed down into Merry's stormy gaze. "I was under the impression that you were choking and in need of some assistance."

"In the future, English, you might wait until your assistance is asked for."

Jeremiah's soft laughter was brought to an abrupt stop, as Nettie jabbed her elbow into his side and quickly led him from the raging Merry and her smiling companion.

"A point well taken, Mistress. In the future I shall wait until asked," he responded, sounding to all ears as though he was thoroughly repentant; but only Merry could see the twinkle in his eyes.

Arrogant beast, she cried silently, as she spun away from his insincere apology. What had she done to deserve the company of this rude beggar, she groaned. She didn't realize until he threw his head back and laughed happily, that she had done so aloud.

Quickly gaining control over his mirth, Jonathan escorted her to her wagon and, with much gallantry, helped her aboard.

His gentlemanly actions only angered her further. In truth, Merry was growing sick with the intensity of her feelings about this man. Her head ached. She trembled as if fevered when he touched her. She had to get away from him. She had to think, to clear her mind, to forget his existence, if only for a short space of time. But such was not to be.

Jeremiah and Nettie were pulling away, as Jonathan lifted the reins and snapped them over the backs of the horses. Slowly, the wagon moved away from the farm. Again his hand came to rest familiarly around her, as the rutted road caused her slight form to nearly bounce from the seat.

Merry removed his hand from her waist. "Kindly keep your hands from me, English." Watching Jeremiah's wagon gain distance, she continued, "And please hurry the animals. I've no wish to be on these roads after dark."

Jonathan chuckled at her fury and asked, "Would

you prefer to find yourself thrown from the wagon and injured in the process?"

"I'd sooner suffer being thrown into hell than enduring your company for even a moment longer than necessary."

"I take it, then, you are not in sympathy with the King."

"Are you mad?" she snapped back, all caution gone. "I've no doubt, sir, that your country is superior over all in the growth of blockheads, but even a captain in George's elite force should be capable of seeing what any child of five would know as fact!"

Merry couldn't prevent the small groan that slipped from her foolish lips. Never before had she lost all control. For years she had suffered the abuse of the Englishmen while swearing to be in sympathy with them, and now, after a few teasing words, she had allowed him to know her as no other Britisher did.

"You speak bravely, Mistress, to this blockhead," he grinned, as he forced his laughter under control. "I've cause to doubt your father would be pleased were it known where your loyalties lie. You chance to lose much by being so honest with me."

Merry knew he spoke the truth and she bit at her lip, feverishly thinking how she could repair the damage her overactive tongue had wrought. Why did she lose all control in his presence? What was the purpose of signing loyalty oaths to the accursed British, if she was foolish enough to allow her temper to guide her tongue.

She forced a smile and lowered her voice to a soft, husky tone, "Have I judged you falsely then, Captain? Would you be so ungallant as to report a weak, defenseless woman of her sharp tongue?"

Jonathan gave a deep, hearty laugh at her obvious coquetry. "Only a mile back I was a blockhead, now I am a gallant gentleman. The improvement is astounding, would you not agree?"

Despite herself, Merry could not prevent the twitching of her lips, and turned her head lest he see she was not duly sorry for her outburst.

"And as for being weak and defenseless," he taunted slowly, his grin nearly lecherous, as his dark eyes took in the softness of her curving figure. "I've cause to wonder."

Merry reddened at his flagrantly bold stare. She might be proficient in the art of intrigue and fearless as she led a group of Rebels on nightly excursions against the British, but she was an innocent in the ways of men.

Jonathan smiled, her reddening cheeks giving him cause to wonder at her innocence. Surely, the girl who returned his kisses last night was not a novice, although now, as he thought of it without desire clouding his mind, she had seemed virginal at first, but she had soon left him without a doubt as to the depth of her passion.

What was she, he wondered? She was the leader of the Rebels who had waylaid and robbed him. Her exquisite eyes and telltale scent of lemon plus the huskiness of her angry whisper had left him without a doubt of this. Could a young woman lead such a life and remain an innocent? He chuckled softly, and looked forward to discovering for himself the answer.

Keeping her voice soft, despite the urge to snarl, she simpered, "What have I done, sir, to convince you that I am any stronger than the rest of my gender, or that you have a need to feel fear of me?"

"Oh, lovely," he sighed almost to himself, "I've not a doubt I've much to fear from you."

For a long moment their gazes held. "It comes as natural as breathing, does it not, this ability of some of your gentle gender to procure all and still more from the ignorant male species."

A smile touched the corners of her full lips, and Jonathan gave a sharp gasp at the startling beauty the smile lent her. Her topaz eyes tilted up at the corners and she gazed enticingly from beneath dark brown lashes. Her gaze, though in reality quite natural, looked to be as practiced and worldly as that of the most elegant ladies of court.

"Do you believe yourself such an expert on women, sir?"

He gave a long sigh and waited a full minute before he dared speak, lest his voice quiver and betray the depth of his feelings for her. "Nay, Mistress, in fact the opposite is truth. The more I learn, the less I know."

Merry couldn't prevent the soft laughter that bubbled from her throat. His admitting to his insecurity suddenly gave her a feeling of power and she dared to allow her gaze to linger on his.

Her husky, low laughter caused Jonathan to swear silently, as he longed to take her in his arms and taste again of the sweetness of her mouth.

Merry lowered her eyes again, her mouth thinning, as she recognized the same look on Jonathan's face that she had seen last night the moment before he had kissed her. She had no wish to bring about that occurrence again. It was enough that the disgraceful incident had happened once. It never would again. God in heaven, how was she to bear this man? It mattered not at all that he tried to make himself pleasant to her. He was a Britisher! And she could not fathom a deeper hatred than she felt toward them.

They had been traveling for close to an hour and had long ago lost sight of Jeremiah and Nettie. No amount of prodding could convince this English beast to hurry his pace. Suddenly, the wagon hit a particularly deep rut and tipped crazily. For a moment Merry thought they were going to turn over. She felt herself being propelled forward, unable to stop, and she knew she was going to hit the harness of the horses and land amid their prancing hooves.

Instinctively, she cried out and lifted her arms to protect her head, when she suddenly stopped in midair, her ribs aching as if entrapped in steel.

A low, growling curse sounded close to her ear, as she was pulled back and enfolded within Jonathan's strong arms. She was disoriented, her body momentarily pliant and soft against him, and it took her some minutes to realize she was in his arms and not lying on the ground.

"Are you all right, my love?" he soothed, his voice low and shaking with emotion, his breath warm against her suddenly chilled skin.

Merry remained still for a long time, her aching ribs making it uncomfortable for her to breathe.

"My ribs hurt."

Jonathan smiled, "Truly, I am sorry if I was a bit too rough."

"A bit too rough! You big oaf! Do you not realize your strength?" She tried to push away from him, but was unable to break his hold. "Unhand me! You've caused me enough pain. My ribs will ache for a week."

Jonathan chuckled smoothly, ignoring her demand for release, pressing her close to him while taunting her lack of gratitude, "You are indeed welcome, my love. No effort is too great to see you unharmed."

"Had you any knowledge in the ways of handling a wagon, Captain, we would not have hit this ditch. If it is beyond your capabilities, I will gladly control these animals."

"I've no doubt that you could, Mistress, but I fear t'was not a ditch but the loss of a wheel that has caused this mishap."

Merry groaned out a word she had no business knowing and only realized when he laughed that she had spoken aloud.

"'Tis refreshing to find a young woman who speaks her mind."

"No doubt," she snapped, her face pressed into his throat, her hands pushing against his chest, as she tried to gain her freedom from his steely hold. Lifting her face, she licked nervously at her dry lips and asked, "Will you please release me?"

Jonathan gave a silent curse at the stirrings her closeness caused him. What was it about this chit that enticed him so? He felt a sudden terror that she could cause him to feel such helpless yearning.

"Aye," he breathed, his mouth hovering only inches from hers.

The scent of his clean breath filled her senses and caused her heart to race madly and her breathing to quicken noticeably. She didn't want this. She didn't want to feel these new sensations only he seemed to cause. She felt herself softening against him, molding herself to his hard, lean form and tried to stop it. *No! I don't want this!* And yet, she knew in her heart, somehow she did.

His long fingers traced her brow and high cheekbones, slowly moving over her small, slender nose to her full mouth. The tip of his finger slid between her parted lips and caused her to take a sharp gasp.

Jonathan felt a trembling such as he'd never before known, as his fingers traced the loveliness of her face. He had thought of nothing but touching her since last night. Her breasts were pressed against his chest and left him breathless with longing. My God, she is so beautiful, he mused silently, his heart racing, his loins tightening with a yearning so strong, he toyed with the idea of taking her here and now.

Steady, man, he admonished himself, this one is too special for a quick toss. This one needs gentle coaxing. Later, he promised himself. Not here in sight of anyone who might happen by.

Slowly, her face lifted closer to his. Her mouth suddenly grew soft, yearning to be touched. A long, ragged sigh escaped him, as she felt herself being released and heard his voice deep and smooth with just the slightest trace of suffering at its core, as he tried to smile. "'Tis best, I think, to first see if the wheel can be repaired."

Merry sat atop the wagon as dazed as though she had been slapped. How could she have allowed his teasing to upset her so? Her face flamed at the thought of how she had invited his kiss and the mortification of being refused for her effort.

Standing, she quickly lowered herself to the ground. But her sudden angry movements made her careless, and she felt herself beginning to fall. Too late, she tried to grab hold of the wagon. An instant later, with a soft expulsion of breath, she found herself sitting on her derriere in the middle of the dirt road.

With each moment she remained in his company she became more of a clumsy, awkward ninny, she thought. What was the matter with her? Coming to her feet, she groaned at finding she had fallen into fresh horse droppings. The dismal tone of her voice caused Jonathan's cheerful face to look over the top of the wagon.

"Have you a problem, Mistress?"

"Nay, fool," she snapped, as he came around the wagon, a grin splitting his handsome mouth nearly ear to ear. "Must you stand their gawking like some lunatic? Have you never seen a soiled skirt before?"

Jonathan laughed out loud. "That I have, Mistress. But to my recollection, never with such an unusual and outstanding aroma."

"Obnoxious bore!" She scoffed at his overbearing laughter.

"Can I be of some assistance?" he offered, while taking a step toward her. "Perhaps if you remove the skirt."

"Touch me, English, and I swear I'll see to it you are put out of your misery."

"Am I in a state of misery?" he asked, his brows raising with puzzlement, his laughter only barely under control.

"Your very existence is a state of misery," she snarled to his echoing laughter, as she turned and stomped down the road.

Chapter Four

"HE SCARES ME."

Merry looked at the young girl with pure amazement, unable to comprehend how the man could instill terror in anyone. "In truth?"

Rebecca nodded her small head in short, rapid movements. "He's different from the others. He's always smiling, but his smile denotes no humor. Rather, it makes him look dangerous. Especially when he looks at you. There is something in that look that I cannot define. It brings to mind my brother when he smells plum pudding and can't wait to take a bite. I don't want him to look at me that way."

Merry gave a weary sigh. She knew the young serving girl was right. The blasted Britisher had a smile that she supposed could be interpreted as hungry, which sent a thrill of excitement down her spine, and he did look at her with an expression that closely resembled starvation. It was the same look she had seen before he had first kissed her and then again in the wagon when she had wantonly offered her mouth to him.

Since that day, more than a week past, Merry had been careful not to be alone with the doctor. Actually, she had no wish to see the lout under any circumstances. Still, that had not deterred him from making his presence known to her at every opportunity. Much to her annoyance, she rarely found herself with a moment of privacy, lest she retire to her room.

From across the taproom their eyes met and held for a long moment before Merry managed to pull her gaze from his. Finally, she sighed, "Nonsense, Becky. 'Tis naught but your imagination. He's a man, plain and simple, no more, no less, and he'll bring ye no harm."

"Nay, Merry," the serving girl shook her head and handed Merry the tray that held two plates of hot, sliced roast beef and potatoes. "He be no simple man, that 'un and I'd not be wantin' to serve him."

"Very well," Merry groaned, as she balanced the heavy tray in one hand and reached for two tankards of ale with the other.

Jonathan's blue eyes grew wide with appreciation watching the graceful swing of her long gray skirt as she walked to his table. As always, the sight of her inspired wild fantasies, and he felt the familiar tightening of his loins at the delicious thought of bedding her.

His companion, a certain Lieutenant Harris, had just taken a pinch of snuff and sneezed delicately into a lace handkerchief. Unbeknownst to him, his sneeze had caused his powdered wig to tip at a peculiar angle, and Merry couldn't resist a genuine smile as the young officer looked up at her.

Quickly, she placed the tankards and plates before each man. Wanting to spend as little time as possible near the officers, she hurried, and as sometimes happens when one moves too quickly, her hand knocked against the full tankard and it fell into Jonathan's lap.

As he jumped to his feet, Merry's look of astonishment turned to soft, husky laughter once she spied the cause of his sudden movement.

Even with the shock of the cold liquid, Jonathan could feel his body respond to the low sound of her laughter, and it was with a good deal of control that he managed to keep his hands from her.

A small towel hung over her shoulder, and she snapped it into her hand and offered it to him with a look that left little doubt as to the truth of her apology. Barely controlling her laughter, she managed to groan out, "Oh, sir, pardon me, please. I had not realized the tankard was so close to the edge of the table."

"'Tis nothing, Mistress," Jonathan smiled, as he took the towel and began to wipe off the excess liquid. "Worry of it no longer."

Of that you can be sure, she thought.

In the meantime Lieutenant Harris was engaged in whispered conversation with a fellow officer at the table behind him. "Hey, Jonny," the young Lieutenant called out without thinking, "you want to go over to Laine's house later?" And since Laine's was well-known to be a house of ill-repute, he had the good grace to blush crimson when he realized Mistress Gates was still standing at Jonathan's side.

Jonathan gave Merry a lopsided grin and watched with much appreciation as her cheeks pinkened. God, she was a delight to watch. He wondered if more than her cheeks colored so prettily when she was embarrassed, and swore the time was fast approaching when he'd find out for himself.

To say she intrigued him was a gross understatement. The woman was a mystery. She was capable of leading a gang of Rebels, yet there were times in his presence when she was as shy as a young girl, and still others when she might rage like a young colt, daring him to try to brake her.

An instant later, she turned from him and retrieved another tankard of ale. For some unfathomable reason, she was suddenly angry.

A moment later, she put the pewter vessel before Jonathan with such force as to nearly empty its contents.

Jonathan lifted his gaze from the now wet table to her fiery golden gaze. He took a deep breath, as her tawny eyes left him nearly breathless, and finally answered his friend, "Nay, Jamie, such sport is not to my liking."

Merry continued to glare at the English doctor. Had she given a moment's thought to her anger, she would have realized she was being irrational, for she had no reason to care whatsoever what he did with his evenings. When she spoke, she was just as amazed as he at what she uttered. "Why, not?" And then gasped at her own effrontery, her hand touching her lips too late to prevent the words.

Jonathan's eyes widened with surprise, and laughter lurked dangerously close to the surface, as he valiantly fought to contain it. He knew from her look of confusion and her groan of horror that she hadn't meant to speak out and, therefore, invited no answer from him.

An instant later, she was gone from the taproom.

How was it that he always managed to upset her, she thought, as she entered the tiny linen room off the long hall that ran the depth of the building. Can you not be in his company more than a moment that you do not make a complete fool of yourself?

Trying to take her mind off the ghastly occurrence, she busied herself by folding the linen that had recently been taken from the line. The warmth of the sun and the clean, crisp scent of the sea still clung to the fabric, as she shook out the towels and began to fold them into a neat pile.

Suddenly, he was there. She knew it even though his footsteps made not a sound and he uttered no words. His woodsy aroma overcame the scent of the linen. He said nothing, yet her body became sharply alive, and she almost moaned out loud at the thought of him standing behind her.

Taking another towel, she pressed the fabric to her face, as if that could blot out his scent and make him disappear.

It did not.

"Would it cause you distress if I should join the men at Laine's on this night?"

Her whole body stiffened. Desperately trying to seem nonchalant, she snapped the towel in the air and folded it in a few quick movements. "Pray tell, sir, why anything you do should distress me?"

Jonathan chuckled softly, his gaze moving along the slim, stiff line of her back, to her tiny waist, and then to the wide flair of her hips. He wondered how much of that flair was petticoat and how much longer it would be before he found out.

"You should not be in here," she finally managed.

He ignored her statement, while taking the last two objects from the basket and flinging them on a shelf behind him.

Merry, with nothing left to fold, was at a loss as to what to do with her hands, and she nervously ran her fingers over the many folds of her full skirt; yet she would not face him.

"In truth now, Merry," he gently preceded his question, "would it cause you distress should I join the men?"

She gave a long, ragged sigh, but could honestly offer no objection as to why he should not, except for the fact that she did not want him there, and the very thought of it was about to drive her into a murderous rage.

She said nothing.

He moved closer now; his warm breath stirred the short tendrils of golden hair that had slipped from her cap and lay curled at her neck.

"Will you not answer me, Mistress?"

Merry's voice trembled noticeably as she answered, "Sir, I've not the right to tell you where you may or may not go." Giving a long, breathy sigh, she continued, "What you do is entirely your business."

"Agreed," he commented, "but t'was not my question."

She shivered and took a quick step closer to the shelves, as a lone finger reached out and touched the nape of her neck. A soft sound that spoke of pain escaped her, and she took several long, deep breaths, trying to dispel the sudden dizzying weakness that threatened to buckle her knees.

"Will you not answer my question, Merry?"

She silently shook her head for a response.

His long arm reached out and slid around her small waist, pulling her back to rest securely against him.

Her soft gasp was the only sound in the room as his lips suddenly found the nape of her neck to be irresistible. His mouth moved to the side of the smooth golden column, and she couldn't prevent the low groan that sounded deep in her throat.

She trembled in his arms and had to use all of her willpower not to turn in his embrace and offer her mouth to his.

Oh, God, how she wanted to feel that mouth on hers. She was shaking as if palsied, suddenly having no control over her muscles. "Please," she whispered in a low, pleading voice; but she knew not whether she was asking for him to stop or go on.

And then she tipped her head so he might more easily reach the flesh of her neck, and she knew, no matter how she might hate him, no matter how she might distrust him, she only wanted more of this.

His long fingers were moving with deliberate slowness up her ribcage and down to her flat stomach and then to her waist. Wild, irrational thoughts were surging through her mind. She was suddenly sure his plan was to drive her crazy with longing and thereby take full advantage of her when she could no longer refuse him.

Without thinking, she turned in his arms. Their eyes met and held for a long moment before his mouth crashed down and covered her own. Her head was pushed back, her neck felt ready to snap, and yet she welcomed the strength of his kiss; while leaning into him, she allowed his tongue to penetrate her mouth. Weakly, she swayed closer.

Suddenly, her arms were around his neck and she was pressing her mouth equally hard against his, answering his probing tongue with her own.

Gasping from the lack of air and the sudden breathless force that had sprung to life between them, he pulled his mouth away and panted, "An answer, Merry," just before he covered her yielding sweet lips again.

Desperately she clung to him, wishing away his question, wanting only to go on touching him, breathing his scent, kissing his warm, hard lips, feeling his tongue rub roughly against her own.

His mouth left hers and slid to her ear. Tugging aside her cap with his teeth, he nibbled tenderly on the lobe, his breathing harsh and quick as he murmured, "God, you taste so good. I cannot wait to taste all of you."

His words were an aphrodisiac to Merry's senses and she gave a low moan, nearly swooning with the thought of his warm, moist mouth moving over the length of her body.

"I'd have your answer now, my love."

"Nay," she cried softly, just before his mouth joined to hers again. She couldn't tell him she would go mad if he touched another. She couldn't.

But he was unrelenting in his need for an answer. Whenever his mouth left hers he pressed for the words he longed to hear.

Finally, she could bear his teasing no more. She needed that mouth against her own. She'd admit to anything to taste him, to feel him against her. "Aye! Are you satisfied, English? It would cause me distress."

And as his mouth continued to taunt her with short, hot flicks of his tongue, she breathed her total surrender, "Oh, God, it would, it would," until his mouth prevented all further speech.

Jonathan was fast losing control. He had never wanted a woman so badly. Almost past the point of rational thinking, he was dangerously close to taking her here on the floor of the linen closet.

Suddenly and with superhuman effort, he tore his mouth from hers. Merry wobbled as he left her and his hand reached out to steady her. How he wanted this woman!

His chest heaved as he fought to gain control of his emotions. Quickly, he stepped back, as if he feared to be near her any longer. His eyes never left her as he moved away. At the door, he finally managed, in a raw voice that was barely audible, strained with a yearning so strong it nearly choked him, "Not here . . . not now."

Merry stood frozen in place as she watched him leave her. Her hands clutched at the shelves behind her lest she fall; so shaken was she. A mixture of terror and longing flooded her eyes as tears blurred her vision, and she turned with a choking, muffled cry to bury her face in her hands.

She had admitted all to him. In her entire life she had never felt such shame. She groaned with the enormity of what she had done. How was this happening? She hated him and his kind and yet she had not the strength to resist the pull she felt toward him. God in heaven, how was she to go on?

Chapter Five

MERRY PUSHED OUT HER LOWER LIP AND BLEW A WHISP OF golden hair from her sticky forehead. The kitchen was stifling and, even though the door stood ajar and the windows wide open, the air that trickled in brought little relief. The long summer months had stretched far into the month of September with no end in sight to this unbearable heat.

Suddenly, from outside the window arose the loud shrieks of a terrified woman and bawdy male laughter. "What in the world is going on out there?" Merry asked. Receiving no answer, she turned from the workbench. While wiping her small, floured hands across her apron, another shriek came clearly through the window.

"Becky, what is it?"

Rebecca's back was ramrod straight, as she turned from the window and faced her employer. Her face was white, her brown eyes grew huge with fear, as she answered in a small, shaking voice, "'Tis Miss Nettie. The soldiers are . . . are . . ."

Merry knew well enough what the soldiers were doing. It bothered them not that they terrified the young women of the town. How often had stories filtered back to her of one abuse or another. Complaints of ill treatment were less than useless and only to be ignored by those in command. In truth, these hated English thought themselves above the law and, in fact, they were.

A long growl erupted from her lovely mouth, "No more, dammit, no more! 'Tis more than enough."

Without thought of the consequences of her actions, Merry grabbed the thick handle of the broom and ran outside. Ready to do battle, she lunged at the group of young soldiers who surrounded the sobbing Nettie. Not one of the four saw her approach. Nor did they hear her shouts above the laughing of their comrades and the cries of the terrified woman clutching at her ripped dress, while being pushed to and fro within the small circle they had formed.

The sight of her friend's terrified eyes brought on a rage such as Merry had never known before. The thick handle of the broom came whistling through the air and smacked the closest soldier with a dull thud, hitting him just below his knee. The blow caused his leg to buckle instantly, and a howl of pain erupted from his startled face.

Barely had he time to utter a sound, when another felt the full force of her fury, and he too hit the ground. The surprise on his face was matched only by the pain that filled his eyes.

By now, the two remaining men realized what she was about. In an instant the broom was torn from her hands, while her arms were pinned behind her in a vicelike hold.

The leering, livid face of the last soldier came close, as he spoke out his hatred. "You dare lay a hand on an officer of the King's Dragoons, Mistress?" His teeth clenched as he spoke, his voice barely audible above the terrified screeching of Nettie and Rebecca.

Suddenly and quite unexpectantly, his fist slammed into the side of her face. With no little disgust, she heard a sound come from her throat which distinctly resembled that of a grunting animal being led to slaughter. To her further mortification she felt her knees wobble and, had it not been for the brute who held her upright, she knew she'd have fallen to the ground.

Vaguely she heard the moans of the two officers she had felled and fought valiantly not to add her own sounds of agony to theirs. She'd not allow these animals the knowledge of her suffering. The next punch split her lip, the one after hit her squarely on the temple, and she gratefully welcomed the blackness it brought.

Jonathan returned from the fort, dismounted his horse and tied the leather reins to the hitching post at the front of the inn.

A crowd was forming at the side of the building. Anxious to see the lovely proprietress, he was bent on ignoring the commotion.

Bounding up the two steps that led to the inn's front door, he was almost run down by a white-faced Noah Gates as he came charging out.

Jonathan had no time to ask what the matter might

be as the man sped past him. The only sound he uttered was, "Merry!" Now totally puzzled, Jonathan followed the agitated landlord to the side of the inn. Even with his height, he could not see the cause of the gathering; but, for some unexplained reason, he suddenly felt a cold wave of fear clutch at his heart.

The now silent crowd parted, as the landlord roughly pushed his way through. Jonathan, although afraid of what he might see, moved quickly in his wake.

His worst fears confirmed, he was instantly filled with a wide variety of emotions; not the least of them being a rage toward his countrymen for hurting the lady, whose face was barely recognizable as the soldier delivered another blow.

Jonathan never realized the bellow of rage that erupted from his throat as he charged at the officer and swung him about. It happened so fast that he never noticed that one swing of his mighty fist had caused the man to slump at his feet. From all around him could be heard sounds of moaning and cries of fear, but nothing at all came from the tiny lady, whose slumped form was still held by the last standing officer.

Enraged and about to lunge at him and give him some similar benefit of his anger, it was Noah Gates's steady and calm presence that brought some sanity to Jonathan's mind.

Mr. Gates took his daughter's unconscious body from the now terrified young man. Jonathan watched, his heart breaking with pity, as Merry was held in her father's arms. Her eye was already swelling, her jaw and cheek growing bluer as each second passed.

Tearing his gaze from her, he faced the soldier, the

temptation to strike him so great, he felt his whole body shaking with the effort it took to restrain himself.

Jonathan's voice trembled with rage as he coldly ordered, "Take your friends and be gone from here. Should I find you've returned, or hear a word of this has reached our Colonel's ears, you'll find yourself up on charges. Do you hear me, Mister?"

"Aye, Captain," the terrified young man responded quickly. "He will hear naught of this," he promised, saluting.

The crowd parted again, and the two men, limping ahead, led the way for the soldier, who struggled as he dragged his semiconscious friend.

Becky stood sobbing with her apron covering her face and jumped sharply as Jonathan spoke. "Fetch water and clean linens. Bring them to your mistress's room. Then go to my room and bring my bag." And when the girl stood looking at him in a stupor of terror, he bellowed, "Immediately!"

Her big brown eyes were wide with fear as she darted around the back of the building and disappeared into the kitchen.

Jonathan wasted no time. He barely remembered moving, as he took the stairs three at a time, and suddenly found himself outside Merry's bedroom door. Taking a deep breath, he steeled himself and entered.

Mr. Gates was kneeling beside the bed, his fingers gently pushing her blood-soaked hair from her face as he coaxed her to answer him. "Merry, 'tis Father. Can you hear me? Can you speak?"

"She cannot hear you, Mr. Gates," Jonathan said from behind him. "Be thankful. At least she feels no pain. If you've no objection, I'd like to assess the damage done."

Noah Gates was torn between the care of his daughter and the rage he felt toward all those who pledged their loyalty to George. After all, one of his kind had just inflicted this abuse on her. Could he trust this doctor to do his best?

Reading the indecision in the man's eyes and knowing its reasons, Jonathan reassured him. "Fear not, Mr. Gates. I am not ignorant of your dislike for us. And I know you include me in your hatred, but I care for her. Can you not put aside for a time the fact that I am loyal to the Crown? I'd not see her suffer. I swear it."

Noah studied the young man's face. He could see nothing but sincerity and caring in his dark blue eyes. Somehow he knew his daughter would be well again, if this man had anything to say about it.

He nodded and slowly came to his feet, leaving room for the doctor to administer to her.

Jonathan was not aware that the lady's father had not left the room, nor did he realize he spoke his words aloud. His voice broke with emotion as he bent over her still form and choked out, "Merry, oh Merry, my love. What have they done to you?"

Leaning his head to her chest, he listened for her heartbeat and breathed a long sigh of relief as he heard it beat a steady, strong rhythm.

"Where in God's name is that wench?" he muttered, as he began to loosen the blood-soaked bodice of her dress.

No sooner had he spoken than a timid knock sounded at the door.

Immediately, Mr. Gates opened the door and saw his

serving girl weighed down with a bucket of water and clean toweling plus the doctor's bag.

Quickly, he moved a table from the far corner of the room and placed it near the bed. He took the washbasin from the dry sink, filled it with water and placed it on the table.

Jonathan worked quickly; his long, steady fingers never shook or showed the slightest hesitancy, as he cleaned her face and hair of blood.

He gave a sigh of relief to see the damage was less than he had expected.

"Get your mistress a clean nightdress," he ordered, never stopping his ministrations.

"Yes, sir," she whispered shakily and hurried to do his bidding. With the fresh nightdress folded neatly at the foot of the bed, she took Merry's slippers from her feet and pulled down her stockings.

Merry moaned in pain and Jonathan raged unreasonably, unable to control his own private suffering any longer. "Get the hell out! Can you not see you are hurting her?"

Noah Gates felt a warm wave of relief at hearing his daughter's cry of pain. Her face was free of blood and the damage was less than he had first thought. He smiled, knowing Becky had caused her mistress no added pain, but that the doctor snapped at her due to his own concern for his patient.

Watching him work and listening to his tender words, he had no doubt the young man loved his daughter. A grin split his mouth, knowing her feelings for the English and the battles the young man was sure to face.

She moaned again and opened one eye. Spying Jonathan working over her, she tried to push his hands away. "Nay," she said. "I need not your ministrations, English. Leave me."

"Let it be, Merry," her father's voice sounded from across the room. "You've been sadly abused and are in need of care. No doubt you are aware Captain Townsend is a doctor. I believe you'll fare well in his care."

"'Tis only my face that was battered, father. I need no one to care for my injury."

"Allow me to be the judge of that, Mistress," Jonathan replied. "It may have been your face that has taken most of the abuse, but we know not if you've a concussion or broken bones to worry over."

"I've not!" she insisted, and then grimaced at the pain her speaking caused to the side of her face.

"Mr. Gates," Jonathan sighed helplessly and turned to the man who now stood at the foot of the bed. "Can you not reason with her?"

"In the past, I've found Merry does not often respond to reason, Captain. I think a direct order is more to the point."

For a quick moment, she forgot her pain and felt her body stiffen with annoyance. How dare they discuss her as if she were not present? She tried to rise from the bed, but fell back with a low oath, as her arms were suddenly so weak and shaking, they could not do what her mind ordered. A soft moan escaped her as her head rested once again on the pillow.

"Headache?"

"Aye," she sighed.

"'Tis as I thought, Mistress. You'll be in need of bed rest for some days to come."

She started to object, but he interrupted with, "It

matters not whether you are willing, you have no option but to do as I say."

"Father?" she asked, her voice pleading for help.

"Daughter," he returned, "you will do as you are told. I'll hear no more of it. You may proceed Doctor."

Merry breathed a long sigh of martyred submission and allowed him to continue his ministrations with a mumbled, "Very well."

Mr. Gates smiled at his obstinate daughter as he turned to leave. "I will return once the doctor is finished."

"Nay," she cried out more sharply than she had intended. "'Tis no need for you to leave, Father."

Noah Gates grinned at his daughter's sudden agitation. There was more here than met the eye. "You'd not be afraid, Merry?"

"Of course not," she snapped. "I simply see no reason for you to leave."

"Do you think Becky so nimble-witted as to cope with the noonday meal without my aid?"

"Nay," she sighed reluctantly.

He nodded his gray head as he spoke. "Rest easy, daughter. I will return before long."

Jonathan grinned down at his patient. It was obvious she didn't want to be alone with him and he wondered as to the true cause of it. Could it be she felt more than she'd admit? Could it be his presence disturbed her as much as hers did him? Should he allow himself to hope it was not hatred she felt, but an emotion more terrifying and tender?

As Mr. Gates left the room, he had cause to wonder if Merry did not return some of the doctor's obvious feelings. He laughed softly and murmured low, "Oh, God, this will be something to see."

Perhaps she did care for the doctor, he mused silently. Although he knew she'd never admit to it, it would surely explain her erratic behavior as of late. He couldn't remember when he'd seen her so happy, and the very next moment plunged into the depths of a sorrow he couldn't comprehend.

He gave a low chuckle as he descended the steps, sure in the knowledge that she was being well cared for, and surer still that this war just past was nothing compared to the battles that lay ahead between these two spirited young people.

Jonathan applied a cool compress to her lip, until the bleeding stopped completely. Thank God, there seemed to be no broken bones. Her left eye was swollen shut and would surely discolor, but there was apparently no permanent damage. The left side of her face was one large dark bruise running from temple to jaw. He cursed the bastard that had done this to her, sorry now he had not picked him up and hit him again.

Rinsing out the cloth in clean water, he held it to her face again, hoping to prevent any further swelling. Leaving the cloth against her cheek, he finished the task of unbuttoning her bodice. The chemise beneath her dress was wet with blood and he was loath to pull the items over her head.

Reaching into his bag, he took a pair of shears and cut the material at her shoulders and down the length of her. A moment later, he pulled both dress and chemise from beneath her.

Merry gave a soft gasp as she felt the material slide away and the warm air of the room rush up against her naked breasts. The injury she had suffered did not cloud her mind and she knew very well what was happening. Closing her uninjured eye tightly, she said nothing. She knew he was looking at her. The rapid change in his breathing told her how her half-naked state was affecting him.

He said not a word, but went about the business of cleaning the blood from her breasts. Merry stiffened noticeably and gave a soft murmur for him to desist.

"Easy, love," he soothed above her in a voice that trembled despite his efforts to control it. "I'd not see you upset, but this needs to be done."

Had his hands not begun to shake, Merry would not have guessed the extent of his suffering, for his expression was stony and solemn.

Their gazes met and held and she read within those dark blue eyes a yearning so powerful, she feared she had not the strength to resist his silent plea.

A long, shaky sigh escaped her as she felt his hands move almost reverently over her. She grunted as he touched a bruise on her ribs, and his hand came instantly away.

"'Tis possible you have a fractured rib. Can you take a deep breath without pain?"

Merry tried and found her chest tight with pain. "Nay."

Jonathan nodded at her reply. "If I bind it you will have less discomfort," he promised, and then set about to do so.

His fingers worked quickly, and Merry soon found some relief as a linen cloth was tied securely around her ribs. It did not go unnoticed by either of them that, as he tied the cloth, his fingers often brushed against her breast, and Merry tried unsuccessfully to deny a longing for him to never stop.

He loomed hugely above her. His dark eyes bore into hers, and she couldn't be sure if it was the effect of his gaze or the tightness of the cloth around her chest, but she was suddenly unable to breathe. Her pain forgotten, her lips parted as she struggled to breathe. His dark gaze searched her face adoringly. The silent question she read in their depths was soon obvious, as she felt his long fingers reach inside the waistband of her lace-trimmed cotton drawers.

Her small hands came to cover his, but offered no resistance as he began to tug them down to her hips. Both knew it to be an unnecessary action. She need not be naked beneath her nightdress, but she never objected to his unspoken plea. His eyes never left her face as his large warm hands caressed her quivering thighs, and she felt an undeniable longing, even injured as she was, for him to touch her, to look at her, to love her.

He is a doctor, she silently reminded herself. This has no meaning for either of us, she lied, for she knew in her heart it was not so.

His gaze left her face and wandered the full length of her tiny frame. His voice came as a hiss to her ears as he muttered a tormented, "Oh, God, I knew you'd look like this."

Amazingly, Merry felt not a moment's embarrassment as his eyes roamed over her. Her breathing increased to panting and she could have sworn she felt his gaze as if a caress.

He was torn between his desire to touch her and the knowledge of her injury and how he would be taking advantage of the situation. Not ignorant of her reaction to his gaze, he knew that were she unhurt and he were to do what his body craved, she'd offer no objection.

A low oath escaped his throat as he saw her shiver. What had come over him? Was he so low as to take advantage of a totally helpless lady? He sighed with disgust that he should allow such a lapse in professionalism. His patient needed his care and here he was mooning over her like some love-starved adolescent.

Gaining some control, he asked in a shaking voice, "Are you chilled?"

Equally shaken, she replied, "Nay." For she had trembled at the look in his eyes, not at the temperature of the room.

He smiled down at her. Sitting at her side, he gently guided the nightdress over her head and down her body. "Had anyone told me I'd be foolish enough to be covering you, I'd have laughed."

She gave a hesitant, shy smile, unable as yet to feel comfortable that he should tease her about his desire for her.

His voice was deeply husky as he held her to him in a tender embrace, his fingers caressing the uninjured side of her face as he soothed, "Rest easy, my love. No further harm shall come to you. I am here now. I will always care for you."

He was trembling as his fingers closed the last of her buttons, and the effort it caused him not to reach inside her gown was not to be borne.

"It hurts," she sighed as she felt the stiffening of her swelling face.

"I know. I will give you something for the pain."

Quickly, he opened a packet and poured the white powder into a glass. Adding water, he mixed it and lifted her to a sitting position so she might drink.

She made a face at the first sip and groaned again when the pain in her face increased. "'Tis bitter."

"Aye," he agreed, "but the laudanum will allow you to rest more comfortably. Drink it all."

For once Merry offered him no argument and did as she was told.

Lying her back against fluffed pillows, he covered her with a sheet and began to clear away the mess he had made of her clothes and the rags he used to clean her. Spying what was left of her dress, she groaned, "You've ruined another. 'Tis three you owe me, English."

Smiling, he opened her two windows and covered them with the dark blue curtains that hung at their sides. A gentle breeze puffed out the material, but the heat of the day did not penetrate the room.

Still smiling, he sat on the bed, not unaware that his hip was touching hers and gazed down into her bruised face. "A doctor in the King's Dragoons can count little as his own, Mistress. Would you call in your debt?"

"Nay," she sighed sleepily, the laudanum already taking effect, "Perhaps the debt should be canceled in lieu of services rendered."

Jonathan chuckled happily, content to sit at her side and see her comfortable.

Just before she drifted off to sleep, she heard his voice whisper low, "Nay, my love, if it be a dress you want, then a dress it shall be."

Chapter Six

MERRY AWOKE THE NEXT MORNING TO FIND JONATHAN sitting in a chair at the side of her bed. His chin rested on his chest and his lips were parted in sleep.

She was amazed at the sudden rush of happiness that left her breathless. He was magnificent to look at. No matter her dislike, she could not deny his handsomeness. His dark hair fell softly over his forehead, while his features, relaxed in sleep, gave him an appealingly boyish appearance. Had he sat here all night, she wondered. She could see from the one eye that would open, his clothes were rumpled, and a dark shadow had formed on his cheeks and chin.

What had possessed him to stay with her? Surely she was not that seriously hurt that she needed constant attention. She felt herself grow warm as she remembered last night and what had silently passed between them. He had touched her so tenderly, almost lovingly as he examined her, that, despite her injury, she had felt something stir deep within her.

Her face flamed as she remembered how she had been so bold as to allow him to gaze upon her naked body. His eyes had scorched her with their flaming intensity. He had wanted to touch her, to make love to her. Of this she had no doubt. For a long moment he had looked upon her body, not as a doctor, but as a man. A man who desired a woman.

Forcing her thoughts from last night's happenings and careful of her aching ribs, she rolled to her side and lifted herself slowly to her elbow. Trying to sit up she inadvertently groaned as she felt the pain seize her chest.

Instantly, he was awake. "Where the hell do you think you're going?" he bellowed and then saw her give a start at the sound of his voice.

"What business is it of yours, English?" she returned sharply. "You scared me with your blasted booming. Can you not speak in normal tones upon awakening? And what are you doing in my room in the first place?"

Jonathan gave a soft chuckle at her rising temper, suddenly happy that she was once again her normal fiery self. Her face was a mess. Damn the bastard who hit her, he thought. No wonder she hates us, he groaned silently, if this was a taste of what she could expect from those loyal to the King. How could he make her understand that treatment such as this would never be tolerated under a fair and just British commander.

She couldn't see that the English were no different from others, and like others, could be guilty of injustice. She believed them all to be heartless beasts and he felt powerless to convince her otherwise.

Suddenly, he realized he didn't want her to see him in the light. He wanted her to believe not all English were women beaters and drunken louts. Least of all, himself.

"Lie back, Merry," he soothed, as he sat on the bed and pressed her shoulders gently to the bed. "If you rise with a possible fractured rib, you could cause yourself some harm."

"Might I," she snapped a bit sarcastically. "Am I not already harmed?"

"Further harm then," he corrected.

Helpless to fight against his superior strength, she gave a weary sigh and allowed his order to stand.

"Are you hungry?"

She gave a small nod. "A cup of tea would fare well, but I think it's too early. I doubt the kitchen fires are lit as yet."

"It matters not. I will light them. Do not try to get up until I return. Can I do anything for you before I leave?"

Merry blushed that he should hint at so personal a matter and whispered with lowered eyes. "Send Becky to me."

"'Tis not necessary," he answered. "You cannot leave your bed. I am capable of bringing you the chamber pot."

"Oh, please," she groaned in obvious misery.

Jonathan chuckled. "Mistress, you need not suffer so. I am not ignorant of the body's functions. Have you forgotten I am a doctor?"

She raised her one good eye to him and repeated with a definite note of desperation in her voice, "Send Becky to me."

"As you wish, Mistress," he conceded with a tender smile as he left the room.

Nettie came for a visit later that morning, just as Jonathan was taking a tray of dirty dishes from the room. As he passed her, he asked if she might not like a cup of tea.

Closing the door behind her, she found herself laughing as she asked, "Have you acquired new help Merry? Merry! My God, look at your face!" Her blue eyes growing wide with horror at the sight of her dearest friend's injury.

Merry smiled at her expression. "Nay, I fear to look upon the destruction caused, lest I seek out the culprit and return the favor."

Nettie smiled at her friend's tenacity. "After yesterday, I'd believe no less of you. Where did you find the courage?"

Merry gave a sheepish, if painful, grin. "I fear t'was not courage that spurred me, Nettie, but anger coupled with the simple lack of common sense."

Nettie bit at her lower lip and whispered guiltily, "'Tis my fault."

"Nay," her friend returned vigorously, "'Tis the fault of the damned British and none other. In truth, they are a hateful, barbarian lot."

"Not all, Merry," Nettie reminded her with a gentle smile. "Captain Townsend seems to be most agreeable. Your father has told me he hovers over you like a mother hen, seeing to your every want, and until now, allowing no one but your father entrance to this room, lest you be disturbed. Has he not sat through the night with you?"

"'Tis guilt, is all," she sighed.

"I think not," Nettie insisted. "No matter the shame he feels toward his countrymen, he need not have taken your care upon himself."

Upon seeing the disbelief in Merry's face, she asked, "Was it guilt that caused him to lay low the officer who hit you? I think not. All in all, Jeremiah and myself believe him to be a most likeable fellow."

Merry's attention was riveted to her friend's face and, when she spoke, her voice was wispy with awe. "He hit him?"

"Aye," Nettie smiled at Merry's astonishment, "and the roar of rage he gave should have easily been heard some miles away."

Merry gave a small smile, her expression one of confusion. Why would he chance court martial? To strike a fellow officer was a serious offense. She couldn't understand his reasoning.

The subject soon turned to more pleasant matters and, when Jonathan returned with tea for Merry's guest, the gentle laughter that filled the room brought a lightness to his heart and a gleam of tenderness to his eyes.

After the midday meal, which he delivered, served and joined them in, Merry began to show signs of fatigue. Nettie soon left her friend to Jonathan's care, promising to return on the morrow for another visit.

Alone with Jonathan, Merry followed his every movement, as her thoughts returned to her newly acquired information.

"Before you sleep," he remarked, unmindful of her

close scrutiny, as he filled a bowl with water and dipped a clean cloth into it, "I want to bathe your face and check the bruises on your ribs."

He worked quickly and brought her no added pain, as the cool wet cloth moved over the damaged half of her face.

Upon inspecting her ribs, he adjusted the sheet so that the lower portion of her body remained covered, while his fingers probed the injury. His expression registered nothing unusual as his fingers grazed the soft golden mounds of her breasts. "It appears 'tis no more than a bruise. Still, I want you to stay abed a day or two longer."

"Why did you hit him?"

Jonathan's eyes lifted to her gaze and he flushed slightly beneath his tan. Knowing it was too soon to reveal his growing feelings for her, he simply stated, "Nettie should not have told you."

Gently his fingers moved to lower her nightdress once more.

"But she did. Why did you hit him?" she insisted.

Jonathan gave a long, weary sigh as he adjusted the sheet and sat beside her, his fingertips brushing against the uninjured side of her face in a tender caress. "I know you consider the English, on the whole, to be little more than animals, but I promise you, 'tis not so. The drunken lout that hit you was no better than swine and deserves your contempt, but you must not believe, no matter your loyalty, that all Englishmen are so lacking in honor as to strike a lady."

"Is that why you feel you must care for me? To show me all are not so inclined to brutality?"

"Nay, Merry," he soothed with a tender smile. "I

care for you simply because I wish to see you well again. Is there another here about spirited enough to dare to shoot me evil sneers or growl at my comments? Already I miss our heated discussions."

Merry laughed and then groaned at the pain it brought both her face and chest. "You find enjoyment then in my anger?"

Jonathan chuckled at her taunting grin and gave her a decidedly leering look, "It will suffice till more enjoyable confrontations make themselves known."

Chapter Seven

MERRY'S LAUGHTER, SOFT AND SLIGHTLY ECHOING IN THE predawn stillness, mingled sweetly with the sound of small white caps brushing a delicate kiss of water against the rocky shoreline.

The sun was just then sending its brilliant glow over the horizon, as Jonathan stood at his window, relieved that another night of sleeplessness had finally passed, watching as the object of his torment raced along the shore, the shaggy gray puppy giving short squeaking barks in her wake.

The five days he had nursed her had been pure torture, for it had drawn him closer than ever to the lady. He had been hard put indeed to resist his baser instincts.

Turning abruptly, he watched as she welcomed the charging little beast with open arms, laughing happily as the furry creature scrambled up her small form and licked wildly at her face. Jonathan couldn't prevent the twinge of jealousy he felt. If only she'd open her arms thus for him.

He had been here two months and with each passing day, he grew more and more obsessed with the need to possess this woman. No longer did he bother to deny his feelings. He wanted her, aye, but he wanted more than just her body. He wanted everything she had to offer.

He'd not have thought it possible to so love another. Thoughts of her occupied his every waking moment. How many more nights was he to lie sleepless in his bed? How much more torment was he to bear before she was his? How often had he heard her light footsteps above him as she walked the floor of her own room? Could he dare to hope she wanted him as well? Did she too pace away her longing, far into each night?

"Oh, God," he groaned aloud, what was to come of this? At times he could see no future for them. Were she to admit her desire . . . what then? Would she come with him? Would she leave her beloved colonies?

His place was in England. He could not, would not abandon his family and what waited for him upon his return home. Since his older brother's sudden death two years past, the weight of the family's responsibilities had fallen directly on his shoulders.

His mother ran the estates in his absence, but once he returned, he would be expected to take his rightful seat in the House of Lords as the new Earl of Hampshire. Would she be happy as his Countess?

Good God! She hated the English and above all the

aristocracy. Had he not often heard her spout of the equality of all men? Did she not continuously turn up her beautiful nose ⸢ class distinction?

Jonathan stiffened at his own thoughts. What was he thinking? Did he truly want her so badly as to offer for her hand? He watched her a moment longer, his loins tightening at the mere sight of her. His chest constricted at the sound of her laughter, and he knew. Aye, he'd offer that and more. For the first time in his thirty-three years, he found himself wanting a woman more than life itself, and he'd stop at nothing until he had her.

A low oath slipped past his firm lips as he promised himself an end to his suffering. No matter her objections, she would be his.

He smiled as he envisioned the fight she'd give him. She loved this country and the whispers of freedom that floated in the wind. He had to admit, he too had taken a liking to this new land and its promise of all that is good in mankind. Perhaps they could return often. He'd not see her unhappy and, if she wanted to see her father and her friends, he'd find that to be of no hardship.

Nay, he reasoned, that was no obstacle. Uppermost in his mind now was how to convince her to admit she wanted him as badly as he did her. His firmly chiseled lips split into a tender smile as he remembered her reaction to his kisses. Each time it had been him that had called a stop to their passion-filled, intimate moments. Nay, he had not a doubt that she wanted him, but did her desire mean what he hoped? Did it mean she cared for him?

He grinned, suddenly sure of himself, knowing full

well he had the power to bring her to him weak with longing, soft, pliant and willing in his arms. Arrogantly, he mused, if she did not care as yet, she soon would.

Pulling on his soft knee-high leather boots, he left his room to join the lovely lass on the beach. Being a man of no little intelligence, he was not ignorant as to the constant wandering of her golden gaze upon his person, and so, it was with a wicked gleam in his dark blue eyes and a taunting smile turning the corners of his mouth that he purposely unbuttoned two more buttons of his white shirt.

Merry laughed again as the little puppy's teeth clamped tightly over the hem of her long skirt. Picking him up, she unhooked his teeth from the material. "One would think you a Britisher, Muffit. No gentleman would sniff so boldly after a lady's skirt." And then she remembered again who had given her the puppy. "Perhaps you are a Britisher, after all. Well we'll soon bring a change to your loyalties, little one."

Sitting on a large rock, she petted the dog, as her gaze wandered out to the blue expanse of calm water. Now, if she could only do the same with a certain English doctor. Would it matter, she wondered? Would she care? Would it make a difference in her feelings toward him if he joined her cause? Did she want that?

Definitely, it would make her feelings easier to comprehend. As they stood now, she was in a state of constant upheaval. In truth, she wanted him, wanted his touch and to touch him in return, wanted his kisses and more; but the very idea only served to disgust her. How could she allow tender thoughts toward her country's hated enemy? She shivered with horror and felt herself truly traitorous.

The shore of Connecticut, just coming into view through the shroud of mist that was only now lifting from the water's surface, brought her a blissful moment of peace from the constant thought of the English doctor who slept just beneath her room. Her face flushed with embarrassment as she remembered his return two night's hence after a week's absence, during which he had gone to administer to an ailing officer at the fort. She knew her eyes had been aglow with an unbelievable stab of happiness to see him again, but, when he had pulled a tiny ball of gray fur from inside his shirt and handed the sleeping puppy to her, she had nearly giggled with pleasure.

At first she had thought it to be a muff, hence the puppy's name, but soon realized it was a living creature. She gave a mournful groan as she remembered her momentary lapse and how she had whispered, "Oh, English, thank you." Then impulsively, with the puppy pressed tightly between them, she had flung herself into his arms and kissed his startled lips.

She hadn't been able to look at him since, that his smiling eyes did not remind her of her bold action. When are they to leave these shores, she asked herself. When would her country truly be at peace? When would she?

Unable to reach any sort of an answer to her dilemma, she gave a long, weary sigh and came to her feet. "Come, Muffit, let us race along the beach. To sit here and wish for what is not will bring neither of us closer to our wants."

A moment later, she was running again with the puppy close behind barking at the flare of her skirts. She was laughing and glancing back at her pursuer, when she suddenly slammed into a wall of warm flesh. She hit him so hard, she would have fallen back, had not strong arms come quickly around her waist to steady her.

Her hands came automatically up to push against his hold and he released her. Gasping with the shock of touching his naked chest, she pulled her hands from him and jumped back, while choking out breathlessly, "Excuse me, Captain, I fear I did not see you. This little mongrel, in hot pursuit, took much of my attention."

"The little one is wise beyond his years," Jonathan grinned. "Perhaps I should do as he, for I have long sought your attention."

Merry, her heart racing at his words, stood flabbergasted and unable to answer in kind. Was he teasing her again? He was smiling, but his smile had suddenly become tender and . . . and . . . and what? Why was he always causing her such confusion?

Her voice was stilted and unsteady when she finally spoke, "Pray, excuse me, Captain. I did not realize the hour had grown so late. I'll be needed in the kitchen."

"Nay, Merry," he responded. "The house still sleeps. I, like you, left my bed early to seek a breath of fresh air and a bit of sunshine."

Her golden hair whipped about her head in wild disarray, as she had yet to secure it and cover it with her cap. Jonathan grasped a long, curling lock between his fingers and brought it to his mouth. Slowly, he inhaled the clean, lemony scent that clung to it, the same scent that had haunted him since their first meeting. "You should never secure your hair, Merry. 'Tis a thing of beauty and far too lovely to hide."

Merry gathered her waist-length hair and twisted it into a large knot, as she took her cap from her apron pocket and covered the golden tresses. "Nay, sir, 'tis most unseemly. A lady does not leave her hair down but in the privacy of her chambers."

"And yet you had it unbound."

She smiled a quick, shy response to his question and Jonathan's heart hammered wildly in his chest. He barely heard her as she answered, "Aye, but I was alone."

Her eyes wandered the length of his tall, lean frame and she gave a sharp, silent curse that the sight of this man should cause her such distress. Why was he never in uniform? Why did he always have his shirt unbuttoned? Good God, did he not realize how much of his chest was exposed when the wind took the material and parted it still further? And his pants! It was positively indecent the way the material clung to his lean hips, leaving almost nothing to the imagination. The muscles of his thighs rippled, as he shifted his weight and turned to gaze out to smooth water, and Merry felt herself grow light-headed with an emotion she had sworn did not exist.

Annoyed, she tore her gaze from him and joined him in looking out across the Sound. Why should she care how the rutting cad chose to dress? In truth, he dressed no different from any other man. Why did it cause her such anger to see him strut in these disgustingly tight pants?

For a long moment they stood in silence, as the puppy, not yet giving up hope of further frolicking, yelped at her heels for attention.

Jonathan chuckled as he bent to pick up the dog. "Has your mistress abandoned you, little one?"

Gently, he cuddled the dog in his arm, and Merry watched in silent horror as the puppy sought out his new companion's warmth and burrowed his face beneath the shirt to the bare, furred chest, pushing half his body inside.

She couldn't breathe. For how long had she wanted to do just that? She was almost jealous of the helpless little puppy, that he should have what she craved.

Her face grew pink and her breathing labored as she watched. "He seeks the warmth," Jonathan said, as he glanced first at the puppy and then at Merry's mesmerized gaze.

Unthinkingly, she nodded her head and breathed, "I know. At night he scrambles beneath my sheet. It tickles, but he insists on laying his head on my stomach." Stopping suddenly, her face turned crimson at what she had said.

Jonathan paled beneath his tan and his senses reeled. It took every ounce of control not to grab her and pull her to him, as he realized she had inadvertently told him she slept naked. A low oath slipped unnoticed past his lips. He was positive he'd never sleep again. Knowing she lay above him covered only by a thin sheet was more than he could take.

Goddammit! He had to think of something else, lest he take the girl here in full sight of anyone who cared to look out of the inn's windows.

His voice broke and he found he had to begin again. This time the ragged edge seemed less harsh, as he took a deep breath. "'Tis nearly empty, these waters today.

Last night the comings and goings of your countrymen kept me awake most of the night."

"In truth?" she smiled, breathing a silent thanks that he had ignored her slip. "Myself, I thought they were unusually quiet."

"Did you?"

She gave a soft, husky laugh that was nearly his undoing as she went on, "You've heard nothing, sir, until Caleb Brewster visits these shores. I believe his choice of ungentlemanly epithets, particularly when describing one of your illustrious countrymen, are sure to go down in history as the most colorful additions to the English language since its outset."

Jonathan chuckled and asked, "Is he always so unreserved?"

"Always."

Jonathan didn't miss the inflection of tenderness as she answered and was suddenly filled with a heretofore unknown fear. Unable to resist, he asked, "Is he special to you?"

Merry faced him again, her eyes dancing with laughter as she thought of the rascal. "Aye, that he is. I've known Caleb and his Annie for as long as I can remember. I am honored to consider them my true friends."

Jonathan breathed a sigh of relief. So this Caleb had an Annie. Indeed that was news he welcomed. "One wonders why these shores should be so honored by his visits."

Merry smiled and remarked, "I'm sure one does."

"There be a code, as like as not, between Mr. Brewster and someone on the Long Island shore, for he has become as slippery as an eel and harder to catch. Never does he put to shore in the same place twice. And no matter the amount of guards, he evades us every time."

Merry smiled and lowered her head, lest he read the truth of his words in her expression, for he had already guessed more than enough. Each night a black petticoat was put on the line to dry. Beside it were any number of white handkerchiefs, the exact number to indicate where Caleb could land his whaleboat, that area being free for a time of the English.

It was so ludicrously simple as to be laughable, and yet, the English were unable to guess at the answer. Rather than think they were dense, they had put to Caleb supernatural powers of evasion.

"Caleb brings much needed supplies to our shores, Captain. Without him many would have not survived this winter past and now, with Colonel Thompson's arrival, his services are needed more than ever."

"Perhaps," Jonathan agreed, "but what of the cargo he returns to Connecticut?"

"Of what do you speak, sir?" she asked feigning innocence, knowing full well what he brought to Connecticut. Was she not one of his main suppliers?

"Would you deny, Mistress, that he often returns home with one or more of the King's Dragoons?"

"I cannot say, sir." And indeed she could not.

He sighed softly. "Did you know I was waylaid and robbed on my way here?"

Merry forced herself to act surprised. "In truth? Was anything of importance taken?"

"Naught but a ring. When the Rebels realized I was a

doctor and could offer Washington no information, I was left on the roadside, tied, until the passing of a guard brought me freedom."

Suddenly, he knew he couldn't bear it if she came to harm, and it was with an audible groan that he turned and pulled her into his arms, holding her tight against him, his hand pressing her face to his chest as he choked out, "Oh, Merry, I'd not see anyone hurt. This war is at its end. All that is left is to sign the peace. What can be gained by endangering one's self?"

Snuggling her cheek to his bare chest, she almost sighed with contentment and had to force her mind back to their conversation. "There be much gained, Captain. As yet, the peace is only a promise. I believe Washington does not trust your colleagues and would keep his eyes and ears open for all information regarding the truth of the intended peace."

Relaxing his hold on her, her head lifted from his chest after much effort on her part, for she wanted anything but to leave his warmth. His large hands framed her face and his thumbs slowly stroked her lips and cheek. "In the meantime, I wonder if it is realized how dangerous these nightly expeditions are becoming? Colonel Thompson rages that they are conducted beneath his nose. I fear greatly for anyone caught relaying messages. Even had she friends in high places, it would not go easy for her."

Merry didn't answer him as she stood beneath his tender regard. What could she say? It was obvious he knew of her involvement. It was useless to deny it and just as useless to promise she'd stop. She could not . . . would not.

"Worry of it no more, Captain. 'Tis not as dangerous

as you suppose, I'm sure." She could say no more. In truth, it was not as dangerous as he believed. When a message was passed, it was done either by pasting it face down into the back of a book, so it appeared to be part of the cover, or it was written with sympathetic ink between the lines of an innocent-looking letter.

Washington, of course, knew of the invisible ink and had the needed developer to bring the message to light. Nay, he needn't have worried, for those in the Culper Spy Ring were not known to take unnecessary chances, and, she added with a touch of arrogance, t'was not that hard to fool these swaggering English.

Chapter Eight

MERRY STOMPED OUT OF THE INN WITH THE OFFICIAL-looking document crumpled tightly in her hand. In her rage, she barely noticed the man who nodded his head and gave her a dazzling smile. As she passed him, he stopped abruptly. Turning on his heels, he began to follow her.

In a few quick strides Jonathan caught up with her and matched his steps to hers. He grinned into golden eyes, sparkling with rage. "Good morning, Mistress. A lovely day, is it not?"

She only snorted for an answer.

"And where might you be heading on this fine morn?"

"Since when must I answer to you on my comings and goings, English?" she snarled.

Oh, God, he groaned silently, what the hell had happened now to ruffle her pretty feathers? Was he never to hear a kind word from her? Each time he had hope to believe she was softening toward him, something else happened.

"Merry, stop a moment. What is the matter?" he commanded.

Merry turned the full force of her anger on him, as she pushed the crumpled document into his face and thundered, "This is the matter, English! One of your commander's lackey's has just now delivered this piece of rot."

Jonathan took the offending paper from her hand. Slowly spreading it open, he read it. Colonel Thompson was giving them two days to vacate the inn, after which it would be torn down and the wood used to build a stable at the fort.

Jonathan's fingers ran through his neatly combed hair in frustration. "Bastard," he muttered.

"My sentiments exactly," she snapped. "I was just now on my way to relay that message in person. So, if you will excuse me, Captain."

Jonathan had not a doubt that she meant every word she said, and his body broke out in a cold sweat as he thought of the consequences her temper could bring.

Merry turned away, but her movements were instantly stilled, as a strong arm came around her waist and lifted her clear of the wooden sidewalk. Ignoring her objections, he retraced their steps and brought her kicking and snarling into the inn.

Once inside he released her before an open-mouthed Mr. Gates and a neighbor, Mr. Bach. "See to it the wench stays here or I'll throttle her with my bare hands!"

"Who do you think you are?" she raged. "You cannot treat me thus. I'll not stand for it!"

Jonathan ignored her rantings and faced her father. "See to it you do as I say. It is of the utmost importance." Turning from a flabbergasted Mr. Gates, he flung over his shoulder, "If need be, tie her up."

A glass that was standing on the bar suddenly smashed against the door, sending splinters flying just as he was about to open it.

Jonathan turned and glared at her, his jaw clenched tightly, his voice barely a whisper as he warned, "Take a care, Mistress, and mind what you are about. I'll brook no further tantrums from you or you'll find yourself pulled across my knee."

Standing with her hands on her hips, she sneered, "If you've a care for your life, English, you'll not touch me again."

Jonathan grinned at her fearless stance and assured her. "The time is not far, Mistress, when I'll not only touch you, but have you begging for me not to stop."

Merry gasped aloud and sent an angry look to the four men, including her father whose laughter suddenly filled the room. Her face turned crimson and she was sorely tempted to send another glass sailing, but resisted the impulse, suddenly fearful lest he put his words into action.

Her sharp tongue lashed out the moment Jonathan left the inn. "Do you find your lives so carefree that you can wile away a morning when there is work to be done? Mr. Bach, does Patience know the smithy stands unattended?"

Mr. Bach, muttering as to the interference of females and why God had seen clear to burden mankind with them, made haste to quit the taproom, while the town's carpenter, a certain Mr. Williams, unwilling to meet Merry's furious gaze, meekly followed close behind.

Merry shot her father a look of rage, as she left him to prepare the noonday meal. But she soon found she was helpless to concentrate on anything but what Jonathan might be about.

Finally, after she had cracked six eggs and added them to a huge pot of coffee, rather than the flour she had prepared for bread, she gave up any hope of working in the kitchen.

Finding herself on the inn's front porch, she paced for nigh on an hour before she saw his horse approach. Jonathan stopped his horse before her. Wordlessly, he dismounted and tied the animal to the hitching post. Merry nearly groaned as he walked slowly toward her. Why did the beast never close his shirt? God, the man moved as gracefully as if he were dancing. Why did that suddenly seem so . . . so . . . she refused to finish the thought. Tearing her gaze from his chest, she searched his face for any sign that would bring relief from this torture.

"Well?" she finally managed.

He only grinned as he stood before her.

"Are you going to stand there grinning all day, or are you going to tell me what you've been about?"

He chuckled softly, readying himself for the rage that was sure to come. "Aye, Mistress, that I shall. But first, I've brought you back a message from Colonel Thompson. He sends his best wishes on our impending wedding."

The silence that followed was ominous, as Merry's quick mind digested his light comment. He had told the Colonel he was marrying her. Apparently, that was all this dim witted physician could think of in order to save the inn. She knew the Colonel would not destroy it if it belonged to one of his officers.

He laughed out loud as he saw her expression of shock change to one of understanding and then to anger. "Have you a kiss for your betrothed, my love?"

"Are you insane?!" she asked, her voice breaking with emotion, sounding strangely like a duck. "You cannot believe I would marry a *Britisher!*"

Merry had no chance to speak again, as he propelled her into the inn so fast, her feet barely touched the floor, past the amazed patrons in the taproom, down the long hall. It was only an instant later that he flung her into the small family sitting room at the rear of the inn and slammed the door shut behind them.

"Will you stop it!" she snapped, as she fought to free herself of his firm and not too gentle hold. "Is this a taste of what your wife can look forward to? Release me, dammit!"

"Shut up, you ungrateful little waif," he growled, as his fury mounted with each word she uttered.

"Who the hell do you think you are talking to? You have no right."

"As your future husband, I have every right."

"Never," she spat. "I'll see your rotting soul in hell before I'd marry a Britisher."

Jonathan, obviously unconcerned at her distress,

gave a humorless smile and a minute nod of his head. "Have you a better thought to dissuade our illustrious commander? What reasonings can you offer to prevent the demolition of your father's inn?" When she remained silent, he added sarcastically, "Perhaps you might relate your high opinion of him. No doubt that would do much to aid your cause."

She waved aside his remark with a flippant motion of her hand. "I would have thought of something. I've no need for your interference."

"Interference is it? Very well, I will let Colonel Thompson know there is no longer a liaison between us and he may continue with his plans at will. He was following me and he's sure to have arrived by now."

She watched as he turned and began walking away from her. Merry's mind raced for a solution. "Wait!" she cried out in sudden desperation. "Wait!"

Slowly he did as she asked and returned to face her. His tone was clearly taunting as he asked, "Have you reconsidered, Mistress?"

Merry swallowed her pride and gritted between clenched teeth, "Perhaps you are right, sir. This may be the only way to save the inn."

Unwilling to give him the chance to gloat, she snarled an instant later, "I know not your reasonings, sir, but you cannot believe, should I accept such a magnanimous offer, that we could live as man and wife once the vows are taken."

"Can I not?" he asked with a humorless grin, his eyes hard and cold, daring her to disagree. "Do you believe I would be satisfied to offer you my protection and receive nothing for my troubles?"

She stomped her foot, "Have I asked for your protection? Did you hear me seek it out?"

He raged, disgusted more at himself than at anything she had said, that he should have allowed her rejection to affect him so thoroughly. His voice was barely above a whisper when he answered, "You sought it, Mistress, whether consciously or nought I cannot say, but indeed you sought it."

Her voice held a note of hysteria, her eyes wild with fright, knowing in her heart there was no way out. She would marry him or lose the inn. Yet, stubbornly, she couldn't find it in her heart to meekly accept this. "I've no wish to marry you. Can I make myself clearer? I can barely stand being in the same room with you."

"Lower your voice, dammit. Would you have our beloved commander hear your mewlings?"

"Mewlings?! Because I would refuse you I'm mewling? Damn your black soul to hell, English." Her lip curled over her teeth in a sneer. "I'll marry you to be sure, but I swear you'll find nary a moment of peace for your offer." She couldn't resist shooting him one more look of contempt.

In an instant his hand was on her arm and she was flung up against the wall. "'Tis too much to expect a thank you from an ignorant Rebel."

Her mouth thinned into a sneering line. "Ask not gratitude of me, English. Were it not for your countrymen's hated presence, this would not be necessary in the first place."

"Aye, Mistress, but you've forgotten. I've no control over the policy of my government, nor of the few who take the power they possess to the extreme. In the end I am only a simple doctor, called by my country into service, and I can claim responsibility for my actions alone."

Merry knew he was right. She was being unfair. Yet she couldn't help the suspicions that raged through her stubborn mind. For too long she had hated. For too long she and all she loved had suffered under the brutal hand of their occupiers, and she could not as yet separate the man from his country.

It had been so simple before he had come—this arrogant beast who flashed appealing smiles, who taunted and teased with devilish looks, who caused her stomach to flutter with a swagger, her ire to flare at the cut of his clothing and her knees to weaken at a remembered kiss.

Why did she have to be so confused? He was English, and that was reason in itself to hate him.

"I've no liking for this, English, and I'd not object if you took back your offer."

"No doubt," he nodded, his mouth grim at her total and complete rejection. What the hell could he do to find favor with this little witch and why the hell should he bother to try? He was sick of the whole thing. Since the moment they had met, she had never spoken a kind word to him and, he continued righteously, he had done nothing to warrant this hatred.

So it was with a good deal of sarcasm that he finally finished with, "Fear not, Mistress. I'll wager you'll soon grow easy with the thought once I have you beneath my sheets."

Her hand curled into a fist and she didn't hesitate to give him a quick, clean punch in the midsection. She nearly smiled her satisfaction, when she heard his sharp expulsion of breath at the surprise attack.

"Should you try to bed me, English, you can expect more of that."

If Merry thought, a bit smugly, that that was the end of the subject, she was quickly dissuaded, as his hands gripped her slender arms in a bone-crushing hold. He gave her a shake hard enough to snap her cap from her head and caused her hair to fall in luxurious waves of shimmering gold past her shoulders to nearly reach her waist. His face was only inches from hers as he growled, "Should you be unwise enough to try that again, I'll not promise to refrain from returning the favor."

Merry gasped at the force of his hold. Her eyes widened with fear as the pressure of his fingers increased, yet a moment later her mouth thinned to a straight, furious line, and she faced him as if she had no concept of fear.

"If you have a care for your life, English bastard, you'll unhand me."

Jonathan chuckled, unable to hold his anger, as this little one fearlessly faced him. "More threats, Merry?"

Both of them knew she was helpless against his superior strength, yet she'd not back off. He almost laughed out loud as she began to fight him. Like a little ruffian, her small, slippered feet kicked at his shins, while her balled hands sought to inflict damage, but were hampered by his hold.

"Gawking ass," she muttered at his unmistakable look of delight. And then groaned in frustration, "You gutless swine," as she soon realized she was causing him no discomfort for her efforts.

His hands still on her upper arms, he pulled her to him, lifting her easily from the floor and holding her so her feet dangled in the air and their faces were level.

"Put me down, you cowardly brute!"

"Oh, Merry," he laughed, his eyes dancing with pure enjoyment, his warm, clean breath causing her a flutter she refused to acknowledge. "The mind boggles with the promise of fiery passion of our first coupling."

Merry gasped at his blunt words. "English swine," she snarled, "I'd not believe it possible to hate so thoroughly."

He laughed and answered simply, "Perhaps," just before his mouth took possession of her own.

The pressure of his mouth brought a gasp of surprise from her and, even though her head was pushed back to the point where she thought her neck might snap, she managed to twist her face to the side and free her mouth from his.

"I hate you," she cried, her voice growing a bit breathless.

Slowly, he lowered her to the floor, his hands sliding up her arms to her throat, his thumb tracing an imaginary line to her jaw, sending unwanted chills down the length of her and finally forcing her head back and up.

"Rebel," he murmured low and huskily as his head lowered to hers; his chest twisted with a desire he wished to God he did not feel, for it left him vulnerable and an easy target for her cruel words. "I've not a doubt as to the truth of your words, yet, were you to complete the thought, you'd no doubt say, 'I hate you, English, but like you, I can barely think for wanting you. Sleep is nonexistent as I suffer through every night aching to feel you at my side. Your smile is my happiness. Your tears my heartache. Your scent my life's breath. Your touch food for my soul. And your kiss, aye, love, your kiss,' he groaned softly, 'that for which I thirst, as a dying man thirsts for water.'"

"Nay," she sighed weakly, refusing to admit she too suffered as he, but unable to deny to herself the impact of his words on her senses.

"Aye," he retorted easily, as his mouth covered hers in a kiss so gentle as to take her breath away.

"Stop," she murmured, as his lips left hers and slid to her ear.

"In time," he promised.

She felt him tremble as he fought a battle of control. He wanted nothing more than to take this woman in his arms, bound up the stairs to his room and press her gently to his bed, keeping her there until they both lay exhausted and replete in each others arms.

"Nay," she groaned again, her voice trembling as his mouth slid to her throat. "Nay," she whimpered unknowingly, her conscious thoughts gone, as his hand left her throat and lowered slowly to her breast cupping it gently.

Her back arched toward him as her knees weakened, and she swayed drunkenly, her body leaning full length against his and causing him to groan.

And when his mouth returned to hers, she forgot her resistance, she forgot her hatred, she forgot her disgust that this man was a Britisher. Her small hands reached up his sides to his partially opened shirt. A soft moan of pleasure was torn from the back of her throat, as her fingers spread through the lustrous, springy hairs that covered his broad chest, and she thought she might swoon with the pleasure of touching him.

Tearing his mouth from hers, his breathing harsh and ragged, he held her close against his shaking form.

"Aye, my love," he crooned tenderly, as his lips pressed gently against the top of her head, breathing in the dizzying lemon scent of her hair. "No matter our loyalties, no matter our beliefs in the right or wrong of this conflict, one fact remains. There is no future for us apart. We were meant to come together and that we shall."

For the moment, Merry found not the strength to offer objections and simply leaned her slight frame against his for support.

From far off she heard her name called. She willed the sound away, wanting nothing more than to be held against the man and to drown in his breathless, sweet kisses.

"I thought I'd find you two here," her father's amused voice spoke from the door.

Merry jumped at the sound and flushed with embarrassment, as Jonathan's arm came familiarly around her waist and held the back of her against him. "It seems to me the week's end would not be too soon for a wedding. Do you not agree?"

Merry only lowered her flaming face, suddenly finding the floor to be the most interesting object in the room.

"Agreed," Jonathan replied, as nonchalant and indifferent as if they were discussing a date for a game of whist.

"I've a need of your help in the kitchen, Merry," her father added. "Rebecca, that little dimwit, is nowhere to be found and the hour fast approaches for the noonday meal."

Chapter Nine

LATER THAT DAY, MUCH TO MERRY'S RELIEF, JONATHAN was called to New York, and the plans for the upcoming wedding were postponed for at least two weeks.

Merry gave one continuous prayer that he never return, and yet, she knew she'd not long keep Colonel Thompson at bay. Unrealistically, she clung to the thin ray of hope that the war might officially end and these hated English would forever leave these shores, before it became necessary to prostitute herself. If not and the Britisher returned . . . She shivered, her whole mind and body crying out in protest at the inevitable outcome.

Oh, God, how could she marry him? She was a Rebel. It went against everything she believed in. Everything she wanted. It was a nightmare!

In the meantime, Mr. Gates cheerfully went about

the preparations for his daughter's wedding feast. Having no love for the English, he nevertheless recognized in his future son-in-law an unmistakable quality of honor and knew instinctively Merry would not suffer under his gentle and firm hand.

Hams and sausages were being collected and stored in the smokehouse at the rear of the inn, while bushels of potatoes and corn were delivered from the Hewlett farm.

Of course, the whole town would attend, and everyone was so hungry for a reason to feast and celebrate, that they eagerly offered to take on a share of the work.

Amelia Poke, the owner of the town's general store, was found more often at the inn than attending to her business. The elderly lady of seventy seemed to grow years younger as she took on the task of her friend's daughter's wedding with a loving hand.

Merry had known Mrs. Poke since she was a baby. She would long remember the happy days of childhood when she would visit the store with her mother. In those days her father would often slip a coin into her chubby hand before the shopping began, and her little mouth would water at the promise of the bag of horehound candies the penny would buy.

Oh, God, how she missed those days when there were no shortages of life's simple pleasures, when monsters did not occupy and presume to tell a person how they might live.

Merry, in a black mood, walked aimlessly along the beach, her thoughts never straying far from the problem at hand. In the distance she could see a wagon delivering rum and ale. A few of the townspeople had come to assist the driver, and even from here their jovial laughter was clear, as they strained their backs to bring the kegs inside the inn.

Merry groaned at the happiness that surrounded her. Even Nettie, who should have known better, joined in the festivities by proudly displaying, with a sweetness all her own, the wedding nightdress she was embroidering. Merry had shown just the right amount of delicate shyness upon viewing the garment, but in private she could only roll her eyes skyward at the useless nightdress. She was positive the lusty beast would allow her to wear it but a moment before his insistent fingers raised the thin cambric material over her head.

At those moments, when she thought of what might happen between them, she seemed almost eager to see the end of this waiting. Her palms would grow damp, her breasts tender to the touch of her clothes, while a tightness began to form across her abdomen.

Disgusted with her shameful thoughts, she decided it was long past the time for the nightly raids to begin again. All had been quiet for these past weeks and the English were growing lazy and confident that all was under their control. A smile spread across her full lips, the first real smile she had shown since this mess had come about.

She and her group would take these arrogant beasts down a peg and there was no time like the present to begin.

Merry felt at home astride her horse. The leather saddle felt as comfortable as a chair. She listened with delight to the silence of the dark night. The quiet chirping of the crickets accompanied by an occasional croaking frog belied the danger that lurked in the night.

Excitement bubbled within her and she breathed in great gulps of salty air, as they waited in the brush along the side of the road.

It was after midnight and the moon's glow lent more than enough light to the dirt road to allow her to see anyone else who traveled it. Washington had sent word through Culper Sr. that he needed to know the number of men stationed at the fort and the gun implacements therein.

Were she or any of the townsfolk allowed to enter the fort, it would, of course, be a simple matter to convey the information to the General. As it was, Colonel Thompson distrusted and hated the people of Huntington, a feeling reciprocated at nearly every instance, and did everything within his power to bring them suffering. She had no doubt that, were it not for her impending marriage to one of his officers, she'd not be allowed the amount of food so suddenly available for the celebration, nor would the townsfolk see the relaxation of the many rules as the preparations were made.

No matter, she reasoned silently. It was no great task to waylay a soldier or two and send him on his way to Washington in Connecticut via Caleb Brewster. By the time the soldier arrived, due to Caleb's none too gentle persuasion, he was usually more than happy to comply with his captors and offer any and all information they might seek.

The sound of a lone rider coming at a steady pace snapped her from her reverie and she became instantly alert. Soundlessly, she showed her companions to ready themselves by the simple prearranged signal of her hands. Quietly, they placed themselves amid the thick bushes and trees that bordered the road, exactly as she had ordered, and waited poised for her signal to attack.

A moment later he came into sight. Even in the moonlight she knew him instantly. Tonight he wore a dark jacket and matching trousers, white shirt and knee-high leather boots. She watched as his body moved in rhythm with his mount, his knees pressed to the horse, his long fingers holding the reins. How did one so large appear so graceful? A quick shake of her head prevented the men from stopping him. She felt more than a little surprised at the sudden thundering of her heart.

It was only the surprise at seeing him so soon, she reasoned. He wasn't due back for another week. He had startled her, was all. Nothing more!

His horse, evidently sensing the other animals close by, skittered sharply and pranced sideways, snorting a high-pitched whinnying sound, and she breathed a thankful sigh that everyone had grasped their own horses' jaws and stopped them from answering in kind.

He was talking to the horse, his voice low and deep, but far enough away that she could not distinguish his words. Her breath caught in her throat and she watched as if spellbound how his hands came to caress the animal's neck.

In an instant she was imagining those hands touching her, setting her skin aflame, leaving her weak and trembling in his arms.

What is the matter with me? She looked around, not sure if she had spoken out loud. Apparently she hadn't, for no one had moved or turned to look at her. She breathed a long, deep sigh of relief as she watched him ride out of sight.

She almost groaned out loud as she realized that he'd be at the inn tonight when she returned. She'd have to be quiet as she passed his door. She shivered, imagining him sleeping below her room. What did he wear when he slept? Oh, God, stop it, she cried silently. Stop it now and put your mind to your work. Your life could depend on it.

She almost laughed, so relieved was she to hear the sound of at least two horses coming toward them. They approached from the direction of the inn and, from the sound of their loud laughter, the men were deep in their cups. Merry beamed. This was going to be easier than she thought. These beggars would find themselves aboard Caleb's whaleboat and heading for Connecticut before their hangovers began. And on the morrow, George's Dragoons would be minus a few of their elite.

As always, adrenaline shot through her and her heart pounded furiously. Her senses came alive to the sounds of their voices and the steady clopping of their horses hooves.

She and her four comrades waited silently. At last the soldiers came into view. There were four of them. Usually, she did not attempt to stop so many at one time, but, judging by their condition and the element of surprise that was in her favor, she guessed in this case there was little danger.

But Merry had not taken into account the false bravery that a few drinks can sometimes incur.

At exactly the right moment she gave the signal, and the anxious group of rebels bolted from the brush, guns drawn and aimed with deadly accuracy. In the past riders had tried to flee or reach for their own pistols, but were instantly brought up short in their attempts. Tonight, however, the four English riders were far past the point of common sense and, hampered by an exorbitant degree of alcohol consumed, each thought with drunken confidence that he could handle any and all situations.

So it was when their horses were brought up short, and loaded and cocked pistols were aimed in their direction, each of the four registered no alarm. One of them pulled at his reins with slow, easy pressure, fully expecting he had moved fast enough to escape these ruffians, and he uttered an oath of surprise to find himself knocked on the head and choking on the dust disturbed by his fall.

Each of the remaining three, watching in something of a daze, saw what they took to be the unnecessary abuse of their comrade, and reached in unison for their pistols. Merry wanted to laugh at the ridiculously slow actions, but soon found her smile turned into a gasp of horror, for none of the three listened to the sharp order to desist.

Three of her allies opened fire as the soldiers' guns came into view. Two of the men gaped in silent, openmouthed surprise at the dark holes that suddenly marred the crisp whiteness of their shirt fronts. Their horses reared up on their hind legs, and a hoof hit one of her men and knocked him out of his saddle, while the third Britisher, under the protection of the rearing horses, took aim and fired his gun.

The shout of the blast stunned Merry, and she watched with horror as one of her fellow Rebels clutched at his arm and swayed dangerously in his saddle. An instant later, the soldier was laid low by her men and all four were sprawled upon the dirt road.

Merry hissed a long, low round of curses at her own foolishness to think this would be an easy job. She should have known better than to think these beasts would react as she supposed. Coming quickly to her senses, she snapped out orders to dispose of the two dead officers, for they dared not allow word of this escapade to reach Colonel Thompson's ears, lest all of Huntington suffer.

The bullet in Jeremy's arm had caused little damage, and by the time the remaining two Britishers were securely tied and shallow graves dug, the bleeding had stopped. They worked quickly, as the hour fast approached for the meeting with Caleb.

Their horses would be sent east to Mastic Beach and given to the Rebel forces that headquartered there. Once all was done, Merry motioned to Samuel Hanes to help her bring Jeremy back to the inn. Jeremy argued he was all right, but she knew his arm was in need of care.

In the oak floor of the taproom was a trapdoor that lead to the wine cellar. The damp, cool cellar was perfect for the storage of kegs of ale. Beyond the cellar stood another room entered only by the movement of two bricks that triggered a hidden spring which opened a doorway in the wall.

It was far into the night before Merry and her two comrades stabled their horses at the rear of the inn and silently entered the dark establishment. Soundlessly, the two men entered the cellar, while Merry made haste to reach her room.

No sooner had the door closed behind her than she was tearing the boy's clothing from her body. In a flash she pulled her dress over her head and smoothed it at her rounded hips. She was still buttoning the bodice as she left the room. She had to help Jeremy and knew of no one to go to but the Englisher. The town had long ago lost its doctor, as he had joined the Rebel forces early in the war and had yet to return.

Her hair unbound, she silently descended the few steps to the second floor. Gasping for air, suddenly nervous, her hand shook as she turned the doorknob. Would he help? She had no alternative but to go to him, lest the bullet remain in Jeremy's arm indefinitely. She turned the knob again as she closed the door, wishing for no sound to disturb the men who slept next door.

The room was dark but for the moonlight that entered his opened window and she could easily make out his form. Soundlessly, she moved to the side of the bed. He was asleep, his sheet pushed low on his hips, his naked chest, rising and falling in even rhythm, showed dark against the white sheets.

She leaned down and gently touched his shoulder, "English, wake up."

Jonathan opened his eyes and was instantly aware of the woman who stood above him. He had been dreaming of her and it was as if his dreams had been answered. She was here.

Merry never realized how her words might sound to him when she whispered, "I've a need of you this night."

"Oh Merry, my God, I thought I'd never hear you

say those words," he groaned as his arm reached up and pulled her startled form over him.

It was only the mattress that prevented her cry of surprise from reaching all in the house as she landed on her face. She tried to lift herself, but his arms were around her pushing her legs so that she suddenly lay next to him.

"Wait!" she cried, softly pressing her hands to his naked chest. She tried to tell him what she was about, but his low rumbling, "Nay," against her lips, prevented her from continuing.

"You don't understand," she gasped, as his lips moved to caress her cheek and the hollow beneath her ear. "I understand this," he breathed against her lips and then laughed as he heard her moan when his warm hands covered her breasts. How, she wondered fleetingly, had he opened her buttons so quickly. He had touched her before, but never had he caressed her bare flesh in this way, and the sweet sensations running through her were overpowering.

She tried to think. This was not why she had come to him. "Wait," she tried again, but her voice was somewhat less insistent. "Oh God, wait," she whimpered, as his mouth left her ear and slid closer . . . closer to her exposed breasts. He was going to kiss her there. She was sure of it and was just as sure that it would be wonderful. His breathing increased to shuddering gasps. Her softly murmured, "Nay," was barely choked out, as his mouth formed a burning path to the tip of her breast. His mouth worked over the softness of her flesh, kissing and licking until she arched her back, hungry to feel his mouth cover the tip.

She gave a soft sigh of relief as he finally filled his mouth with her. His hands caressed with a feather-light touch, while his mouth sucked until the nipple rose to a hard bud between his teeth. He slid his tongue to the valley between her breasts and then up the next mound of soft, beckoning flesh.

Merry felt her stomach tighten to a painful knot, and she groaned softly in protest as his mouth left her breast and returned to hover over her mouth. His tongue darted with quick, sharp jabs between her parted lips, and her head lifted from the pillow, eager to feel the hard pressure of his lips on her own again.

Jonathan groaned softly into her opened mouth. God, how long he had dreamed of this. How long he had wanted her. He couldn't believe she had come to him at last.

His hand reached under her dress and slid up her naked leg. He gave a soft gasp, tearing his lips from hers, his eyes wide with wonder and joy, as his trembling hand moved up the length of her.

She was naked beneath her dress and the knowledge brought him to the brink of explosion. "Oh God, Merry," he groaned into her neck, as his hand roamed freely over the taut flesh of her stomach and around her one smooth hip to the fleshy mound of her derriere and down again. "I've longed so for this."

His hand slipped down her legs and prodded them apart. Slowly, enticingly slowly, he moved up her leg and found the warm junction of her thighs. Merry groaned and clung to him, dazed with the urgency that suddenly filled her.

His fingers explored her warmth, as the knowledge of what he discovered filled him with a happiness that held no bounds. He pulled away with a smile of delight spreading across his mouth. "You are a virgin, Merry," he breathed against her lips. "My God, I didn't dare to hope," he continued, just before his mouth closed over hers again with something that closely resembled reverence.

It took a full minute before his words penetrated Merry's dazed mind and she felt herself stiffen in his arms. Why should he think she was not a virgin? Why did he show such surprise? Had she ever behaved any less than befitted a lady? T'was the arrogant English mind that assumed nothing good could be had in anyone who did not claim George for a king.

"Arrogant bastard," she raged, as she pushed him from her and rolled quickly to her feet. Gasping for breath, she clutched the bodice of her dress to protect herself from his penetrating gaze. Her voice shook as she whispered a low sneer, "Be it so important, English, for you to be the first?"

Jonathan was momentarily dumbfounded and unable to respond to her question. What had he said to make her angry? He could not remember. Had he spoken his thoughts aloud? He must have mentioned his happiness that she was a virgin. Why should that cause her such fury?

"Is it?" she righteously insisted.

"Merry, I don't understand. Why should it cause you such anger that I find your innocence delightful?"

"Nay, English, 'tis not your delight I find disgusting, 'tis your surprise that it should be so. Do you believe that only English ladies value chastity?"

"Merry, please listen," he implored, as he pushed aside the sheet and came to his feet, "you've misunderstood. Perhaps I sounded surprised, but I swear it was happiness you heard not shock."

"Why?" she insisted, her voice quivering, as she watched him close the distance between them. "Why should it be of such importance?"

"Ah, my love," he sighed, as his arms closed around her and pulled her to his naked form. His large hand pressed her head to his warm chest as he spoke. "You've much to learn of the ways of men. I compare you to no one, for as God is my judge, there'd be no other, be she English or not, who could come near you."

His hands ran through her hair and he brought a long golden lock to his face and breathed in the clean lemon scent. His thumb caressed the delicate line of her jaw as he held her face and refused to release her gaze. He continued in a husky voice filled with emotion, "Merry, can you not see how much you mean to me? My God, I've such a desperate need to touch you, I'm in torture at our every meeting. Even in my sleep I find no reprieve, for I dream of you nightly. I want you with me always. Can there be any other reason for me to want to be the first, than the simple fact that you know no other man?"

"'Tis pride of possession then," she murmured softly.

He sighed as he pressed his face into her hair. "Perhaps, my love, but it is beyond my power to change the way I feel." He waited a long moment before he dared to ask, "Are you still angered?"

"Nay," she breathed as she nestled her face to his chest.

"Will you come back to bed with me?"

Merry suddenly remembered and gasped, "Oh, my God! I forgot! A man has been injured and I came to get your help."

"What?" he asked. His amazement couldn't have been greater, as he turned from her and grabbed his pants. "Why did you not tell me sooner?"

"You gave me no chance," she answered demurely, her eyes lowered, her voice no more than a whisper as she remembered these last moments.

Jonathan gave a low chuckle. "My pardon, Mistress. I am unused to lovely ladies visiting my room in the wee hours of the night. And I fear I forgot to inquire why I awoke to find you leaning over me."

Merry, her face flaming at his gentle teasing, gave silent thanks for the dark room.

Grabbing a shirt and his bag, he motioned toward the door. "Where is he?"

"Follow me," she answered as she led the way.

If Jonathan was surprised when she led him to the taproom and opened the trapdoor to the cellar, he showed not a sign of it. Preceding her down the steps, he waited at the bottom for her to join him.

Where the hell is she going, he thought as he watched her walk to a solid wall and press two bricks down. Amazingly, a doorway appeared in the wall and she entered. Jonathan, bending low to fit his tall frame, followed.

His look of amazement was obvious, as he entered the room and saw an injured man lying upon a long, rough table. There was another with him, who quickly checked the scarf that covered the lower half of his face.

"What took you so long?" Samuel Hanes growled

low, so the English doctor might not recognize his voice as the town's miller.

Merry's cheeks burned, and she lowered her head as Jonathan lied. "It took her some time to wake me. I've been riding most of the day."

Merry stood opposite Jonathan with Jeremy lying between them. After a quick look at the man's injury, he raised his head and glared at her. "This man's been shot!"

"Aye," she acknowledged with a quick nod of her head.

"Goddammit, Merry!" he raged. "Were you involved in this?"

"It matters not how you rage, English," she spat back, her brows lifted in disdain that he should dare to question her. "The man is in need of your help. Do what you must."

Jonathan gritted his teeth, his face flushing with rage as he imagined her in a gun battle. "We shall speak of this later, Mistress," he promised, his voice cold with suppressed fury.

The blood on Jeremy's shirt had dried to a dark brown stain, and his arm was stiff and aching, as Merry assisted Jonathan in cutting off his sleeve.

From his bag he took a large pair of tweezers and probed the wound. Merry felt herself grow light-headed, as the steel instrument was pushed beneath the surface of Jeremy's arm. When it began to bleed again, she gave a soft moan.

Her knuckles were white where she clutched the table. Jonathan raised his eyes to her face. It was obvious the lady was suffering, yet she did not walk away. Instinctively, he knew it would be less than useless should he order her to sit, nor could he stop long enough to try to gently convince her. Having no wish to see her sprawled upon the floor in a dead faint, he forced his voice to harden with a great deal of sarcasm, "'Tis true then, Mistress. You can shoot them easily enough, but seeing the destruction you've caused abuses your delicate sensitivity."

Merry's head snapped up and she glared into his cool gaze as she snarled contemptuously. "'Tis your presence above all else that abuses a lady's sensitivity."

Jonathan chuckled as he saw her color return in an angry flush, while Jeremy's head twisted from left to right as he watched the two combatants in silent amazement.

"'Tis naught but a lover's spat, friend," Jonathan remarked to the puzzled patient. "Do you suppose a hearty kiss would soothe her temper?"

Now the three men, much to Merry's chagrin, joined together in teasing laughter. Was no one immune to the man's charm? Shooting each in turn a deadly glare, she managed to stifle their laughter.

A few moments later, a round steel ball was extracted from Jeremy's arm. The wound was tightly bandaged and Jonathan ordered the standing man to see his friend home.

Merry purposely stayed behind, as Jonathan helped Samuel bring Jeremy to the taproom and out of the inn. She waited, busying herself by cleaning up the bloodstains, having no wish to face him this night. Too much had happened between them and she refused to question her reaction to him. It meant nothing but that she enjoyed his touch. He was nothing to her, nor could he ever be. It mattered not in the end, she mused in silent conversation. He was a Britisher and that fact could not be altered.

With a weary sigh, Merry left the cellar and entered the taproom. All was dark and silent. Tired now, she forced herself up the steps to her room. She hesitated as she passed his door, and breathed a sigh of relief at the silence therein, before going on.

Chapter Ten

SHE SAW HIM IN THE SHADOWS AS SHE MOUNTED THE LAST few steps. He was sitting against the wall, his head resting on his arms. She prayed he might have fallen asleep and that she would be allowed to enter her room with no confrontation. But such was not to be, for no sooner did her hand touch the doorknob than she heard him stir behind her.

"Merry," came the husky, low sound out of the dark.

"Be gone, English," she breathed, leaning her head weakly against the door, having no mind to face him now.

His voice came from above her now as he silently stood, "We are going to talk. I've not a care whether we do it here or in your room. The choice is up to you."

"Lower your voice, English!" she snapped. "Would you have the whole house upon us?" And when she realized he was not about to give up, she sighed wearily as she opened her door, "Very well, come in."

Merry lit a candle in the far corner of her room and placed it on the small, round table that separated a rocking chair from a larger comfortable armchair. Picking up her earlier discarded clothes, she flung them into a corner and turned to glare at him. "What is of such importance that it could not wait till the morn?"

"I want to know what you were about tonight?"

She gave a short shrug and a quick shake of her head. "'Tis none of your concern."

"Woman, a man was shot! Tell me now there is no danger in what you do."

"T'was an accident, is all. It will not happen again."

"Your damned right it won't happen again. There'll be no more nightly raids. Do you hear me?"

Merry couldn't control the rage she felt that this man should presume to tell her what she may or may not do. Controlling her urge to strike him quite admirably, she gave him a cold smile, "Indeed I hear you, sir, for I have yet to lose the use of that sense."

"Well?" he questioned, insisting on hearing her agreement to his demands.

"Well?" she mimicked in return and watched with glee as his lips thinned in anger.

"Have a care, Merry, lest you push me beyond my limit," he warned softly.

"Am I to cower in fear at your lordly manner, sir?" she asked, her voice dripping sarcasm. "I know not the usual reaction to your threats. 'Tis best, I think, if you tell me how you wish me to act."

He sighed with disgust, "Mistress, you are easily the

most stubborn woman in these colonies and I curse the day fate brought us together."

"Ah, sir, at last we can agree."

Ignoring her statement, he reiterated, "Are you going to give me your word these nightly jaunts will end?"

"The only thing I'd give you, English, is the tip of my boot."

Jonathan, despite his anger, chuckled at her fearless words. His eyes gleamed with humor, his fingers tucked into his waistband as his feet spread in a casual stance. A taunting smile curved his lips as he asked, "Would you?"

"Try me, English," she sneered, all caution gone in the face of his unbearable arrogance.

"Perhaps I'll take that challange, Mistress. It would, I think, be an unforgettable experience." Stepping closer, his arm suddenly snaked about her waist and he pulled her to him.

Merry gasped at the sudden movement, while her fisted hand came, with no little force, smashing into his cheek.

"Why, you little vixen," he snapped, as he grasped at her flaying hands.

Merry felt a beam of pride as she got in two more punches before he pinned her hands to her back. She bared her teeth and reached up on her toes, hoping to inflict more pain and force him to release her.

"Bite me Merry and you'll find it painful indeed to sit for these next few days," he vowed. "I've yet to hit a woman, but I've noticed you've no aversion to violence."

Her lip curled in a snarl of hatred, "Release my

hands, English, and I'll show you just how averse to violence I be."

Jonathan was not unaffected by the close contact of this woman and cursed himself soundly for the unwanted stirrings he felt in his loins. How was it, no matter how angry he became, she could still cause him to want her? And God, how he wanted her!

He pulled her tighter against him. His hand went roughly to her hair and pulled it so her head tipped back and her eyes smarted with unshed tears.

Denying his closeness was the cause of the fluttering she felt in her stomach, she seethed fearlessly, "I hate you. No matter what you do, you can never change that fact."

"Mistress," he growled, just before his mouth closed over hers in a hard, punishing kiss, "I've come to wonder whether I would want you quite so badly any other way."

Tears blurred her vision and she tasted blood in her mouth, as the brutal kiss came to an end. A low sob tore at the back of her throat, as she felt him swoop her into his arms and suddenly fling her on her bed. He was furious; his body fairly shook with rage and Merry couldn't control her own cry of anger.

His dark form loomed menacingly above her, his voice ragged as he growled, "You've no need to fear me, Mistress."

"Fear you, English?" she cried coming to her knees. "I'd wager I'd see you in hell first."

Ignoring her interruption, he continued, "When I take a woman, I do it for her pleasure, as well as my own. Right now the thought of taking you is as tempting as contracting the pox," he lied and gave silent thanks that his voice did not tremble with the desire that flooded his being.

He gave her a long, cold look just before he turned and left her, closing the door softly behind his departing figure.

Merry didn't know why she cried. She should feel nothing but relief that the beast didn't want her. Why then did she burst into tears at the slightest provocation? For the past three nights she had cried herself to sleep. What the hell was the matter with her? Today had been the worst yet! She and Mrs. Poke were in the kitchen preparing the potato salad for the next day's wedding festivities. Mrs. Poke was reliving the romantic details of her courtship, more than fifty years past.

"Ah, yes, Mr. Poke was quite a gentleman. He quite literally took my breath away in those days, and I've never had a moment since that I haven't thanked the good Lord for sending him to me."

She brushed a tear away as she continued, "It's been nigh on fifteen years since he passed away and never a moment since that I haven't wanted him back."

Merry couldn't stand it. This lady had married the man she loved and she had been happy for the remainder of their life together. Even now, left with only her memories, she was quite content.

What did Merry have to look forward to? A forced marriage to a man she hated? Untold years of torture living with him, or perhaps he would leave her once the English were ordered home.

A sob tore from her throat and the old lady's head jerked up with surprise at the heart-wrenching sound. "Dear me, little Merry. Have I said something to upset you? Why are you crying? Tomorrow is your wedding day. You should be the happiest girl alive. 'Tis no doubt your handsome beau loves you dearly."

The old woman was totally confused, as her words seemed to bring on a torrent of fresh tears. Merry couldn't remember a time when she had cried so bitterly. If only . . . if only . . . she couldn't finish the thought, for she knew not what she wanted.

"I'm all right, Mrs. Poke," she choked out between hiccupping sobs, "I've not a clue as to why I keep crying."

"Listen to me, dear, I know well enough. You're nervous and perhaps a bit frightened. I promise you your wedding night poses little threat. Your man will surely be gentle with you."

Merry smiled at the old lady's words of reassurance and fervently wished that was the total of her problem.

Merry turned on her side and lay still, alert to the sounds of activity in the kitchen. Oh, God, she groaned softly, how could she get through this?

She had a sudden urge to run. But to where? She breathed a soft sigh as she realized her running would accomplish nothing. If she didn't marry him, her father would lose the inn. And no matter her arrogant assumption that worse things could befall them, she knew they'd be homeless and hungry, depending upon handouts of others to survive. Her father's pride could not withstand such a trauma.

Finally, she threw off the sheet and came to her feet. How did you let this happen to you, Merry, she asked herself as she studied her face in the small mirror above her dry sink. How can you let him affect you so, to sway your moods, to cause you to cry over anything and everything? You, who never cried, have suddenly turned into a spout of water.

She groaned with disgust. All right, she mused. Perhaps you have no option at the moment, but you'll not allow yourself to become some sniveling, weak female. Nay, Mistress Gates, you have more to you than that!

Today is your wedding day, Merry. Let him not think you so cowardly that you will not face him and answer his arrogance in kind. You'll show a weakness toward no man.

She smiled in truth now. "Nay, Merry, you'll not cower before him," she promised, as she felt herself grow in strength. "He'll get more than he bargained for here."

There was a soft knock at her door and she called out for Becky to enter with more cheerfulness than she had felt in days.

Merry stood beside her father, her hand resting lightly on his arm. Her eyes were on the man who stood at the Reverend Bower's side.

She heard little of the ceremony. Suddenly, her father was gone. As she stood beside Jonathan, she tried to listen to the words the parson spoke, but nothing seemed to register upon her dazed mind.

Jonathan smiled, as he took her icy hand and slipped a ring upon it. She looked down at the heavy weight to see the widest gold band possible, stretching almost to her knuckle, and heavily encrusted with rubies.

Her eyes grew huge with surprise. How had he gotten it? On his trip to New York, of course, she immediately reasoned. It was beautiful, but why should he have taken such care to purchase something so lovely? What was it he felt for her?

It was her turn now to give a ring. With a devious smile, she took the ring Nettie offered and slid it on his finger. It was the very ring she had taken from him at their first meeting.

At his tender chuckle, she raised eyes feigned with innocence to his knowing gaze.

A moment later the minister announced they were man and wife and Jonathan was taking her stiff form into his arms. Before his mouth covered hers, he smiled and whispered low, "I admire your taste in rings, Madam."

"And I yours," she answered brightly.

Due to the destruction of the church, the wedding feast, like the wedding itself, was held outside. Merry sat with Jonathan at her side at a long table and surveyed the gaiety. Surely there was not one of the townsfolk or regiment missing. Dozens of tables laden with enormous amounts of food dotted the area behind the inn. A man was playing a fiddle, another a guitar and many were dancing.

"You look lovely today, Madam," Jonathan ventured smoothly, as he leaned his mouth close to her ear. And in truth she did. Her mother's cream-colored lace veil covered a maze of golden curls piled high on her head and fell over her shoulders to her waist. Her dress, the very one Mrs. Poke had worn on her wedding day, had lost none of its loveliness over the years and, although it had to be altered considerably, still shimmered with gold thread entwined in a fabric of pure gold silk.

Merry allowed her gaze to rest upon his person and it was impossible not to return the compliment, as she took in his dark hair glistening with health in the strong sunlight. His tanned face was made to appear more so by the sharp contrast of a brilliantly white cravat tied expertly at his throat. She could find naught to complain of in regards to his black jacket and pants and her admiring gaze left little doubt as to her appreciation.

"How is it, Captain, over these past months, I have yet to see you in uniform?"

"Would you prefer it Madam? Should I don the red coat you feel such hatred for?"

"Nay," she responded quickly, and she couldn't prevent the touch of disgust she felt from entering her voice. For no matter how she tried, these redcoats were her enemies and she could think of them in no other light.

Giving him a rueful glance, she remarked, "At least you've managed to keep your shirt closed today."

He laughed and lifted a dark brow, while shooting her a teasing leer, "Has my opened shirt caused you distress, Madam?"

Her eyes grew huge as she forced herself to face him and swear innocence, "And, pray tell, why should your shirt, opened or closed, cause me distress?"

Jonathan only chuckled at her denial, knowing full well she lied. She could deny it from now until forever, but he'd seen the hunger in her golden gaze.

He knew from their few encounters that she possessed a passion that easily matched his own. He would not push her further. The time had come for her to admit her need for him. He'd take no less than total surrender and it had to be she who initiated this coming together.

He had every right to take her tonight, but he would not. Nay, he would wait for her move and he knew he wouldn't be disappointed in the end.

Never before had he waited for a woman as he had for her. She was his now, his to love and cherish forever. His body cried out with the pain of his desire, but he'd not allow her to know of his suffering. And with any luck his waiting was nearing its end.

As dusk settled over the festivities, the party grew loud and boisterous, as many with stomachs pleasantly full grew deeper in their cups. Merry soon became the brunt of much friendly teasing and, as their voices grew louder with each drink taken, the advice offered to Jonathan became increasingly lurid.

Jonathan's arm came familiarly around her waist, and he held her close to his side as they spoke to Nettie and Jeremiah. From the corner of her eye, she saw Caleb Brewster approach. Beyond the hulking man was the small, plump form of his Annie.

The area teamed with soldiers. Colonel Thompson would be absolutely livid should he be found here. Why did he chance coming?

Jonathan felt her stiffen at his side and turned an inquiring eye in her direction. But when the big man swooped her from his arms and spun her about in a joyful greeting, while planting a lusty kiss on her startled mouth, it was all he could do not to rip into him and lay the giant low.

A small lady was attempting to bestow her well wishes by the time Jonathan managed to excuse himself from Nettie and Jeremiah and join his wife.

Jonathan caught Merry's words as he silently approached, "Oh, Annie, why did you let him come?"

"Merry, you know nothing could have kept him away. Besides . . ." she stopped when she noticed Jonathan. "Will you not introduce us to your husband, Merry?"

Merry turned to find Jonathan behind her. His hands came to rest possessively on her waist. But the introductions were unnecessary, as Jonathan suddenly realized who they were.

Extending his hand, he smiled his greeting. "Have I the honor of meeting Caleb Brewster and his Annie, at long last?"

"That you have, sir," Caleb boasted proudly, as he too offered his hand. "Although I'd not be pleased should others hereabout know of my presence."

Jonathan grinned at the swaggering young man. His reputation for fearlessness had preceded him and his appearance had not put to shame his audacity. In the midst of a regiment of the King's Dragoons, he calmly made his appearance and dared any to recognize him.

Soon after, Caleb swooped Merry off to join the dancers. Alone with the happy giant, Merry berated him for his foolishness.

"Naught will come of it, Madam Townsend, for I am here and no one the wiser."

"My husband realized who you were," she insisted.

"I think the average Britisher has not the intelligence of your husband," he answered. "How is it you married one of them, Merry? I could not believe it when your father sent word."

Merry could not bring herself to admit this marriage was forced upon her. She shrugged her shoulder and answered lightly, "'Tis not always possible to direct one's heart, Caleb."

"But a Britisher!"

Merry laughed, "Aye, but he is not the usual. Once you get to know him, I'll wager you'll agree. I've yet to find a soul who dislikes him," she admitted begrudgingly, "no matter what side they fight for."

Merry soon returned to her husband's side and Caleb and Annie blended into the crowd of merrymakers.

Finding themselves alone for a moment, Jonathan urged Merry from the lively crowd to the dark, deserted beach. In companionable silence, they walked some distance along the shore. The moonlight bathed them in a glow of silver light, while a warm breeze drifted over the calm water to caress their bodies and soothe their frazzled nerves.

"'Tis nearly October, yet the weather belies the month," she sighed, as they stopped to gaze out over the smooth surface of the Sound.

"Aye," Jonathan agreed, "'tis a lovely place, this country of yours. I've found naught to dislike. One could almost wish to stay forever."

"Will you not?" Merry asked, as she lifted her gaze to his, unable to resist, knowing she must hear his intentions. "Others of your country have made this land their home."

"Aye 'tis the truth, Merry, and I will always feel a tenderness for this place, but 'tis not possible for me to stay. Nay, the time soon approaches when I must return to England."

She nodded slowly, her shoulders slumped with resignation, as she turned away, blinking back the tears that threatened. What was the matter with her? Good

God. First she wanted him, then she didn't. You were nearly crazed when you realized you'd be forced to marry him and now, knowing that he plans to leave brings you sorrow. What is it you want? "Shall we divorce before or after you return to England?"

Jonathan was taken aback. What the hell was she thinking? "Divorce?" he asked in amazement. "I doubt there be many thinking of divorce on their wedding day, Merry."

"Surely, you'll not wish to remain married while you live in England and I here?" she reasoned, the idea of leaving her home never entering her thoughts.

Jonathan laughed. She thought he was going home without her. What a little spitfire he had married. God, how he loved her. Wisely, he decided not to dissuade her of her erroneous thoughts. 'Tis best, he reasoned silently, that she not be told as yet that she would leave with him.

"Let us speak of more pleasant matters on this beautiful night, Madam," he answered, as he turned her and guided her into the warm circle of his arms. "In truth, I have yet to see a lovelier bride," he whispered into her hair, "and I'd be remiss indeed were I to allow this moment to pass without the pleasure of tasting the gentleness of your kiss."

His long finger lifted her chin and their eyes met in the clear night. Merry felt saddened beyond belief. He was going to leave her. He preferred his homeland to her and there was nothing she could do about it. She sighed softly. Or was there? Could she persuade him to stay? Could she convince him to adopt this country as his own? She wondered as the idea took hold, and she finally realized just what it was that she wanted.

Merry never realized how clearly her thoughts were betrayed in her eyes and, as she came to a decision to keep him at her side, Jonathan nearly laughed out loud, anxious indeed to see what lurked behind the sudden sparkle in her golden gaze.

Later, they accepted the well wishes from the crowd and made their escape to her room. Jonathan led the way up the stairs and closed the door as she followed him inside.

Suddenly unable to think of anything to say, she stood in the dark room and watched as he made himself at home. Lighting a candle at the far end of the room, he took off his jacket and flung it upon the rocker. Sitting in the large, comfortable armchair, he pulled off his boots and stretched his long legs out before him.

As he began to unbutton his shirt, he nodded toward the table and asked, "Would you care for a glass of brandy, Merry? I believe 'tis usual for the bride and groom to share a toast on their wedding night."

Merry looked to the table and noticed a bottle aside two brandy snifters.

"I've yet to taste the brew, sir," she smiled, as she watched his fingers finish with the task and pull his shirt free of his pants.

Jonathan smiled, as he managed to open the bottle and pour a small amount into the glasses. "Then sip it slowly, my love. 'Tis a nectar to be savored. Its nutty taste is most pleasing to the palate."

Merry sipped at the strong amber liquid and smiled her appreciation.

"Is it to your liking, Merry?"

Her eyes were upon his open shirt, her gaze devouring the naked chest that was almost close enough to touch, and when she answered, it wasn't the brandy of which she spoke, "Aye."

"Shall I help you with your dress, Merry?" he asked.

"Aye." She turned her back so he might reach the small buttons that secured the gown.

Jonathan's fingers worked quickly and Merry's wedding dress soon fell from her shoulders. His hands were warm at her neck, sliding to her shoulders, pushing the dress from her.

A moment later, her chemise followed and she stood in only her under garments. Her corset had pushed her breasts high and the removal of her chemise left them bare.

"Would you have me finish?" he asked, his voice growing lower and more ragged.

"Please," she whispered, feeling shy at the thought of standing before him naked, yet knowing the truth of her need to do just that.

His hands reached for the pins in her hair and it soon fell in soft, heavy waves over her shoulders and back. "In truth, 'tis the loveliest sight on earth," he sighed, as his hands greedily clutched at the soft tresses and held its sweetness to his face. Pushing her hair aside, he slid short, tantalizing kisses at the base of her neck to her shoulder. Her eyes closed and she gave a soft moan, as she leaned back, savoring every touch of his mouth.

From over her shoulder, his gaze fell upon her bared breasts, and he couldn't control his sharp intake of breath and the sudden shaking that seemed to wrack his body. He turned her in his arms, his gaze hungrily sweeping over her as he choked out, "Oh, God, I lied, for this beauty easily surpasses all else."

His hands were behind her, untying the corset, and when it fell free of her, his fingers moved to her sides, spreading hot waves of pleasure up her ribcage. Her back arched, her eyes closed, her lips parted, willing his mouth to hers as his fingers teased her flesh.

"Merry," he groaned, just before his mouth covered hers in a searing kiss that left both of them gasping and breathless. "My God, Merry, you can't know what you do to me."

"Tell me," she purred, as she ran her hands up his chest to circle his neck. "Tell me what I do to you."

He tried, but he couldn't prevent the shudder that overtook him at her silken touch, nor could he stop himself from pulling her close against him, or the groan that bespoke his untold suffering from escaping him.

This was not what he had planned. Nay, he groaned silently, he was telling her of his need. It couldn't happen this way. She had to come to him. She had to make it clear she wanted this, wanted him.

Forcing his mind free of his mounting desire, he released her and stepped back. He smiled as he moved away and watched her confusion turn to shock.

"I know you be tired, Merry. I'll not inflict myself upon you this night. Sleep well, my love."

Merry was still standing there gaping, as the door closed quietly behind his departing figure.

What was happening? She had no doubt that he wanted her, not when he held her to him as he had only moments before, not when he kissed her with such sweetly controlled passion that he literally shook from the force of it. Nay, he wanted her, t'was no doubt. Why then did he leave her on their wedding night?

Slowly, Merry discarded the remainder of her clothes and slipped beneath her sheet. Unable to sleep, she watched the candlelight flickering a shadowy dance across her ceiling. What game was the beast about now? There was something afoot here, something she could not comprehend.

She turned on her side and snuggled her head comfortably to her pillow. More relaxed now, her mind seemed to clear. Abruptly, she sat up straight, as she suddenly realized what he was about. He meant to have her come to him! The rogue! The devious beast! He meant for her to admit her desire for him! He meant to take away the last of her pride.

She laughed softly as she fell back. What arrogance! The audacity of the man was not to be borne. Did he truly believe himself so desirable that she'd go to him? She laughed again and whispered softly into the darkened room, "English, t'was folly, I fear, this plan of yours. I see not a chance of it coming about." But even as she spoke them, she wondered if the words were as hollow and empty of meaning as they sounded to her own ears.

Directly below Merry's room, a man paced the floor in an endless pattern of frustration, as he muttered, "Were there ever a more complete fool, Townsend, I've not a clue as to who that might be."

She was willing, so luciously soft and inviting. She was more than willing; she was hungry and fully expected you to stay with her. She was yours for the taking and what did you do? Like some imbecile, you bade her good night! "She has to come to you. She has to!" he groaned, as he slammed his fist into his leg.

As if speaking to another, he sighed, "God in heaven, I pray this plan of yours works."

Fully clothed, he fell across his bed with a hard bounce, too overcome with black depression to bother to disrobe. His tortured thoughts kept him awake long into the night.

Chapter Eleven

MERRY HUMMED A GENTLE TUNE AS SHE MOVED THE COLD, wet cloth over her smooth skin. She smiled as thoughts of this morning drifted back to her. She had been married a week. One solid week of pure torture. Her spirits soared and she almost laughed out loud, for tonight the suffering would end.

After a week of teasing smiles and taunting looks, she thought she had won today. She was positive he'd not be able to resist, but he had. She knew she'd met her match in this one. What other man could have borne the temptation and let the moment pass. She knew he had wanted her. She could see it in his eyes. His hands had begun to reach for her, only to be pulled back at the last moment.

She sighed softly, "But not tonight. Nay, he'll not stop tonight."

She laughed as she remembered how cleverly she had planned it. She had left her room at daybreak, taking care to make enough noise outside his room so as to disturb him.

Purposely, she waited downstairs for him to dress. When she heard the slight sound of his door opening, she left the inn and walked in a rapid pace down the sandy beach. It would not do for him to catch up with her. It had to appear as if she did not expect to be found.

Giving him ample time to find her lone figure on the empty shore, she began to hurry her pace, praying he'd become suspicious of her actions and continue to follow her.

By the time she reached a thick growth of shrubbery that nearly bordered the Sound, the buttons of her dress were undone. An instant later, the dress was flung from her. Her slippers discarded, she ran from the privacy of the woodland over the short stretch of beach and into the gently moving water, clad only in a thin chemise that barely reached her knees.

Jonathan heard the noises outside his door. He had been awake for some time, tortured yet another night by his need for her. The steps creaked beneath her light weight as she made her way below.

He cursed and turned his face into his pillow. How much more will you take before you succumb to her. Jesus, had he ever felt such torment?

Unable to resist her silent call to join her, he left the bed and dressed quickly. He heard the back door of the inn close as he reached the bottom step.

By the time he too had left the inn, she was some

distance down the sandy beach. Where the hell was she going? I'll ring her pretty neck if she's involved in another of her Rebel jaunts, he promised.

She was picking up speed, nearly running as she approached a thick growth of woodland. What in God's name was the chit about? Was she to meet another?

Jonathan felt an unexpected surge of fury at the thought, and the intensity of the emotion left him white faced and filled with breathless pain, as he too hurried his steps.

He was within a hundred feet of the woodland when, to his amazement, she came flying out and dashed almost naked into the water.

Jonathan groaned. Had she planned this it couldn't have brought him more pain. He knew he had not the strength to walk away. He stood at the water's edge and waited for her to finish her swim.

She saw him there. A smile of anticipation teased the corners of her mouth, as she gave silent thanks and dove beneath the surface, lest he see the gleam of victory in her eyes.

A short time later, she emerged from the water, and Jonathan nearly doubled over with the pain that knotted his stomach as she calmly came to stand before him. The pain he felt was obvious in his eyes, and she almost laughed out loud, knowing he was powerless to hide it.

Soaking wet, her chemise appeared totally transparent and clung to her breasts and hips. He could not tear his eyes from her.

For a long, silent moment they stood facing each other. Jonathan nearly groaned aloud, seeing quite clearly how her breasts rose and fell with each breath she took and how the dark tips had hardened from the cold water and now protruded the thin material.

Merry felt not a moment of shyness beneath his hungry stare. She threw her head back and met his dark blue eyes with her own taunting gaze.

He almost reached out for her then and had to forcibly bring his hands back to his sides.

Merry did not miss the movement and gave a silent curse, knowing the moment had passed. Her hands on her hips, her anger rising as she silently raged at his stubbornness, she dared to taunt him further. "Have you nothing better to do with your time, English, than to spy on a lady?"

Jonathan's mouth turned up at the corners, but his eyes denied his humor, as his gaze bore dangerously into her own. "Be thankful, Madam, 'tis your husband who watches you and not another of the hated breed. I fear these days of public bathing are at an end. I'll not have others see you thus."

"You take much upon yourself, English," she snapped. "I've often swam these waters, and I feel no inclination to stop as yet."

"Would you prefer it if I insist?"

She gave him an incredulous look and shrugged, "Insist, if you must, but I shall continue to do as I please."

Moving to stop her as she made to pass him, he touched her shoulder. Angrily, she shrugged his hand away. An instant later, she was brought up short as his hand grabbed her hair and he pulled her back to face him. He tugged hard, so her gaze was forced to lift to his.

"Has no one informed you as yet that a wife is to obey her husband?"

Ignoring the pain in her head, her lip curled over her teeth as she snarled in disgust, "Are you about to show me the consequences should I not?"

"There are many things I could show you, Madam," he taunted wickedly. "Would you have me begin here?"

"Were I to have my way, English, I'd have you begin in hell," she raged, as she tried unsuccessfully to free herself from his hold. Her hand covered his, as she sought to pry his fingers loose. "Release me."

"And if I feel no inclination to stop as yet?" he taunted, using her exact words.

"English swine," she growled, as her hand came flying to his cheek. Finding her swing suddenly blocked by his arm, she tried to hit him with her other fist and found that too blocked.

Her hair released, her arms were now pinned behind her, and he laughed as she struggled to free herself. "Will you never concede me the superior in strength, Rebel?"

"Never!" she said, as she strained to break his hold.

He laughed again as she called him every name she could think of, until his lips interrupted her tirade. He almost laughed when he heard her startled gasp. Barely an instant later, she breathed a long, low groan, as her lips parted against the insistent pressure of his mouth, and he pulled her tighter to him as he felt her soften.

His hand released hers and he nearly cried out his pleasure as her hands came to touch his face, his neck, her fingers threading through his hair.

He tore his mouth from hers and breathed a ragged groan against her ear. "I want you, Merry. Oh, God, I can't believe how much."

He was lowering her willing form to the sand, as he pressed hot, fevered kisses to her neck.

Her groan of longing was unmistakable, as she felt his hand slide up her damp thigh and reach beneath the wet chemise. Her body jerked, as his mouth covered hers at the exact moment his hand reached the warm moistness of her desire. A drumming sounded in her ears and the sky spun dizzily overhead. She tore her mouth away and sucked in a lungful of air. Beyond reason, she didn't know she spoke her thoughts. "Love me, English. I've waited so long."

"Come to my room tonight," he groaned, just before his mouth covered hers again.

She strained her body against his, her hands moved frantically over his neck and shoulders, as she sought to bring him closer. She never wanted this to stop. He had to touch her, to keep touching her.

He made to pull away; his control threatening to break. Still she clung to him, her mouth planting hot, moist kisses to his neck.

He didn't want this. A moment of unleashed passion stemming from anger meant less than nothing. Nay, he wanted her fully conscious and admitting to her need for him.

Taking huge, calming breaths, he finally gained back his control. His voice was gentle and low as he spoke, "I want you, Merry, more than I've ever wanted a woman." As he made no further move to touch her, she came slowly to her senses and released her hold on him. She moved back, her eyes lifting to his in confusion.

His voice was husky with emotion as he continued, "I want you. I've never felt a need like this in my life. Can you say the same?"

Merry couldn't bring herself to say it. Her eyes grew huge and blinked, as giant tears spilled and rolled down her cheeks. Her throat closed and she nearly choked as she tried to swallow. Say it. Say it!

He's English! a voice countered.

He's your husband, said another.

"I'll be in my room tonight, waiting for your answer," he said smoothly. His fingers brushed away her tears as he continued, "Tonight and every night, for as long as it takes."

He left her then with a smile that told her he knew of her suffering. She watched him as he returned to the inn. A soft groan of pain escaped her. What does he want of me? Didn't he realize I was willing? Why must I come to him? Why?

She tried to deny it, but she knew why. He wanted her to put her desire for him above love of country. Could she do it? Could she consciously and deliberately go to him, knowing he represented the enemy?

She smiled as she answered her own question. Merry, 'tis a fool you be. Has he not done as much?

Chapter Twelve

MERRY SAT IN HER BATH, TRYING TO IGNORE THE NAGGING doubt that assailed her. Would he leave her once she confessed her need?

The war was nearly at its end. More than a year had passed since Cornwallis had surrendered at Yorktown and peace talks were now in progress in Paris. When it was over, the English army would leave this country, never to return. Would he leave with them?

Berating herself, she snapped aloud, "Have you so little to offer him, Merry? Can you not hold your man?"

Stepping from the tub, she rubbed the linen towel briskly over her cool skin. A moment later, she was pulling the cotton chemise over her head. God, it was hot. When was this heat to end? She flung open the window with a desperation of one who is starved for breath. Even though the rear of the inn bordered on the Sound, she could find no relief. Already, her skin felt as though it were on fire.

As she moved her head against the window glass, she gave a soft gasp, as the thought of him came in a rush to weaken her knees and tremble her whole being. She could feel it as if it were happening again, how warm his hands had been against her shivering awakening flesh!

"Oh, God," she groaned weakly. His mouth, the taste of his skin, the touch of him against her. Her stomach tightened and her face flushed, as she remembered the sweet pleasure his every touch brought her.

Tonight you'll know it all, Merry, she promised herself.

Without another conscious thought, her feet took her from her room. A moment later, she found herself standing outside his door, turning the knob. Silently, she entered and stood unseen just inside his room.

A lone candle was lit beside the chair in which he dozed. His hair was mussed, as if he had run his fingers through it many times. Short black wisps of it fell boyishly over his forehead. His white shirt was pulled from his pants and left to hang open. The sight of his chest, thickly covered with crisp black hair, caused her to quiver slightly, as she pressed herself against the door.

His head lifted at the sound of the door clicking shut, his body instantly alert to her presence. As if in a trance, she watched him swallow and run his hands over his eyes, as if he couldn't believe what he saw.

Merry was unable to do more than draw each breath deep into her lungs and expel it. It seemed she had come this far only to find her legs unable to move a step farther. She leaned weakly against the door, realizing too late, as she watched his gaze lower and heard his sharp intake of breath, that the chemise showed more than it covered and she had completely forgotten to wear a robe.

It seemed forever before he came to his feet and an eternity more before he stood before her. His eyes darkened as his fingers reached out and touched her hair. Tentatively, as if he feared she might bolt from him, his fingertips grazed her cheek and ran along the delicate line of her jaw and down her neck, baring her shoulder.

Merry's head fell back, her eyes closed with the sensuous pleasure his touch brought her, as she brazenly taunted, "Is this the best you can offer a lady, English?"

A tender chuckle sounded from deep within his chest, as his mouth came to nuzzle the hollow beneath her ear. "Madam wife, you are easily the most bewitching temptress in these colonies. You'll not admit your desire for this English bastard, yet I find you in my room taunting me to do my best. Will I ever understand you?"

Merry gave a soft, throaty laugh that brought a growl of desire from the man who pressed her tiny form close against him. "Need you understand, Captain? Can we not, just for this one time, forget all but what we want?"

"Can you give me what I want, Merry?" he asked, his chest suddenly twisting with pain, as he waited breathlessly for her answer.

"For a time," she sighed, as his hand slid from her waist to gently cup a heavy breast. "Ask no more of me, English," she cried as her mouth lifted to his jaw. "I am here. 'Tis enough for now."

"Nay," he groaned, as he lifted her chemise up and over her head and let it drop to the floor. "'Tis not enough. I want more than this from you."

"Would you not take what I offer then, English?" she asked, as her finger trailed a taunting pattern over his exposed chest.

"I'll take it, dammit. I'll take all I can get," he growled, as he lifted her and brought her to his bed.

Standing beside her, his eyes devoured her smooth golden flesh, as he quickly discarded his clothes and joined her.

"Oh, English, you do know how to kiss," she sighed, as his lips moved from hers, leaving her wanting and trembling for more of the taste of him. Her arms came around his neck and tried to pull him back, but he resisted.

"My name is Jonathan, Merry, use it."

"Nay," she shook her head. For some wild reason she couldn't understand, she knew if she used his name, it would make this moment too important, and she was afraid she'd not be able to bear it if it became that meaningful.

"Nay, is it?" he smiled, as his mouth lowered to her breast, teasing the tip with a sharp flick of his tongue, and moved past it leaving it yearning for more. A moment later, he bit, not too gently, into the soft flesh of her stomach. Satisfied to hear her soft groan of pleasure, he slipped between her parted thighs and, resting on his elbows, he promised, "I'll wager you'll scream it out before this night is done."

"And I'll wager you have much work ahead before you'll find this Rebel screaming," she returned with a taunting smile.

"Perhaps, Merry," he agreed, and then promised softly, as his hands gripped her waist and turned her over so that her breasts hung before his mouth, "but scream it you will."

A soft moan came easily to her lips as he sucked her flesh into his mouth. "Would you wager a repeat of this night, Merry?" and then smiled, as she was obviously unable to answer him. The taste of her skin was enough to drive him wild, but he had waited so long for her to come to him, he'd not rush. No, this delectable, ripe and eager sweetness was made to be savored with a slow, deliberate taking. He knew now, no matter her beliefs, no matter her loyalties, she'd no longer deny him and their need for each other. Tonight he would secure his hold on her. He almost laughed aloud, knowing full well that after this night they would rarely part.

He slid her down the length of him. Her golden hair fell around them, curtaining off a tiny, private place for two lovers to share. Every nerve ending registered the touch of his warmth, as she gazed down into his smiling eyes.

"Kiss me, Merry."

She smiled and gave a low, throaty laugh. "Shall I do everything, English? It was I who came to you."

Ignoring her question, he jeered tenderly, "Has it been so long you've forgotten how?"

"Oh, 'tis the height of arrogance," she smiled wickedly, joining him in his game. "'Tis not unusual for you

English dogs to think the rest of mankind to be dim-witted.''

Jonathan laughed and then repeated, "Kiss me."

"Very well," she gave a slight shrug, "since you are the occupying force, I've little choice but to obey a direct order."

"And just this once," he teased, his eyes glittering mischievously, "do you think you could put some feeling into it?"

"English," she laughed softly, her lips grazing his as she continued, "in truth, 'tis a rogue you are."

Her soft lips covered his mouth and found him oddly quiescent beneath her. She realized he was to let her make the exertion and she willingly allowed this heavy chore to fall to her slim shoulders. Moving her head, she twisted his lips to part and ran the tip of her tongue along the sensitive flesh just inside his lips and then along the smooth surface of his teeth. God, he tasted so good, so clean, so very much a man.

He held himself still. Were it not for that unmistakable and definite hardening of his maleness pressed against her belly, she would have believed she was having no effect on him. Her lips tore themselves from his with a deep groan and she breathed heavily into his neck as her teeth nibbled and her tongue soothed a path back up to his ear. With quick, stabbing movements, her tongue darted into his ear and she smiled victoriously as she felt him jerk beneath her.

He trembled, as her lips moved against his again, this time to gleefully find his mouth greedily accepting her tongue, while answering her movements with his own. It was wonderful, this power she felt.

With a deep groan he turned her so she lay beneath him and sighed, "Woman, have you no knowledge of the pain you cause me?"

"You asked me to kiss you. Have you forgotten?"

Propped on his elbow, he gazed down at her, a gentle smile teased the corners of her mouth, as he gave a shuddering breath. "Ah, temptress, how is it in so short a time you've become a master of the art?"

She smiled, her eyes half closed as she lifted her face and pressed her mouth to his neck and whispered, "'Tis no dimwit here, English. Are you sorry now that I follow your lessons so eagerly?"

He laughed tenderly. "It will be a sorry day indeed, before you hear this man complain."

Her mouth slid lower and nibbled at his collarbone as she ran her fingers lightly over his chest, and Jonathan thought he'd not be able to bear this pleasure. He knew when he first saw her she'd be an equal partner in this act of love. Oh, God, how he wanted her! He knew he'd never let her go. This beautiful, spirited lady had unknowingly sealed her fate the moment she had stopped him along that deserted road.

Her soft moaning as her tongue licked at his skin nearly drove him wild and he was greatly tempted to take her without further coaxing. In truth, Merry needed no further coaxing, but Jonathan had no wish to make this a quick coming together. Nay, he wanted to prolong this pleasure, prolong it until she could no longer deny her desire, until she was wild for him, until she sobbed out her longing and cried out his name.

Looming above her, his eyes trailed the length of her body, his breathing growing labored and shallow, his need for her showing clearly in the hungry glow of his eyes. "Merry, my God, I've not the words to tell you how I feel."

Their gazes met and held for countless moments. Her eyes, glazed with desire, grew bold as they took in the mirrored, desperate need in his, and she managed to whisper, "Then show me, English."

Her words were only just past her lips when his mouth was there again, sipping at her sweetness, drinking of her scent, devouring her essence, until he felt himself losing the battle of control. Leaving her mouth he sampled the smoothness of her cheek and throat only to return again, leaving her breathless and dizzy with every delicious assault.

Jonathan laid his full weight upon her, nearly exploding at the exquisite pleasure of her silken body beneath him. His groan sounded closer to pain than pleasure and he wondered if he had the strength to hold back. The aching sound of his sigh stirred Merry to move in the most tormenting erotic motion against him. "Nay, Merry," he warned. "Do not move!"

He lifted himself from her, a tender smile teasing his lips, as he gazed down at her suddenly frustrated expression. "If you continue to move thus, my love, this time we have together will be short-lived indeed."

"'Tis not to your liking, English?" she asked, while smiling up at him, only just now realizing the power she had suddenly gained over him.

"'Tis your liking I fear for, Merry," he said, while smiling in return. "Should we rush this you'll not gain all the pleasure possible, my love. And more than anything I want you to remember this night for all times."

"Will it hold such wonder?"

"It will," he swore tenderly. "The night before us promises more than your wildest dreams could conjure."

She shook her head; her eyes taunting, her teasing smile and daring look brought a devastating twist of pain to his chest. "I'm not ignorant to the boasting of the English, sir."

Jonathan's short burst of delighted laughter stopped abruptly, lest he awaken one of the sleeping officers. His grin was wide as he asked, "Impertinence again, Rebel? Will you forever question the natural superiority and honor of an English officer?"

"Humph," she murmured, her body stiffening beneath his. "No doubt you are laboring under the misconception that such a possibility exists."

Jonathan smiled, his teasing obvious in the rapid rise and fall of his eyebrows. "Shall I prove my expertise first hand?"

She gave a slight shrug, "And when done, how shall I know the superiority of it? Have I another to compare you to?"

"You'll need no other, Madam," he growled against her full, soft lips. "You will know. On my life, you will know."

Hungrily, Jonathan's lips probed hers until she was floating and dizzy. Barely had she a moment to breathe than his mouth would cover hers once more.

"Tell me," he gasped between burning, breathless kisses, "tell me true. Tell me you want this as much as I."

"Did I not come to you?"

"I want to hear you say it."

There was nothing that didn't add to her excitement.

She was defenseless against his kisses, the sound of his voice, his manly scent. Unable to resist his urgings, she moaned, "I want you, English. Oh, God, aye, I want you."

His fingers twisted into her hair and he gave a hungry growl into her mouth, as the sensuous golden thickness filled his hands. Greedily, his fingers spread through the luxurious tresses, bringing the softness to rub tantalizingly against his mouth, as he breathed in the sweet, clean, lemony scent.

"Merry, my God, Merry," he managed in a breathless whisper, just before his mouth took hers again.

Merry gave a soft moan, as the sound of her name repeated again and again finally filtered through the fog of desire in which she floated. His moist breath against her skin sent chills down her back and, when his mouth sought hers once more, she parted her lips and allowed him to pass the barrier of her teeth.

Slowly, his tongue penetrated the sweet, warm hollow of her mouth, discovering again every dark honeyed crevice. Soft sounds of delight were escaping from deep in her throat as she responded to the hot, wet thrusts of his tongue and answered in kind.

Breathless and dizzy, she fought a heated duel, reveling in the exquisite sensations his rough tongue brought her, as he rubbed it against her own. Instinctively, her neck arched to him, as his mouth left hers to run along the smooth column of golden throat. Nibbling gently at her shoulder, he soothed the tender area with soft, flickering movements of his tongue, and she thought she might swoon with the pleasure of it.

Her soft moans of delight urged him on as his mouth lowered further. "Ohhh," she sighed, once his firm lips took the tip of her breast into his heated mouth. Her back arched unconsciously, her hands at his shoulders crept up his neck to his face. Cupping the sides of his face, she pressed him to her, greedy to learn more of this ecstasy.

"Is this to your liking, Rebel?" he murmured against her skin, his mouth moving again, intent on capturing the other beckoning mound of flesh.

She didn't answer, but squirmed impatiently beneath him, sighing out her pleasure while urging him on, wanting to taste all of this delight.

His mouth was suddenly satisfied with the results incurred and, with a delicious smile, he once again captured the softness of her lips. Warm breaths mingled and left her trembling, suddenly overcome with a yearning so intense, it seemed only to cause pain. His breathing increased to short, jerking pants, stealing the air from her lungs, only to return it again.

Everything he did brought her another thrilling sensation, and Merry wondered how it was possible that this man could do such lovely things to her, to bring her such pleasure, to cause her to float just above this earth.

Jonathan groaned softly, as her hands moved from his shoulders and ran slowly across the wide surface of his chest and down his flat stomach. God, how he wanted this woman. How long had he waited? This yearning was tearing him apart. He couldn't foresee of a time when he wouldn't want her. A tender smile covered the corners of his mouth as he heard her say unashamedly, "Love me, English."

"Aye, Merry," he agreed, while pulling away from her wandering fingers, lest she bring to an instant close these moments between them. He ran his mouth across the tip of both breasts and then down her ribcage to her stomach. Gently his mouth explored the sweet soft flesh of her belly, his tongue licking the clean taste of her skin.

Moving to the hollow of her hip, he smiled at the low groan of pleasure that escaped her and then, sliding lower, he heard her cry out as he found the sweet warmth at the junction of her thighs.

Lifting herself, her hands clutched at his hair. "Nay, English," she pleaded softly. "'Tis wrong."

Jonathan smiled, as he lifted his face from her warmth. "Nothing is wrong if it brings you pleasure."

Merry wasn't sure that the strange sensations she felt were pleasure and the doubt she felt was clear in her voice, "I don't think . . ."

"Don't think," he repeated her words, while conveying a totally different meaning. "Only let yourself feel. I promise you'll not be sorry."

He gave a long, muffled groan of delight as his mouth found her again, and he breathed against her moist flesh. "I've waited so long, my love. I want to give you all the pleasure I know."

Merry denied the wave of jealousy that invaded her mind at his words. She didn't care how he had learned to do this. It mattered not, she swore.

A moment later, she forgot her doubts, as her body relaxed and her head swam dizzily with each movement of his tongue. She tried to stop the sounds her throat emitted, but was helpless to do so. Without thinking, her hips lifted so he might more easily reach her burning flesh, while an unbearable tightening formed across her stomach.

"Oh, God," she whimpered softly. Each word was an effort to utter, while at the same time she was unable to stop them. Her head twisted back and forth over the pillow as she groaned it again and again.

"Oh, English, please. I can bear no more. Help me!" she cried, as she sought to pull his face away. She knew she was babbling, but she seemed to have suddenly lost all control as to either her response to him or her soft, seemingly ceaseless, chatter.

"It hurts," she gasped, speaking of the tight yearning she felt spread painfully across her abdomen. The tension was unbearable. Why should she feel such urgency? What was it she wanted? Why could she not name it?

Her hips were off the bed now, her body as tight as a bow string. She whispered disjointed, meaningless words of sweet torture. His hands spread over the softness of her belly, finally closing tightly over her breasts as it came. Her moans were low and ragged, sounding close to suffering, as each ecstatic wave of pleasure spread over her body. She barely noticed he had moved away.

Her legs still parted, he gripped her hips and held her. His voice was strained and husky as he fought for control. "I'd not see you hurt, Merry, but I'm afraid this cannot be avoided."

Not really hearing him, she groaned an intelligible sound, as she tried to bring him close to her.

Jonathan groaned, her eagerness nearly breaking through his iron will. His mouth reached down to nuzzle into the softness of her mouth, and she was floating with the new sensation of tasting herself on his lips.

With strong, warm hands, he lifted her hips higher and guided her body to his throbbing manhood. She felt the probing hardness of him between her legs. Only gasping breaths could be heard, as they stared silently into each other's eyes. The slight wince of pain that flickered in her eyes was gone a moment after the delicate tissue of flesh broke and he passed the disposed obstruction to fill her to overflowing.

They both lay perfectly still. She not knowing the needed movements, while he waited for her body to stretch and accept him. He breathed against her lips, his voice sounding tender and low, when he asked, "Did I hurt you, Merry?"

Blinking quickly, her face a mask of confusion, having already forgotten the slight pain. She sighed a breathless, "Nay."

Slowly, his hard body began to move above her, his dark eyes leaving her breathless as they bore into hers. For a time she laid still, enjoying the texture of his skin, as it rubbed against her own, and the exquisite sensations his movements instilled within her.

Soon her hands moved hungrily over his chest, her fingers threading through the thick mat of black hair that covered it. His muscles flexed and rippled beneath his taut flesh, as her fingers lightly traced over his shoulders and down his arms.

Seeing the effect her touch brought and remembering the pleasure just now experienced, she felt a need to share that delicious sensation. "I want to bring you pleasure. Show me, English. Show me what to do."

He gasped at her words, his mind spinning with joy that she should care of his feelings. Unable to answer her, his hands guided her to the needed movements.

"Oh, Merry, Merry," he groaned, as he deepened his penetration and brought a gasp of pleasure from her. He was spinning out of control. Having wanted her so desperately, he no longer had the strength to hold back. His pace quickened and he groaned again, as she met each thrust with wild abandonment.

Her hands were twisted around his neck and refused to allow his mouth to part from hers. Merry felt as if she were drowning in sensual pleasure. She couldn't breathe and didn't care. She couldn't think and found she had no need to. She wanted only to feel this exquisite torture forever.

"English!" she cried, instinctively knowing the end was near, her body tensing again to where she thought she might snap, as she arched her back, straining to bring him closer.

"Help me, English," she cried, "'Tis tearing me apart."

"Call me Jonathan, Merry."

"Nay," she cried out weakly, and her body tightened further, as it approached a new threshold of wonder and joy. "English, please!"

"Jonathan. Say it, dammit. Jonathan," he gasped, as he deepened his penetration more so with each word spoken.

Suddenly, it was there again, but different and more exquisite, as waves of aching pleasure swirled them into a vortex of exploding sensation. Together they rode each wave, allowing them to guide their bodies to peaks of pleasure only a few could ever know.

"Oh God, oh God, Jon-a-than!" The words were torn from her throat, she was unable to stop them as she crested one wave and was pulled into another.

Jonathan heard her ragged cry and covered her lips with his own, lest the sound be heard by other ears. In truth, t'was no more than a muffled moan, but it mattered not, for he had heard it clearly.

For a long moment, she was so still, he thought she might have fainted. Her lips were relaxed and parted, her thick, dark lashes lay still against her high cheekbones. Her flushed cheeks and shuddering breath were the only signs of life.

A soft smile soon teased the corners of her mouth. Her eyes remained closed as she whispered, "I will not look at your victorious grin, English dog."

Jonathan had to catch himself, as he nearly gave a roar of laughter. Instead, a strangled sound erupted as he murmured against her cheek and ear, "Rebel, witch, enchantress. 'Tis no wonder the war is lost. What chance had we with the likes of you against us?"

"Much heartache would have been spared, Jonathan, had you been able to convince your countrymen of that truth."

He smiled at her unconscious use of his name, "'Tis not the time to talk of these things, witch. The night is far from over and we've much more pleasure yet before us."

"Oh," she sighed, as she lifted her arms over her head and stretched languidly beneath him, "these boasting, arrogant English."

Jonathan chuckled tenderly above her. "English I am, my love, and I'm no doubt arrogant, as well, but boasting? Shall we wager which of us will last this night?"

"Nay," she laughed huskily, "would I not be the fool to wager with you again?"

Chapter Thirteen

MERRY SNUGGLED HER HEAD FURTHER INTO THE SOFT down pillow, trying to forestall the coming morning, when she'd be forced to leave the comfort of this warm bed. He had kept her awake until the first light of dawn had crept silently over the horizon, the morning sun stirring the birds from their nests to lull her asleep with their happy chirping.

She smiled as she realized his mouth was moving over her hip. Sliding lower, his tongue flicked out and tickled her thigh.

"Be all you English so poor in perception as to confuse a lady with a pillow?" she asked sleepily.

His low chuckle was muffled beneath the sheet, as he pushed her to roll over on her stomach and bit into the soft flesh of her backside.

"Ow! Jonathan, dammit, that hurt!" she snapped as she came fully awake. Turning, she snatched the sheet from him, sat up and faced him fearlessly, while giving him a not too gentle punch on his shoulder.

"That will teach you, Rebel, to show some respect toward an officer in the King's Dragoons." His eyes dancing with humor, he caught her hand in midair as she sought to inflict further damage. She bared her teeth, attempting to answer in kind as he pinned her to the bed.

"That's better," he grinned down at her. "I like my women with a bit of life in them."

"Do you?" she snapped. "You've my permission then to find one of the others."

"What others?" he asked, his confusion obvious.

Still struggling, she muttered, "You said women, the plural of woman. If I'm not mistaken, that means more than one."

He laughed. "If I'm not mistaken, you sound jealous."

"Me?" she asked incredulously. "Impossible."

He laughed softly, his eyes alight with teasing, as he gazed down at her lovely face. His voice was low, his body hardening at the urgency that suddenly filled him yet again. "I believe I've met my match in you, Rebel. Would you wager I can convince you to admit to it?"

She grinned as thoughts of last night came to pinken her cheeks, "Nay, English, I've no doubt you could convince me to admit to fathering your king, had you a mind."

He laughed again, his eyes freely and most lecherously moving over the length of her. "'Tis highly unlikely, Madam, that such an occurrence could have come about."

"Agreed," she smiled a bit breathlessly, feeling her

body respond to his obvious growing hunger, "but, nevertheless, I'd more than not admit to it."

"Have I attained such power over you then?"

"At times," she willingly admitted while watching his face, delighting in the hungry look she could so easily bring about. She giggled and then flushed at her own daring as she added, "And in some positions."

Jonathan flashed white teeth in a happy grin. "'Tis a bold wench you've become, Rebel."

"No bolder than my husband, English," she sighed just before his mouth claimed hers in a hungry kiss.

Much later, his skin glistened with sweat as she laid her head upon his shoulder and ran her fingertip over the damp mat of hair that covered his chest. "I think I could grow to like this," she admitted softly.

He gave a tender chuckle. "Be you unsure?"

"Nay," she grinned, lifting her mischievous gaze to his. "I am positive, I could grow to like this."

"In truth, Madam, I fear I've not the strength, should you grow to like it more."

"Oh, no!" she mocked in feigned shock. "'Tis not so! One of George's finest is admitting defeat?"

He grinned as she propped herself on her elbow and gazed down at him, wide-eyed with supposed amazement. "Shall we notch the bed, Merry?" He chuckled at her puzzled expression. "'Tis possible proof is needed. I'd not be accused falsely of being remiss in husbandly duties." And then, when she continued to give him a doubting look, he added, "Surely, even a Rebel can count."

Realizing what he was about, she commented dryly as she raised one decidedly feminine brow in a look that belied the seriousness of her tone, "Sir, a child of five can count to two."

He laughed at her teasing and grabbed her as she tried to escape, tickling her until she was gasping and breathless, shrieking for him to stop.

Finally able to speak again, she managed, "In truth, the manly ego is a delicate substance. Why even the least bit of disrespect can lead to the most dire consequences."

Laughing a low, husky sound, she allowed him to drag her back. Nuzzled against him, she breathed a soft sigh of contentment as she listened to the sounds below. "The house stirs, Jonathan. I will be expected to help prepare the morning meal."

"Can they not do without you for one morning?" he groaned, as he held her closer, while running his hand over her hip and waist. "We have yet to spend a full day together."

"And what would we do, sir, were I to manage a day free of drudgery? Shall we loll about in bed for the entire day?"

" 'Tis not the worst of happenings, my love, but I was thinking perhaps we might go for a ride and mayhap enjoy a picnic."

Suddenly, there was loud arguing outside the door. Two men were shouting over the favors of a certain lady and they sounded enraged enough to come to blows.

Jonathan leaped from the bed.

"Where are you going?"

"There be a need to stop this before more comes of it than a few angry words."

By the time he reached the door, the sound was already disappearing down the hall as the two men went below. Opening it, he peered outside, his gaze scouting the empty hallway and stairs.

Barely controlling her laughter, Merry followed him soundlessly. Coming up behind him, she suddenly wrenched the opened door from his hand and gave him a push that sent him stumbling into the hall.

Catching a glimpse of his startled expression an instant before she slammed the door, she fell against it in a fit of soft laughter and drove the latch home.

"Woman," he growled, trying to keep the laughter from his voice, "I've cause to believe the opinion of my countrymen may have not been ill conceived in regards to the sanity of these Rebels. Let me in, you maniac!"

Merry's laughter was obvious as she replied, "Have a care, English. 'Tis not I who stands unclothed in the hall of a public establishment. I believe a measure of cajolery is in order." Examining her fingernail, she continued, "Perhaps I'm mistaken and you feel no need to enter this room?"

"Merry, dammit. Enough of your games." He tried to feel anger, but could not. Giving up, his whisper was low and filled with laughter as he spoke through the closed door. "Open this door, witch. When I get my hands on you . . ." he warned, leaving the sentence unfinished and pregnant with meaning.

"Oh pray, sir," she giggled, "do not stop now. When you get your hands on me, then what?"

"Merry," he warned.

She returned his low whisper with an evil snicker, "Have I cause to fear you, sir?"

"Would that I gave you cause wench, I'd not be here begging to reenter my own room."

Suddenly, a piercing screech permeated the entire inn and the loud crashing sound of a heavy tray went banging down the steps.

Merry quickly unlatched the door and wrenched it open.

Jonathan stood within inches of her. His eyes twinkling mischievously as he entered and closed the door behind him. Stalking her slowly, she found herself forced to back away.

"I fear you were moments too late, Madam. By now, Becky has most likely reached New York, if the speed of her flying feet be any proof."

Merry gave a low, husky laugh, as her fingers reached for his chest and tangled themselves in the curling black hair that grew there in abundance. "I fear Becky is more dim-witted than imagined, should she run from one such as you."

"Mmmm," he murmured, fully enjoying her touch, "If memory serves, until most recently, you were not anxious to abide my company, clothed or not. Have you had a change of heart, Madam?"

She smiled as she boldly allowed her fingers free will to run over his chest, stomach and hips, sliding up to his shoulders and then around his neck. Content to hear his quickening breath and the soft grunt of pleasure, as she leaned her naked form to his, she raised smiling, wicked eyes and whispered against his chest, "Until most recently, I'd had no knowledge of what could transpire between a man and a woman, if they be so inclined. In truth," she shrugged, as she released him and turned away reaching for her shift, "you wore away at my resistance until I found myself unable to quell my curiosity."

"Curiosity is it?" he growled, as he pulled her back to him, lifted her and fell across the bed still clutching her in his arms. She gave a short yelp, as she landed along the length of him, laughing as they bounced. "Have you been using me, Madam, to quell your curiosity?"

She gave a short shrug and conceded, "Perhaps a bit, sir."

"Tell me then, Rebel, now that you know the whole of it, what keeps you in my bed."

She shrugged again, "Mayhap 'tis no more than the pure enjoyment of it, English."

"Be that all?" he questioned, unable to stop his words, while cursing himself for playing the fool. What did he expect? Professions of undying love? Damn you, Jonathan, enjoy your bride. Enjoy her until you both lay gasping from the ecstasy of it and question no more.

Merry recognized the seriousness in his voice and wondered at its cause. Why did he question her feelings? What did it matter? He planned to leave, did he not? Would she not be the fool to admit . . . admit . . . What had she to admit? What was it she felt? Forcing aside her confusion, she smiled above him and responded to his question. "Be there more, English?"

"Nay, Rebel," he sighed wearily, unwilling as yet to disclose his deepening love for her, lest she abuse him further. "'Tis no more than this," he agreed, as his long brown fingers slid from her waist down to the fullness of her hips, "And this."

* * *

Merry was still nibbling at a biscuit, as they mounted their horses and swung them about, heading down the dirt road that led to the eastern portion of Long Island. Side by side, they trotted their horses as she grumbled, "I know not why we could not have enjoyed a leisurely breakfast. Was it necessary for you to drag me from the table before I could down the last of my meal?"

He raised a black brow and grinned, "Perhaps I should have kept you abed, Madam. Surely, your humor fared better when otherwise occupied."

She shot him a wry grin. "Have I been complaining unduly?"

"Nay," he reassured. "I did rush you overmuch."

She smiled gently and asked, "Why?"

"'Tis a simple fact that I've waited an eternity for you, and now I find myself hard pressed to exhibit patience when I cannot hold you near me."

"Are you so greedy, English? Were last night and this morning not sufficient in sating your appetite?" she teased, as she glanced sideways and up from beneath thick dark lashes.

"Watch yourself, Madam," he warned with easy humor, "I'd not be adverse to a quick tumble on the roadside, should you provoke me further."

"Are you threatening severe punishment?"

"Aye, Madam, the worst."

She laughed happily and taunted as she pushed her heels to the sides of her horse. "For that, sir, you must catch me first."

Having optioned to ride astride her horse, Merry's dress was draped over the animal, and the force of the wind did little to retain her modesty, as it lifted the thin

159

cotton material to show tantalizing glimpses of slim, shapely legs.

Jonathan set his horse at a gallop and soon pulled alongside, but Merry only laughed, as she pulled at the reins and directed her horse to the left, across a wide plane of waist-high grass that bordered a thin strip of rocky beach. Laughter floated in her wake as her bonnet flew from her head and bounced against her back, and her golden hair tumbled in wild disarray. She bent low over the horse's head and gave the animal free rein.

It was some time before Jonathan managed to come alongside of her again. This time, he did not wait for her to pull up; rather, he leaned to his right and reached out a long arm, snaking it securely about her waist. An instant later, amid short shrieks of surprise and gales of laughter, she was pulled across his saddle.

In a moment the animal was brought to a halt and Merry's weak form pulled from it. Laughing so hard, she found it difficult to remain standing. Forcing herself to adopt a degree of composure, she willed away her giddiness. "Indeed you are a wretch, English," she cried with mock rage, while poking her finger into his hard chest. "Will you always abuse me so?"

Jonathan smiled at her feigned anger, but his tone belied any of the merriment of the moment, as his dark blue eyes grew almost black as they searched her own, "Only should you attempt to flee from me, Rebel."

Merry's cheeks flushed and her eyes widened with total confusion. He spoke of keeping her with him. Had he changed his mind? Did he now plan to stay?

Suddenly, feeling shy and unsure of herself, she decided she'd not question him further. She had time yet to convince him to remain, if he was as yet undecided. It would not do to pressure him.

Merry refused to answer the question that was nagging at her. Why was it so important to her that he stay? She groaned a silent curse. Enough! You want him. Why complicate matters by asking why? You were not sorry to have him touch you. Indeed, you craved it. He is your husband, she reasoned. Take from him what he offers and think no more on it!

Jonathan didn't miss the confusion that flickered in her eyes. He knew, as yet, she did not love him as he loved her. At least, she couldn't recognize her feelings as such. Unwilling to press her, he smiled reassuringly as he took her hand and coaxed, "Walk with me, Merry."

The time was not far off when she would recognize her feelings for him, he believed. He knew her better than she supposed, this woman who had denied her desire until they were both suffused in a void of unending pain and despair. Surely the end result had been well worth the suffering.

Smiling down at her, he was flooded with beautiful, vivid pictures of last night. Suddenly, filled with a love so overpowering as to leave him giddy, he pulled her to him and held her close for long minutes. Her golden hair lifted softly in the gentle breeze. His large hand grasped a long tendril and brought it to his face. "Since our first meeting, I've been haunted by the scent of you," he breathed.

Merry laughed. "One hopes then 'tis a pleasing scent, sir."

"Delectable," he grinned. "Definitely one which would tease the appetite and cause a man to yearn for a taste."

Merry flushed and lowered her eyes, knowing full well he spoke of the intimate moments they had shared the previous night and remembering how he had done just as his words hinted.

"In truth, it stirs the senses as powerfully as any touch."

Merry giggled. "Come near me after a day spent toiling in the kitchen. I promise you a scent not half as sweet."

He laughed as she pushed herself free and wrinkled her nose as if smelling a particularly obnoxious odor.

As they continued to walk, she sighed with contentment, as the sun beat its warming rays upon them, belying the winter winds that would soon rush across these waters.

"Would you always want to live here, Merry?"

"Always."

"Have you never hungered for adventure? Perhaps to discover what it might be like to live elsewhere?"

"Never! My only thought, since I can remember, is to live free of British tyranny. The war is nearing its end. 'Tis nearly time to enjoy this longed-for dream."

Jonathan gave a silent groan. Was this woman so closed minded that she could see nothing beyond her own hopes and desires? He had to convince her to see things his way. Lord, wouldn't she put up a fight should he suddenly haul her aboard a ship and inform her they were to spend their remaining days in England.

"Is it not possible to see this dream of yours to reality and then search out other horizons?"

She shrugged and gave him a quick glance. What was he hinting at? Surely, he'd not believe her so shallow as to have joined these forces for the pure sport of it? She meant to stay and enjoy the fruits of her labor. "Since I've married a Britisher, Jonathan, I've come to believe anything is possible," she replied with a gentle smile.

He grinned at her, remembering her adamant insistence that that particular circumstance should not come about. "Be you happy, Merry?"

"Indeed, sir," she smiled brightly. "I've fared well these past years and at present find naught to complain of."

"Not even a Britisher for a husband?"

"Have you knowledge of any situation that boasts perfection?" she teased in return. "One must accept the good with the bad." Laughing happily, she launched into a fast run, as if expecting retribution for her words.

She was some distance down the shore before he brought her up short with a not-too-gentle tackle that knocked her off her feet and left her gasping and winded.

"You little wretch," he groaned, as he turned her effortlessly to lay on her back, pinning her arms above her head and leaning his weight on her to stem her continued efforts to escape. "Is it not possible for that delectable tongue of yours to utter even one remark that does not wound?"

"Aye, husband, 'tis possible," she laughed from beneath him and teased. "For instance, should you wish to hear a kind word regarding your king, simply have him remove his forces from these colonies and I shall sing his praises."

"Madam, I was in mind of more personal matters, myself in particular."

"Oh, that," she sighed and then grinned wickedly. "Have you a need, sir, to inflate your mammoth ego further?"

Jonathan laughed.

"Perhaps I was mistaken, sir, but I believed arrogance such as yours was not subdued by a lone disparaging remark. In truth, I have not the means to wound, merely to prevent your head from swelling further."

Jonathan nearly grunted aloud. So the chit believed her words to have no effect. T'was best to let her continue this thought, lest she do her best to abuse him further. Forcing aside his serious thoughts, he grinned down at her, "T'would bring little harm, Rebel, should you reverse your course and set out to capture my heart."

Merry's heart pounded at the truth of his words. What would he say if he knew that was exactly what she planned? Forcing herself to appear flippant, she kept her words light, "Would it not? Pray tell, sir, would you return to your homeland with your heart left behind? Nay, I believe it would bring great harm should either of us begin to feel more than we do at present."

God, he groaned silently, as a wave of black depression enveloped him, unable to believe he could feel more than he already did and beginning to wonder if it be possible for her to return even a portion of it.

He shrugged noncommittedly and managed to remark, "At least it would offer each of us an enjoyable interlude, until I must leave."

Merry braved a tentative smile as she digested his words. He did plan to leave, after all. Good God, he must never know how desperately she wanted him to stay. He must continue to believe she cared not if he left. Should she act the fool and beg him to stay . . . what then? Nay, Merry, you must keep your senses about you. To entice this man you must profess to abide his company because you have no alternative. No clinging vine would appeal to this one.

Purposely changing the subject, she smiled and then remarked, "The season draws to a close, English. I've a wish to sample these waters once more before the winter comes."

She glanced to her right, out and over the calm water. "'Tis no one about. Would you keep guard or join me?"

"I've kept guard once. To do so twice would make me double the fool," he grinned, as he rolled from her and began to pull off his boots.

Merry discarded her bonnet and shoes. Her simple brown dress proved to be no problem, as she quickly undid the many buttons and slid out of it. Next came her frilly drawers and petticoats and she was ready.

Facing him, she was not sorry to see the admiration that glowed in his eyes as his gaze slid over her. Her chemise barely reached her knees and clung to her in the gentle breeze.

"Were you always to dress thus, Merry, I'd not object."

Merry laughed. "Perhaps, sir, but this garb is most inappropriate should I wish to leave my room."

"I told you once, Madam, that the bed was most appropriate for you."

She laughed. "Aye. You were a wretched beast that day. How did you dare speak to me thus?"

"I was besotted, Merry," he replied honestly. "Never before had I seen a lovelier vision."

Kneeling before her, he managed to snag a button on a thread and was unable to open it.

Merry leaned over, unconscious of the low neckline of her chemise, nor of the fact that it gaped wider still, leaving nothing to his imagination as she helped untangle the button. "Indeed, sir," she commented as she finished, "I believe you have need of a wife, if only to see to your clothing."

"Nay, Merry, I can think of a better chore for a wife."

She smiled as she recognized the growing hunger in his eyes. "Can you, sir? Pray tell, whatever can that be?"

"Kneel before me and I shall show you."

"Mmm, this sounds most interesting. But I fear should I do as you suggest, I may never reach the water." An instant later, she was gone from sight, her happy laughter the only evidence of her presence, as she bolted out of the tall grass and into the water.

"It's freezing," she called, as he stood unashamedly naked on the shore. Suddenly breathless, her heart hammered wildly at the sight of his tall form, as he casually placed his hands on his hips and grinned at her. God, she groaned silently, he was a sight she could feast on and never tire of. His wide shoulders tapered smoothly to narrow hips, and she could feel her heart thud alarmingly as she allowed her gaze to lower to long, firm thighs. She trembled as she remembered the touch of his warm, hard body against hers and wondered how it would feel wet and slippery and cool.

Calling a halt to her fantasies, she called again, "Mayhap you should reconsider. I'd not see one of George's elite shiver with goose flesh."

Grinning threateningly, he ran toward her, splashing huge amounts of water, until he dove sleekly beneath the surface.

It took a long moment before he surfaced and Merry gave a start to find him so close. She yelped as he dragged her under. An instant later she squirmed free of his hold and escaped.

Taunting him to catch her, she called out as if a child at play, and again evaded his grasp. From beneath the water a hand grasped her knee and she squealed as she fought to free herself. Laughing happily, she hit his shoulder as he surfaced. "How do you do it? I know you can see nothing and yet you continue to find me."

Answering her only with a daring grin, he pulled her leg closer, treading water as he did so. "I will always find you, Merry," he stated simply.

Her laughter turned to a soft moan, as his free hand ran up her leg to brush wet, exploring fingers against her parted thighs. "'Tis naught else on your mind, English?" she asked weakly. "If you persist in this lewd behavior, the residents hereabout will surely find our bodies washed up on shore."

"Nay," he contradicted, as he guided her to where he could touch bottom. "'Tis no chance of that, Merry. I stand."

Briefly, her body slid against his, as the easy but firm pressure of the undercurrents caressed their bodies and caused them to flow with the continuously moving water. From that one fleeting touch she knew his passions raged again, and she longed to run her hands down and over him, to feel his body come hard against her own.

She floated beside him, a tender smile touching her lips, as the salt water held her effortlessly near the surface. Her chemise was floating above her waist and it took little effort for him to reach beneath it and run his hands over her wet, yearning flesh. His one arm slid around her waist and held her so she'd not float away again, while the other hand between her legs continued to work a dreamy magic over her.

Needing no persuasion to respond to his advances, she reached her hands to his shoulders and held herself against his cool, hard form. Her back arched, as she pressed the lower half of her body closer to him. Sighing softly from the pleasure he instilled, she gave a shaking moan of yearning, "Oh, Jonathan, 'tis pure magic in your hands."

Jonathan smiled as he whispered low and huskily near her ear, "You should warn me before you bestow a compliment, Madam, for I know not if I can bear the shock of it."

She gave a low, husky laugh and then a strangled groan, as his fingers entered her. Trying to answer him, she found she was forced to shake her head to regain lucidity. "I shall remember in the future, English." Her mouth was at his shoulder, drinking in the taste of seawater and clean skin. His fingers penetrated further and she gave another gasp, dizzy with sensation. "Think no more of it. Indeed," she cried, "I'd do much to ward off a shock to your senses."

"Merry," he groaned against her full lips, "'tis best I

think to continue this on shore. I've a hunger to see what I touch."

Merry felt only the slightest shyness at his bold words. Pulling away from him, she tried to answer sternly, but failed miserably, "You've managed to ruin my swim, English. I now fear 'tis hopeless to escape your lechery."

He laughed as he gathered her small form into his arms and began to walk toward the shore. "Have you a wish to escape?"

She laughed, but only snuggled closer, giving him no answer, as her lips slid smoothly over his neck and jaw.

"Have you?"

Still no answer.

Suddenly and quite unexpectantly, he dropped her and she slid beneath the water.

She came up choking and sputtering water. "Damn it, Jonathan! Must I suffer the water torture till I answer you?"

Taking her again into his arms, he laughed as she slapped his shoulder. "Never mind, little Rebel, I've more delightful forms of torture in store for you."

Amid the tall, waving grass, they reclined, sipping at glasses of port. Having quite thoroughly made love, they had started upon a leisurely picnic of cold chicken, meat pies, cheese and fruit.

"Decadence, 'tis pure decadence," she sighed happily.

"Are you complaining again?" he asked as his fingers slid through a length of golden hair.

"Nay," she smiled, "I could easily grow to enjoy this

new world you've introduced to me." After a long moment, she continued, "Still, 'tis most indecent, this." Her head resting against his naked stomach, she raised her leg, turning her ankle as if inspecting it. "Should someone come across us, I'd not be able to show my face hereabouts again."

"Should someone come across us, Merry, I doubt they'd notice your face overmuch," he chuckled, as his hand played with the long golden hair, gathering the now dry curling locks and bringing the tumbled tresses to cover her naked breasts. "Is that not better?"

"Oh, indeed," she laughed, examining his attempt to cover her. "Now I feel confident that no one would notice my state of undress."

It was late before they returned to the inn. Merry felt lazy and satiated, while a smile twitched at her lips. God, he was a lusty beast. She had lost count of the times he had loved her. Between last night and today, it must total a dozen or more.

In her entire life she had never felt such utter contentment and happiness. For the moment, she refused to question why he should be capable of bringing about such feelings in her. It was enough that he did. She'd question it no further.

As they entered the inn, Jonathan ordered Becky to bring roast beef dinners and a bottle of port to his room.

Merry grinned as they mounted the steps. "I've come to think, 'tis not the worst of happenings being married to a Britisher."

She laughed out loud at his look of astonishment and shrugged as she replied to his look, "As long as you stay, I'll be guaranteed a full stomach."

He laughed at her teasing and then grabbed her close to his side and whispered just as he shot her a wicked leer, "That's not the only thing I guarantee will be filled, Madam."

Upon entering the room, she came to a sudden stop as she noticed two large trunks and a dozen boxes of various sizes spread about the room and bed.

"What is this?"

Jonathan shrugged, "Perhaps in your absence your room has been rented and Becky brought your things down here."

"Nay," she smiled, "I've not enough to fill these boxes let alone the trunks. Seth must have made a mistake and brought someone else's belongings to your room."

She made to leave in order to inquire where they might belong when he stopped her. "Nay, Merry, 'tis no mistake."

She looked up at him, her face a mask of confusion.

He grinned down at her and answered her silent question. "I've ordered them."

"Have you a need of so much, English?" she smiled and then continued, "I've been laboring under the apparent misconception that the King's forces traveled with little more than the bare essentials."

"I ordered a few things when I was in New York last," he replied with a flippant shrug. Sitting in an armchair, he began to remove his boots as he continued, "See to the unpacking, will you, Merry?"

"Humph," she retorted, "now comes the truth as to why you wished a wife. Would you not have fared better to secure the service of a manservant?"

Jonathan laughed, "Nay, wife. The nights are lonely

and overlong and the bed huge and cold to lie alone. I think I did well, in this instance. Both chores are accomplished at the price of one."

Merry laughed, turning her back to him to open a box. "English and tightfisted to boot. Two admirable qualities to be sure."

She laughed out loud as she managed to lift the first lid and flounces of pink lacy material fell out. She pulled at the garment and held a thin lace-trimmed negligee in front of her and faced him. "Oh, Jonathan, indeed, I have a need to see you in this."

Jonathan grinned as he watched his wife unpack another. This time a sheer gown of black silk was pulled from the box. She laughed again. "Here's another, Jonathan." Facing him, she continued, "Apparently, the shop has made a mistake and shipped the wrong order."

He shrugged, obviously unconcerned. "No doubt they'll take them back."

She answered with a shrug of her own. "No doubt," as she began to refold the sheer fabric.

"Unless, of course, you can think of someone who might want them."

"Would you give them away?"

"Are you suggesting I use them?"

She laughed again. "Mayhap you should try them on before you decide."

He made as if to think on it and then, as if the thought had just occurred, he suggested, "I seem to remember a debt I owe."

She sat on the bed, listening silently.

"A lady once told me I owed her three dresses. Do

you think this would suffice for payment?" he asked, as he waved his arm toward the trunks and boxes.

Merry didn't answer, so totally dumbfounded was she. Her eyes grew huge and she blinked slowly, as she finally managed a hoarse whisper, "Did you buy these for me?"

"Merry," he admonished with a gentle shake of his head, "would I, a married man, buy them for another?"

Merry was filled with a wide range of emotion, astonishment not the least withstanding, as huge tears rolled down her face.

Coming from the chair, he knelt before her and wiped away her tears. "Had I known a simple present would cause you to cry, I'd have thought twice on it."

"Simple indeed," she remarked as her finger moved over his firm brown jaw. "Simply wonderful. Thank you, Jonathan," she whispered throatily against his neck as he held her close to him.

"Do not thank me, Merry. You are my wife, are you not?"

She nodded.

"All I have is yours, is it not? I am not a poor man."

"Aye," she laughed and then teased, "we shall fare well on your salary."

"Would you mind?"

"Would I mind being poor?" She laughed again. "Jonathan, I've never been rich and yet I find nothing to complain of about my station."

Chapter Fourteen

"JONATHAN!" SHE CRIED, AS SHE SHOVED A CRISP LOAF OF bread into his hands. "How in God's name is one to eat these cursed loaves with the mark of the dead encrusted upon them? There are no words to explain the disgust I feel. 'Tis fitting he calls the fort Golgotha, since it rests upon our burial grounds. Damn him and his lot to hell. I pray the poor souls he disturbs haunt him for eternity.

"Be warned, Jonathan. Your fellow compatriots may laugh over this, but the town fumes. I'd not be surprised to see an insurrection in the near future."

Jonathan nodded his head in compliance, as he examined the loaf to find the tombstone engraving plainly legible upon its surface. "I've no words, Merry, to find excuses. I agree 'tis abhorrent. I know not what Colonel Thompson is thinking."

"Oh, I know well enough what the bastard thinks,"

she stormed furiously. As she paced the kitchen, she added, "'Tis merely his way of showing his high esteem of the colonists. God," she groaned, "how much longer are we to abide this treatment? Winter is at our door and already a shortage of food exists. At this rate, most of the townsfolk will perish before the new year."

Jonathan knew she was right, but he was helpless to do more than give what would amount to a feeble protest, for he knew Colonel Thompson would do as he wished, regardless of his Captain's objections.

"Not only has he torn down our church and used the lumber for a stable, but, while he lived in the parsonage, he used the library for kindling." She gave a long, exaggerated sigh as she went on. "How sadly mistaken was I to think the taxes before his appearance to be unsuitable, for he has far surpassed any of his wretched predecessors. 'Tis too much to ask a body to bear. What will become of us?"

"Fear not, my love. I promise you none will suffer overmuch this winter."

"How can you say that? Everyone is forced to give up to those wretches every blade of wheat and rye straw. We are left with nothing to feed the animals and little enough to feed ourselves. Most hereabouts are farmers, Jonathan. How can they plant a crop or harvest it with a starving horse at the plow?

"Do you realize the list of taxes include hay, wheat, oats and rye? It goes on and on. Were it not that my father is the innkeeper and many of the soldiers eat here, I'd surely be joining the others in their suffering. Jonathan, please," she asked more gently, "can you not object? Is there no one in authority you can go to?"

"Nay, Merry, there is no one."

She nodded her head and asked, "Need the tables of the dragoons overflow, while others have naught? I'd wager what is thrown away at one meal could feed these townsfolk for a week."

"Perhaps something could be done, Merry," he offered. "What would you say if we could secure some of the food intended for the dragoons and distribute it among the townsfolk?"

"Would you do that? Would you help our cause?"

"Nay, Merry, to help your cause would label me traitor. I believe in the sovereignty of my king, but I see no reason for the colonists to suffer to such an extreme. The only reason could be spite. 'Tis not necessary for women and babies to go hungry so our Colonel Thompson can grow fatter. 'Tis no traitorous act, this."

Merry was quite ignorant of the fact that certain sums of money mysteriously passed hands. The commissary of forage seemed not to notice the slightly lessening amounts of produce that was accountable as taxes, nor did he miss the emptying of grain bushels once accounted for. But Merry noticed the bushels of wheat and rye that somehow appeared overnight in her barn, only to disappear again before the next dawn.

Merry felt a growing tenderness coupled with a newfound respect for her husband, knowing he was somehow responsible and, although she longed to tell all their welfare was secure, she dared not breathe a word lest her husband's good deeds be found out. He could not help being what he was, she reasoned prejudiciously. He was born in England, after all, and raised with one thought, that the King was the supreme ruler and his word law. Still, for a Britisher, he possessed an enormous humanity, she grudgingly allowed. He truly cared for her people and disliked the suffering they endured. She realized she was helpless against the burgeoning feelings toward him that swelled within her breast and found she was not sorry she was beginning to consider him in an entirely new light, one which would have terrified her only weeks earlier.

The reality of war faded into the back of her mind and she found a happiness she'd not have believed possible. More often at her side than not, she found she missed his company were he gone only a few hours.

And when he was about, a smile was never far from her eyes, while a lightness moved her step. Soft, gentle laughter was often heard through the inn these days, as she began to find all of life most thoroughly enjoyable.

In her newfound happiness, she slowly began to see the English less as an enemy. At last, she realized that they were merely people, and, like all others, some were good, some were bad. Why hadn't she seen this before, she wondered? Why had she hated so completely, so totally, simply because they had not believed as she?

She also came to realize that the King's soldiers were more widely accepted than she had previously thought. Having lived in the colonies for these past several years, many of the soldiers had struck up alliances with the women of the colonies and were either married to them or about to be.

Most of the colonists' animosity was directed at the Tories, rather than at the fighting force sent by their king. Yet, till now she had been unable to separate the two.

It was late November and, although most of the farmers' produce was taken in levied taxes, the townsfolk of Huntington were not ignorant of the fact that they had much for which to be thankful. This year, as none before since this war had begun, they had found they had more food and therefore less to fear of the coming winter.

Nettie and Merry decided a celebration of sorts was in order, and they initiated the plans for a pot-luck feast to be held in the inn. Now that the fort was completed, the large room upstairs that had held so many soldiers stood empty. The townsfolk did not number so many that they could not come together and celebrate.

Merry was alone in the kitchen absentmindedly stirring a huge pot of pudding, as she watched Jonathan outside the window chopping wood for the stove. Although it was cold, he had taken off his shirt and his skin glistened with sweat in the strong sunlight. Feeling her gaze upon him, he turned and gave her a heart-stopping grin.

He was magnificent, she mused and her feelings were registered in her eyes. He turned back to his work and finished the piece he had nearly severed. His muscles bunched beneath taut bronzed skin, as he stretched his arms and brought the ax down again. Merry couldn't contain a shiver of excitement from the sight of his half-naked form.

Throwing down the ax, he grabbed his shirt and ran into the fragrant, warm kitchen. Swooping her into his arms and spinning her about, he planted a deep, hungry kiss on her smiling lips.

Releasing her mouth, he smiled and warned wickedly as she gasped for air, "That's for watching me with those luscious golden eyes. Were you not in the midst of cooking, I'd take you upstairs and give you exactly what you ask for."

She gave a low, husky laugh and exclaimed a bit breathlessly, "Me? Nay, sir, you've misunderstood. I simply worried about your nakedness in the cold air. It was you who came charging into my kitchen, almost swallowing me with hungry kisses."

Jonathan smiled as he slipped his shirt on. "How easily you deny what we both know to be true. Don't you know your denial only tempts me to convince you further. Perhaps you know, after all," he teased. "T'would be like you, Rebel, to tease me and then deny it."

"Be serious, Jonathan," she giggled, as she ran her fingers over his chest, enjoying again the hard feel of him. "I have much work to do and I've not the time to dally with you."

"Shall I leave you then and let you be about your business?"

"Nay, Jonathan," she smiled impishly and gave a small shrug, "I'd not be averse to an extra hand in my preparations."

"Merry, I've little experience in a kitchen. I'm not sure that you'll be thankful for my help."

"Indeed, sir, I will agree that your skills lie in areas other than kitchen service and are best put to use in more privacy." She laughed as he ogled her with a teasing leer, and then swung out of his grip as his hand suddenly found the firm roundness of her backside to be irresistible. "Still, I'm sure a man of your ability can be put to some use. You may stir the pudding while I peel the potatoes."

She laughed softly as she untied her apron and secured it around his waist. "Is that not better?"

And when he turned to allow her to admire his form in an apron, particularly this one, as it was edged in feminine ruffles, she laughed again. "In truth, it suits you, sir."

"Does it?" he asked, while answering her grin with his own.

He took the spoon from her and began mixing the pudding. Suddenly, a choking emotion overcame her as he stood before her, his confidence intact as he grinned over the silly apron, and she knew for a fact what she hadn't dared to think till now.

"Enough nonsense, woman," he ordered gruffly as he moved to swat her behind, while the gentleness in his eyes belied his tone. "Get back to your work. I've a need that won't wait much longer, lest you rather we put the table to the best use it's ever known."

Merry blushed as she realized what his words were about and refused to look at him, knowing her thoughts ran in much the same vein. Growing redder still, she imagined quite clearly what it would be like to make love on the thick wooden table. Her legs wrapped around his hips as he stood before her and she couldn't control the shiver of delight that suddenly ran through her.

Jonathan read her thoughts easily as he watched her gaze move over the clean smooth surface. "Am I correct in assuming the idea is not repugnant to you?"

Merry lifted her eyes to his and smiled as she answered eagerly. "Aye."

Her easy admittance took him totally by surprise, for he had expected maidenly shyness and a cool denial.

Jonathan laughed as he gathered her close to him. The pudding forgotten, he smiled into the open honesty and loveliness of his wife's face. "Woman," he sighed, as his rough fingers moved tenderly over the smoothness of her cheek, his eyes glowing with undeniable hunger, "you'll never know the effort it takes not to bed you at this moment. Still," he murmured, as his lips came to follow in the wake of his fingers, "I'd wager before long I will have made love to you in every position and pose imaginable. Not a room will pass us by without being properly introduced to the hunger we share."

Merry gave a low, sultry laugh, "Would you see me exposed, unmindful of whomever might enter?"

"Madam, all who might wander in generally sleep at night," he grinned.

She gave him a sharp poke in his midsection, while moving quickly from his arms. "Watch the pudding." And then gave a soft yelp as he made a teasing attempt to lunge after her.

Later that day, after carefully inspecting the preparations for the night's festivities, Merry readied herself for a long, luxuriating soak in her bath.

Testing the water with her hand, she bent over the tub. Before she could right herself again and add the much needed pails of cold water, the door behind her swung open. Thinking one of the officers she had just heard outside her door had entered the wrong room, she gave a short shriek and spun about. Completely off balance, she found herself helplessly falling back.

Jonathan stood just inside the door to his room, his eyes wide with amazement, watching the bizarre actions of his wife, with arms and legs flying, as she fell into a tub of water.

At the moment she was totally helpless, as her legs hung over the side of the tub and the hot water burned her rump. "Jonathan," she cried, "get me out of here!"

He laughed as he walked quickly to her, took her hand and pulled her out. She twisted to examine her pink derriere, until she saw that he too was examining her flushed backside. Giving him a swat on his shoulder, she snapped, "Must you stand there gawking?"

Jonathan gave a low chuckle. "Shall I close my eyes?"

She snarled in disgust that he should enjoy her discomfort. "Give me that cloth," she pointed behind him, "and the bucket of cold water."

He did as he was told and watched as she tried to dab at her tender behind. "You scared me half to death. I thought it was a soldier coming upon me."

Taking the cloth from her hand, he turned her and continued to do a more thorough and gentle job of it. "It was."

"You know I mean another," she said and sighed with relief as cold compresses were pressed to the tender area.

He chuckled softly, on his knees now. Her skin was slowly recovering its normal tint.

"The least you could do is knock before entering a room."

"Knock on my own door?" he asked, his humor barely under control, and she gave a low helpless giggle at the absurdity of it.

"Perhaps, Madam, you should limit yourself to cold water. If memory serves, you are quite accomplished with it."

Merry knew he was speaking of the day she had

doused him. "Surely, sir," she replied primly, "you cannot deny you were most deserving."

"Aye, Merry, that I was," he agreed happily, as he stopped his ministrations, satisfied to see the pink skin disappear. He added two buckets of cold water to her bath and tested the water himself. "'Tis safe now, I think," he allowed as his hand reached for hers and he helped her into the tub.

The water offered her no privacy and his warm gaze moved slowly over her, watching with obvious delight as the water came to rest just below her breasts.

"Have you nothing to occupy your time, English?" she asked, while squirming a bit beneath the growing hunger in his penetrating gaze.

"Aye, Rebel, that I have," he agreed and then laughed at her surprise as he began to slowly open the buttons of his shirt.

Her eyes widened further still as he easily removed his boots and pants. Standing naked before her, she had no doubt as to his intentions. "Nay, Jonathan, the tub will not hold both of us. 'Tis too small."

He ignored her protest and slid his long body behind her. She sat between his legs, his knees raised above the water's surface, his hands holding her close against him.

She laughed softly and rested her back against his warm, hard chest. "I'll wager little washing will be done. I can barely move."

"Turn around," he whispered into the golden halo of her hair. "I will see to this heavy chore."

She turned to face him, smiling gently as she leaned back and sat on her legs. "Would you play the servant for me?" she laughed softly.

"For you, my lady, I'd do that and more."

Stretching languidly before him, she shot him a wanton glance, her eyes glistening with pleasure as she noticed his hungry, startled response. Then she sighed with mock weariness and with an air of boredom, her eyes resting upon the ceiling. "Very well, you may begin your labors, servant."

Jonathan laughed at her playacting, although his chuckles contained an underlying sound of pain. Finally, he managed, "How easily you acquire the art of lady of leisure in her bath. The role suits you to perfection."

Merry eyed him suspiciously as he soaped a cloth, ready to set about his task. She tried, but she couldn't control the stab of jealousy she felt, nor could she resist asking, "Have you often watched ladies in their bath?"

Putting her doubts to rest, he responded firmly, "No, and neither have you, I'd wager. Still, you manage to portray the noblewoman easily enough. I wonder if you would enjoy the role had you to play it daily?"

"Have no fear, Jonathan," she laughed softly, "there is no other of fuller pockets that lures me from your side."

"Would you be happier, Merry, had you servants of your own?"

"Nay, I think not," she reasoned, "for were I ever to achieve that station, Jonathan, I would, no doubt, work twice as hard, for I'd not have it rumored that their mistress was of slovenly persuasion."

He laughed gently as he pressed the soapy cloth to her neck and shoulders. "I think that worry would pass in time."

She sighed softly as his hands smoothed the suds over

her shoulders. "If this were the treatment I'd get, I confess I could grow to withstand it."

He smiled at her obvious enjoyment. Cupping water in his hands, he rinsed away the suds and watched, as if mesmerized, how the water ran in smooth rivulets down her silken skin to her full breasts and dripped tantalizingly from the pink tips.

Without thought, he pulled her closer and allowed his tongue to dispose of the last of the scented water that threatened to drop off. His hands beneath the water now moved smoothly over the slippery skin of her back and waist, sliding lower to her hips. Forgetting the cloth, he simply reached to discover again all the joys her body offered.

"Oh, Jonathan," she moaned softly, as his hands finally reached the aching need between her legs, "I would easily allow you to bathe me daily, should you always exercise your duties so expertly."

He laughed tenderly, just before his mouth claimed hers in a wild kiss that caused her to slip wet arms around his neck and hold his mouth tightly to hers.

"Turn again and rest against me, my love," he whispered once the kiss ended.

Merry needed little coaxing, did as he asked and never was she more pleased that she had done so.

Resting her head against his chest, she sighed with delight as his wandering fingers found her again, while the other hand moved deliciously over her, touching her everywhere, until she found she had to bite her lip to keep from crying out her pleasure.

"Oh, Jonathan," she cried, as she tried to twist her head so she might reach his body with her mouth. "I want to touch you, please," she begged.

"I know my love and you will," he promised, his mouth nuzzling the tender flesh of her neck, as his free hand moved over her breasts.

Her moans became desperate as the tightening in her abdomen threatened to rip her to pieces. She turned her face again, hungry to reach his lips, as wave after wave of aching pleasure came to carry her off to a place where nothing but ecstasy existed.

For a long moment she rested against him, her head nuzzled to his warm chest as she tried to control her breathing, and waited for her heart to stop pounding.

"You can turn around now," he whispered from above her.

"I cannot. I have not the strength."

A moment later he laughed, as she suddenly made to leave the bath. "In truth, I think I'm clean enough."

"Not yet, Rebel," he grinned, as he turned her to face him. "Your husband needs much the same cleansing."

"Does he?" she grinned impishly. And then sniffing like a puppy at his neck and shoulder, she wrinkled her nose. "Perhaps you are right, sir. Surely a spot of soap could bring little harm."

Touching a soapy finger to her nose, he remarked, "Spunky little thing, aren't you, once you've been pleasured?"

She grinned as she knelt before him and rubbed the bar of lemon soap over the cloth and gave a small shrug. "There is no one to blame but yourself, English. Greedy for debauchery, wicked to the last."

"I heard not a murmur of complaint while bestowing my debauchery upon a certain young lady."

Ignoring his comment, she smiled into his dark blue

eyes, as she ran the cloth over his neck and shoulders. "You will carry the scent of a lady on this day."

He breathed a long, satisfying sigh at her ministrations. "I care not."

Continuing, she lathered him until all that showed above water was covered with scented suds, her hands moving lovingly over him. "People will sniff at you and give you peculiar looks."

"Let them."

Her eyes glowed with admiration. "I've never known a man so sure of himself, Jonathan. A frilly apron causes you only to smile and appear more masculine, while feminine scents and bubbles leave you undaunted."

He chuckled softly. "Would you believe me to become feminine because I allow womanly things to touch me? Nay, Merry, put your hand beneath this water and I will show you how feminine I've become."

She jumped back, splashing water over the sides while feigning shock at his words, her eyes growing huge as she played her game. "Me! Oh sir, nay, t'would be most unseemly should this maiden adhere to your wishes."

"Are you not my servant?" he responded, unable to keep the smile from his lips.

"Aye, sir, I am," she answered, lowering her head as if at last realizing her place, while a smile teased the corners of her mouth.

"Then you may proceed servant and do not neglect any vital parts."

Sighing tiredly, he leaned back, his arms resting along the edge of the tub as he continued, "Oh, God, I grow weary of telling these wenches what their chores be. I long to find one among you that will do her duties with relish."

"Jonathan," she warned, her eyes lifting to his murderously. "If I thought . . ."

He laughed at her rage, happy to see she could not hide her jealousy, his heart beating madly with joy, knowing deep feelings for him lurked within her whether she'd admit to them or not.

She hit his shoulder with a fisted hand and soap splattered every which way.

Pulling her suddenly against him, he held her hands to her back and caught her mouth with his burning, hungry lips, holding her to him well past the time her anger left her. And when he released her arms, he deepened the kiss and caused a low moan to escape the back of her throat, while her arms circled his neck and held his mouth to hers.

A satisfied gleam danced in his eyes as he released her mouth, and Merry didn't miss it as she gave a low groan and moved back. "Wretched beast."

He laughed at her mutterings, as he tipped her head so she was forced to face him. His wet fingertip grazed her cheek as he spoke. "None other have been here before you, Merry, and I promise no other will follow you, for I want only you above all others."

He waited until her golden eyes softened to a warm, loving glow before he continued. "Come to me, Merry, and let me show you of my need."

Chapter Fifteen

MERRY SNUGGLED DEEPER INTO JONATHAN'S ARMS, WISH-
ing she could keep the creeping dawn at bay, as she
reveled in the touch of his warm body against hers. "I
wish you did not have to go. Is there no other that could
take your place?"

"Merry," he breathed into her golden hair, "you
know I've been taking care of Captain Remington's
wife since the beginning of her pregnancy. She trusts no
one else to tend to her. Will you miss me, Rebel?" he
teased.

She laughed as she buried her face in his neck,
refusing to admit the truth to him. "I'll have no one to
badger. Who will fight with me?"

He chuckled and held her tighter, caressing the
length of her back as he spoke softly, "Is that all you
will miss?"

"What would you have me admit, English?"

"The simple truth would suffice, Merry."

"Perhaps I know not the truth as yet."

"Perhaps," he agreed, "but I think not. I believe you know well enough what is in your heart. Are you afraid to speak it?"

She lowered her gaze, unwilling to meet his eyes as he put some inches between them. "Shall I help you?" he asked.

No response.

"I have yet to tell a woman I love her, Merry. Till now there has not been a need."

Unable to resist as her eyes lifted to his in a searching look, she whispered haltingly, "Do you love now, Jonathan?"

He gave a long, shaky breath, as his voice deepened with the intensity of his feelings. "I fear what I feel goes beyond that simple emotion, Merry. I truly wonder if it be possible to relate the extent of it, for it wordlessly shadows my every waking moment and haunts my dreams. It brings a joy I've not before known existed, a happiness that lifts the soul and quickens the step, a longing that seems never satisfied. No matter how many times I hold you, I find I want you more.

"I respect your courage, admire your loyalty, delight in your rages, am captivated by your smile. At times I need no more than to watch you, whether you are canning fruit, folding laundry, or pouring a tankard of ale.

"And most astonishing of all, I awaken to find you sleeping at my side, and I'm filled with a rush of wondrous happiness that I should be so fortunate, for I know there'd be no other to compare to you."

190

She raised shy eyes to his shimmering, dark gaze. "Will you always consider me thus?"

"Merry," he sighed, as he pulled her to him once again. "I cannot fathom a time when I would not. In truth my feelings for you grow as each day passes."

For a long time he simply held her to him, placing a light kiss on her shoulder and then following it with many more at her neck, while waiting for her to respond to his declaration. When she volunteered nothing, he finally whispered, "Have you nothing to say, Merry?"

She smiled as she snuggled closer. "If I bared my soul, Jonathan, would you promise to forever cherish it and treat it with tenderness?"

"Aye, that I would, Merry."

She breathed a long sigh and forced herself to speak the words she had known these long, happy weeks. "'Tis true, Jonathan. I do love you."

"Oh, Merry," he laughed, as he pulled her tiny form to lie upon the length of his body, his arms holding her above him for a long moment as he reveled in her disheveled, naked beauty. "Was it so hard for you to admit your love?" he asked as he allowed her to rest upon him.

She grinned down at him and gave him a short shrug. "T'was harder to say it than to feel it."

"For how long have you known?"

"I've suspected it for some time, but until recently, I've not known it as fact."

– "When?"

"Do you remember the day you helped me cook for the pot-luck supper?"

He nodded.

"Remember when I tied an apron at your waist?"

He gave a sheepish grin, "Indeed, Madam, for it gave you a particularly good laugh."

"It was then I knew."

"In truth?!" he asked, his astonishment obvious. "Had my lovemaking done naught to sway you?"

"Oh indeed, sir, it did much," she grinned and dared to allow her hands to roam boldly over him, delighted to feel his body hardening in response, "but when you were able to laugh at yourself in an apron, your confidence undaunted, it was then I knew I loved you."

He laughed. "'Tis unbelievable, the mind of a woman. For months I teased and cajoled, deliberately setting out to entrap you, taunting you to deny your desire for me—my pants tight enough to split—while nearly catching pneumonia in my unbuttoned shirts. And in the end, all I needed was an apron."

Merry laughed as she swatted his shoulder. "Oh, you wretch! So you knew what the cut of your clothes did to me. I should throttle you for the torment you caused."

"But you will not," he whispered knowingly, as his hands reached up to cup a ripe breast and brought it to his mouth.

"Nay," she smiled, as she allowed his mouth to seek her out. "I will not."

He gave a low, hungry growl as he nuzzled her breasts with his scratchy cheeks. She made to roll from him to lie on her back, but he countered her movement with a firm hand at her hip. "Nay, stay here. Show me the truth of the words you speak."

Merry greedily sought out the warmth of his mouth,

their breathing becoming one as hot tongues entwined, until each grew breathless and dizzy, longing for all of what their kiss promised. Tearing her mouth from his with a slow, purposeful lingering of her full lips, she taunted him to groan for more.

"Merry, your taste is such a bittersweet nectar that I know not how to bear the pain when your lips linger so," he sighed, as she slid her body lower, eager to touch her mouth to the solid warmth of his chest and stomach.

"Perhaps I should stop. I've no wish to see you suffer," she murmured into his warm flesh.

As she covered his body with slow, luxurious kisses, his body tensed and he cried out with a longing that surely equaled torture. "Oh, nay, Merry. I gladly suffer this torment, for without you it's even worse."

Straddling his hips, she sat upon his hardened maleness, pressing it between their bodies as her lips came once again to his mouth, leaving searing kisses, hungrily drinking in the taste of this huge, dark man who lay so meekly beneath her.

His groans of pleasure were louder now, and Merry nearly laughed out loud; so heady was this new sensation of power. He had never seemed so masculine to her, so confident of his worth that he felt no need to be the master here, so loving, as he allowed her to rub herself over him.

Her knees on each side of his hips, she rocked back and forth. Her eyes were half closed and unseeing as the pleasure swept over her, and her breathing quickened as she intensified her movements. His hands slid along her thighs to her hips and up her small frame to cup her breasts.

"Oh, Jonathan, 'tis so good," she breathed, as he leaned up and took her breast, sucking the tip into his mouth. His teeth nibbled and caused tingling shocks to run the length of her.

She had never felt so achingly alive. A low moaning started at the back of her throat. Her neck arched back, waiting for the coming pleasure.

Suddenly, she was on her back. Her eyes opened with shock at the quickness of his movements. "'Tis coming, I know," he whispered above her. "Fear not, I wish only to make it better for you."

Happiness and love for her clearly showed from his eyes, as they slowly moved over the length of her. "Merry, my love, you bring pleasure of such thunderous magnitude, I begin to fear for my sanity." His mouth brushed whisper-soft against her own and then continued a downward path, tasting every inch of her until she was sure she'd no longer be able to stand the yearning that filled her.

She gave a low, helpless moan as his mouth reached her at last. With building urgency, she held his head to her, as she moved her hips in agonizing motion against him, encouraging him to continue this tormenting ecstasy.

Her head twisted wildly over the pillow, as she cried out her need for him to bring this torture to an end.

Knowing the end was near for her, he suddenly entered her straining, firm body with a powerful thrust, that left her wide-eyed, gasping and shaken.

He brought his mouth to hers in a savage kiss that left her unsure of pain or pleasure, only wanting. Helpless to do more than moan unintelligibly, she felt his hand return to where his mouth had been, as he began to move his hips and fingers in a blinding rhythm of ecstasy.

He could feel the undeniable tightening, the wildly erotic tremors both in and out. He hurried his pace, unable to control his need for her, loving her with every ounce of knowledge he possessed.

She groaned thickly as a new indescribable sensation overcame her. Surely her body and mind would not bear it should this continue. Her back arched and his teeth caught the tip of her breast, biting just hard enough to intensify the sweet suffering, until a cry of aching anguish was torn from her throat and she fell over the edge of sanity, sure that this demented, vicious person she had become was as unreal as this wild act of passion.

It took a long time before she came back to reality and understood his gentle words of love, as he pressed tender kisses to her soft mouth. "I did not hurt you, Merry?"

"Nay," she smiled up at his concerned expression. "Have no fear, Jonathan, I will tell you loud enough should you hurt me."

"Of that, I've no doubt, my love," he returned as a tender chuckle came from deep within his chest. He rolled from her, taking her with him as he came to rest on his back, his arm circling her as he held her possessively to his side. "Ah, Merry, 'tis good this love we share."

"Have there been so many to compare?"

"There's been none to compare."

Unable to prevent the thought that others had enjoyed this act with him, she questioned, "How many have there been?"

He groaned, knowing no good could come of this. "Merry, I think 'tis best if the past lay dead and forgotten."

"The past can never be forgotten, Jonathan. Are we not the summation of all we have done?"

"Aye," he answered reluctantly.

"Would you have such expertise in lovemaking had there not been others?"

"Nay," he groaned, wanting to end this now. "Merry, need we talk of this? I'd not see this moment ruined."

"Are you sorry then that you've learned so much?"

"Not if it brings you pleasure. There have not been so many, Merry. I swear it. My life has not been so work-free to have allowed frequent dalliances. Much of what I know comes from my own imagination and my long withheld desire to have you."

She laughed. "Are you so imaginative, English? I was not aware George allowed such in his armies."

He pinched her backside and laughed as she punched his arm. "I'll have no disparaging remarks toward my King, Madam. 'Tis a matter of pride we English hold close to our hearts."

"Of that I have no doubt, sir. To see the English swagger is to see pride overmuch."

"Perhaps 'tis natural to swagger when an army is such a glorious sight."

"Aye, sir, blazing lobster backs be you all. Still," she lifted her eyes to the ceiling and remarked innocently, "one does wonder how those ragged Rebels could have beaten the mighty English, pretty uniforms and all."

Jonathan laughed and grabbed her, tickling her until she could only shriek for mercy.

Chapter Sixteen

AFTER JONATHAN LEFT, MERRY SET ABOUT THE DAILY chores. Working harder than usual, she strove to be able to fall into bed that night and, due to pure exhaustion, miss him not.

With a bucket of hot, soapy lye water and a stiff brush, she scrubbed the taproom floor, until the wood shone almost white. Finishing the chore, she sat for a time to recover her strength before starting another.

Still sitting, she lifted her gaze and shivered at the gust of cold air that swept through the room just before the front door closed. Her heart began to beat with a sudden rush of excitement, as she spied Austin Roe at the threshold.

Quickly she lowered her gaze, lest others in the taproom notice her interest. Something of importance was afoot, she reasoned, for she had seldom seen Austin show himself in daylight. More often than not, a slip of paper with the numbers 724 would mysteriously find its way to her dressing table. From that she would know to meet him at the usual place and time and he would have information that needed to be passed on.

Coming to her feet, she wiped her hands on her apron as she approached him, "Can I be of some assistance, sir?" she asked, pretending to be unaware of his identity.

"A tankard of ale would be put to good use, Mistress."

She smiled as she turned from him, wishing the others in the room gone, anxious to speak with him.

As she returned with the ale, a soldier at the far end of the room began to relate a tale of his expertise on the battlefield, which allowed Austin to speak a quick word to her. "Jimmy Rivington might find that of interest," he commented, as he allowed his gaze to rest upon a small Bible that was sitting on the table.

She knew he was asking her to deliver it. Thank God, Jonathan was gone for the day, leaving her able to do so. It was obvious Austin could not go into the city. Perhaps the English were becoming suspicious.

She smiled as she looked pointedly at the Bible. "'Tis no problem, sir."

Soon after finishing his ale, he left, allowing it to appear to all eyes as if he had forgotten the book. Merry wiped off the table and placed the Bible in her pocket.

"Father," she remarked casually before the laughing soldiers, "should that man return, tell him he left his book and I have it."

A few hours later, a small, lone figure dressed in the garb of a farm boy left the inn.

Wearing a heavy, coarse jacket to ward off the cold night, he was unnoticed by probing eyes as he spurred his horse along the dirt road that headed west toward Brooklyn Heights.

Merry realized it was impossible for her to dress as a lady and travel without a companion, therefore the disguise. Not being averse to the freedom a boy's clothing brought, she was not sorry to take on this easy chore. This was a simple task indeed. Before her marriage, she had often moved along these roads to relay a message, and it felt good to be about her work once again.

Urging her mount on as the day approached dusk, she knew she'd have to hurry, not wanting to be on the road as night fell. Still, no matter how she hurried, she did not reach the city until well after dark. Lanterns were lit along the cobblestone streets, while soldiers and Tories, accompanied by their ladies, made merry. Laughter echoed along the streets as the couples disembarked their carriages, huddled in heavy coats and flowing capes of fur, to enter eating establishments.

There was almost an hysterical note to their laughter, she mused, as if each knew the end was near, and they laughed all the more seeking to deny the eventual outcome.

Soon Merry was guiding her horse down the familiar side street and entering the darkened alley at the back of Jimmy Rivington's teahouse. Dismounting, she tied her horse to the ring embedded in the brick wall, feeling no premonition of fear, as she moved stealthily through the dark.

Suddenly, a boisterous group of laughing soldiers exited the taproom across the alley. From the light across the way, Merry judged them to be deep in their cups, as they staggered out of the light and closer to her. One of them cursed loudly as he fell over a garbage can. A few leaned up against the wall, as Merry pressed flat to the other.

She dared not breathe, hoping beyond hope that they would not notice her. Her heart sank as she heard one of them. "What have we here? Mates, a moment of your time, if you will. A young lad be cowering here. Mayhaps we should ask him to join our group?"

"Molly likes them young," another ventured. "No doubt she'd give us all a little extra if we bring him along."

Merry wondered how they could not hear her heart pounding with terror. Lowering her voice to a boyish whisper, she answered haltingly, "I've got to go home. My mom will be worryin'."

"His mom!" The man laughed uproariously, as if that was the funniest thing he had ever heard, bar none. "Did you hear him? His mom!"

"Come boy," another said, while clutching at her elbow and leading her from the alley. "A man fears not his mother. 'Tis past time I think for you to find the delights of white parted thighs."

Merry groaned silently as she was pulled along. How was she to get out of this mess? Of all the dastardly luck! Countless were the times she had come to New York and left unaccosted. Why did they have to pick just that moment to leave the ale room? Damn their evil souls!

She was being pulled along the wide sidewalk now, stumbling, as did the soldiers that held on to her, when the leader of the group was suddenly brought up short.

Merry gasped, as two officers suddenly blocked their path. One of the men was none other than her husband! Oh, God, no! she cried silently. Literally thousands of people walked these streets daily and it was her fate to find Jonathan staring down at her.

Thankfully, they were some distance from a lantern and she prayed he'd not see her among the soldiers.

"What have you here, men?" he asked, noticing her immediately among the soldiers. "'Tis no trouble, I hope."

"Nay, Captain," one of the men volunteered. "We be bringing the lad to Molly's. She's always in need of a young stud."

"So I've heard," Jonathan answered as he looked at Merry.

For an instant his eyes registered recognition, but the expression died as suddenly as it had come to life, and Merry found herself relaxing some. "He looks terrified. Is this his first time?"

The men laughed, while one of them teased, "Aye, he be frettin' on his mom."

"If the boy is unwilling . . ." he left the sentence unfinished.

"Oh he'll be willin' enough once Molly gets her hands on him," another boasted.

"I think not," Jonathan remarked casually and Merry gave a silent groan. He *had* recognized her. He wouldn't be interfering otherwise. "If you've no objection, I think 'tis best if you leave him in my charge. The first time for a tender youth should be a moment well remembered and I've a particularly lovely lady in mind."

"No!" Merry grunted, as she pushed the soldier who

201

stood at her side further off balance and watched with no little amazement and a great deal of relief, as he fell into his comrade; like dominoes, they all went down amid shouts of laughter and grunting curses.

Merry was off and running before Jonathan could regain his stance, since the soldier that fell on him seemed to be perfectly content for the time being to rest against his form, rather than the hard, dirty sidewalk.

Merry dared not pause in her escape, as she heard fast footsteps approaching from behind. Ducking into the first alley she came to, she scrambled behind two tins of garbage. Invisible in the dark, she watched as Jonathan paused and peered down the alley and then ran through it to the next street, his muttered curses floating softly in his wake.

For a second he wavered, obviously unsure of which direction to take. An instant later, he disappeared from sight, as he made his decision and ran to his right.

Merry breathed a sigh of relief and then shivered with a sudden chill, as she realized what would be in store for her once Jonathan returned to the inn. With a weary sigh, she left her hiding place, only to jump back again, as the group of soldiers who had followed Jonathan were merrily taking up the chase.

Carefully, she left the alley again as the sound of their laughter and shouting began to fade. As nonchalantly as her stiff, terrified body allowed, she crossed the street and went down another alley, heading back to the teahouse and her horse.

The Bible, with its hidden message, was quickly dispatched and Merry was soon on her horse, leaving the city behind her. Icy night air cut into her face and froze her fingers as she rode her horse hard, desperate to return to the inn as quickly as possible. She knew, unless she hurried, he'd be there waiting for her.

In her panic to be gone, she didn't remember the vial of medicine she should have returned with. T'was as always her excuse to be about this time of night. An ailing mother nearly always did the trick, she mused.

Merry groaned with annoyance when she was ordered to stop some miles from home by a group of soldiers. She knew she could offer no valid reason for being on the road at this time of night. Fearing discovery, she bolted her horse and sped on. Behind her she heard a man roar, "Halt!" She ignored the order.

Shots were fired in the night. No sooner did she breathe a sigh of relief upon escaping her foe, than did she feel a hard, punishing thud hit her right shoulder. For an instant, she was confused, thinking she had hit a low-lying branch, not realizing the thud would have been felt on the front of her shoulder, rather than the back.

She mumbled a low curse as she realized with no little disgust she'd been shot. Dammit! She'd never be able to deny her journey now. Merry was amazed that she felt so little pain. Her right arm and hand simply seemed to go numb and she was forced to move the reins to her left hand.

She groaned as she felt the warm wetness seep down her back and then icy chills, as the cold air stole beneath her coat. She pushed her horse harder. What a mess she'd made of this night. She prayed nothing else would go wrong. At this rate, she wasn't sure she'd make it home at all. She had to keep her senses about her and hurry.

Twenty minutes later, she was numb with the cold as she stabled her horse behind the inn. She cursed helplessly, having no easy time of it, since she was forced to use only one hand. Quickly, she wiped her horse down. Jonathan's horse was already in the barn and she couldn't control the shiver of apprehension that overcame her, knowing he was inside waiting for her.

Silently, she entered the inn, moved quickly past the shadowy forms of furniture downstairs and mounted the steps to her room.

She was inside. Leaning against the closed door, she breathed a sigh of relief, knowing she need not face him this night. She began to shiver. Vaguely, she wondered why. Reaction to this wild night and her injury, no doubt. She struck a flint to the prepared fire in the grate and sighed again, as she sat on the floor before the small, growing blaze. Her fingers were outstretched, searching for the needed warmth. Her cap sailed from her head to the corner with the use of her good arm. After a long time, she came to her feet and managed, with some trouble, to slip her heavy jacket off.

"What is the matter with your arm?" came a voice out of the dark.

She gasped at the sudden and unexpected deep sound and spun around, almost falling into the fire as she did so, while noticing for the first time the dark form of her husband reclining upon the bed.

Ignoring his question, she demanded, "What are you doing here?" Suddenly, she was enraged that he should be watching her all this time.

Coming to his feet, Jonathan lit the candle that stood on a small table beside the bed. He turned to face her and smiled sardonically, his voice icy with controlled rage. "Have you forgotten, Rebel, after only a few hours of separation? I am your husband."

Her eyes caught the disorder of her dresser drawers. Clothing was pulled out and lay every which way. Obviously, they had been thoroughly searched. "How dare you go through my drawers? Being my husband gives you no right to invade my privacy."

He leaned lazily against the heavy bedpost, his casual stance belying the rage that boiled his blood. "In your absence I found myself with some time on my hands," he answered snidely, "and I thought I might learn a bit about the lady I call wife."

"So you took it upon yourself to spy on me, to search my things?"

"Have a care, woman," he warned coldly, his rage only barely under control, as he held up his hand to forestall any further outburst, while stepping closer to her. "Whether you wish to believe it or not, I was worried for your safety, and I thought I might be able to find out where you were or what you were about."

The last of his control vanished, as he suddenly grabbed her arms and gave her a hard shake. "Are you out of what little mind you have? Where were you?" His voice broke as he continued, "Do you realize how I suffered thinking you might have been taken? Do you think your beauty will save you should you be found out? Do you know what they do to pretty little ladies who spy?"

Merry nearly screamed at the agonizing pain that shot through her at his not too gentle touch. With a will of iron, she pushed aside the pain and grated hoarsely, "Get out of my room."

He looked at her as if he didn't know who she was. "I

could beat you, dammit! And if you say another word, I just might," he raged, as he released her with a sudden, hard shove and watched with some puzzlement as she swayed drunkenly before him. "Are you all right?"

Merry felt a hard cramp hit her midsection and nearly doubled over with the force of it. The ache in her shoulder was nothing compared to this ripping pain. What the hell was happening to her?

Lifting her chin in defiance, she denied the wave of dizziness that caused the room to tilt at a crazy angle. "The day I complain of an ailment to an English bas . . ." she got no further, as the blackness that threatened the edge of her consciousness finally overcame her, and she crumbled into a heap before his astonished eyes.

"Jesus!" he groaned softly, instantly flooded with guilt, as he bent over her limp form and gathered her into his arms. "Merry, my God, are you all right?" he asked, his voice shaking with fear, as he laid her on the bed, while waves of sympathy, guilt and terror washed over him.

Quickly, he undid the buttons of her shirt and, as he went about the task of removing it, wondered why she should moan as if in pain. Then he saw the blood. Suddenly, he was filled with such rage that he pulled back his hands, afraid that he might inflict further harm upon her. Gaining some control, he finally rolled her to her stomach and studied the wound, while uttering a stream of curses and swearing revenge upon her for making him suffer so.

He was gone from her for only the time it took to run to his room and return with clean linen and his bag. When he returned she was lucid again.

Stiff and cold was his attitude, as he began to clean the wound. "Here," he offered her a strip of folded linen. "Put this between your teeth and bite on it. This is going to hurt."

She did as she was told, holding back her screams admirably, giving only the slightest moan as he extracted the steel ball.

He thanked God as he examined the extent of her injury. She must have been some distance from the gun, for the ball was lodged against the bone, but had not shattered it. Placing the ball in his pocket, he set about closing the injury. When he was finished, as he had once before, he gave her laudanum for the pain.

While she slept, he washed her tenderly, his face showing little emotion until he removed her pants. Suddenly, his cool composure crumbled at what he saw and he felt a knifelike pain grip his chest. Huge, wracking sobs were torn from him, and he felt an insane need to hold her lovingly to him and choke the very life from her at the same time.

For the remainder of the night he sat at her side and watched her sleep. He was exhausted from the long ride and the additional stress of worry. Now that he had her safely in his hands, he felt the aching tiredness seep into his bones. He swore he'd never leave her alone again. God, he couldn't go through another night like this, for she obviously was not to be trusted.

He had nearly dropped dead from shock, spying her clutched tightly in the hands of an English soldier. For a wild moment he had nearly panicked, as he thought she had been found out. Then he had realized they had thought her to be a boy. A wave of relief had washed over him, as his mind raced to remedy the situation, until the little chit had pushed the drunken louts on him and made good her escape.

He had nearly gone insane searching the streets and alleys of New York for her. He never wanted to live through such panic again.

Finally, he had given up the hunt and sped back, hoping to find her along the road. Instead, he had spent some two hours waiting for her return. He felt the anger flood through him again, and all during the night he wavered between relief and rage.

It was late the next morning when she moaned softly. Still more than half asleep, she tried to relieve the soreness she felt in her shoulder. Forgetting she'd been shot, she thought she had lain on it too long. Finally, the pain brought her fully awake and she spied him sitting beside her, his face closed, his eyes cold with suppressed rage.

In a stilted voice he asked, "How be you faring on this morn, Madam?"

Merry glanced at him sharply, knowing full his knowledge of her injury and his apparent care for her, since a bandage was securely tied about her shoulder. "Well enough," she managed, but unwittingly moaned as she tried to lift herself.

"I'm afraid you'll have to stay in bed for a day or two."

"Nay," she insisted. "My arm aches is all."

"You've lost a bit of blood, be your clothes any proof," he remarked nonchalantly.

She ignored him and continued, until she was sitting at last, her legs hanging over the edge of the bed.

"I am perfectly fine," she snapped fiercely, and if

her voice shook with weakness, she refused to acknowledge it.

Stonily he sat and watched her. Slowly, she came to her feet and swayed dizzily. Suddenly, her face grew white and he knew she was about to faint again.

Muttering an oath, he grabbed her and pushed her back on the bed. She felt less dizzy sitting, but a sudden rage at his rough treatment of her filled her to overflowing. "I said I was all right!"

"Goddamn you and your stubbornness!" he raged, as he pressed her back to her pillows, snapping her quilt over her with no tenderness. His teeth clenched in anger, as he leaned over her and growled into her face. "Do you realize you've aborted our child with your insanity?" Noticing the shocked expression in her eyes, he pressed on, "Yes, Madam, I said aborted, not miscarried, for as far as I'm concerned you cared nothing for the English brat."

He moaned in torment, as he leaned back and covered his face with shaking hands. His voice broke as he went on. "I wonder if I shall ever forgive you? As of now, I think not."

Merry made a small sound, wanting to deny the terrible loss that suddenly filled her. It couldn't be true! Thinking back, she realized she had twiced missed her monthly flow. How could it be that she had not realized her condition? Why hadn't she stopped to think? Surely someone else could have taken her place. She was not indispensable. Good God, what had she done? It was her fault, of course. She could not shift the blame to another. The simple fact was she should not have been out on a mission.

She turned to face him and could not find the words to speak. His expression was one of such raw agony that she could not stop the tears that ran from her eyes.

"I did not know, Jonathan. I swear it," she cried.

"No doubt," he snapped, "all you can think of is your righteous cause. Everything else be damned."

He sat for a long moment before he finally managed to continue in a low weary voice, "Had I known of the pain you are capable of inflicting, Madam, I would have run at the sight of you. As it is I can barely stand your presence. You will, I've no doubt, excuse me," he added as he came to his feet and left her alone with her aching sorrow and guilt.

The next few days passed in slow misery, as she, for the most part, lay alone in her bed, barring an occasional visit from her father or Nettie. Jonathan came once a day to check her wound. His examinations were quick and impersonal. While he worked over her, she found herself studying his handsome face. Never once did he allow himself eye contact with her, nor did he speak unless necessary.

She knew he was hurt, that he believed she had not cared for or wanted his baby, and she was unable to break down the wall he had put between them. She knew in her heart that no amount of pleading would work. He believed her to be the same hate-filled girl he had once known. Only time could heal his pain and give her a chance to make amends.

Chapter Seventeen

Merry sat in the family parlor, a book held loosely in her hands as she pretended to read. Her concentration was nil, and she groaned silently as she found her eyes wandering once again to the tall form of her husband as he poked at the fire that blazed in the grate. She gave a soft, weary sigh and discarded the book. Her injury had healed long ago, she was restless and jittery and longed to be free of this forced confinement.

It had been weeks since they had spoken anything other than niceties to one another. Weeks since he looked at her. Weeks since he smiled. How much longer was this to go on?

She knew he was no longer angry, but his cool indifference was almost more than she could bear. Aye, she'd take his rages any day rather than the cool politeness he now showed her.

Merry noticed her father's puzzled looks, whenever

he was with them. It was obvious there was trouble between them, yet Noah Gates chose to keep his comments and advice to himself, hoping whatever it was would soon right itself without his interference.

Merry was at a loss as to what to do. Twice she had tried to bring up the subject that had caused this rift, to explain she had not meant for it to happen and to ask for his forgiveness, only to be told in no uncertain terms, he'd hear none of it. Since the night she had returned from New York, she had slept alone in her room. If she were to go to him, would it soothe the hurt they each suffered? Would their relationship return to what it once had been if she put aside her pride?

Why should he think he suffered alone? Didn't he realize the child had been hers, too? Did he truly think her so heartless? Of course he did, she reasoned. Why else would he rage so?

Oh, God. How little he truly knew of her. She had been careless and unthinking, in truth, but never did she realize she was to have his baby. If she had known she'd never have gone on that mission. Why wouldn't he listen?

She knew the reason, of course. For too long she had raged against the English. How often had she lumped them together as evil misfits, swearing to hate each and every one until her death? Why hadn't she seen the folly of her words and the damage they were sure to cause? He had believed her wild words were meant for all, including his child.

Merry stirred restlessly. She longed to be gone from here. How much longer was she to bear this deafening silence? Her fingers touched the letter in her pocket.

Her Aunt Elizabeth had written, expressing her sorrow over the loss of the baby and suggesting Merry might come to her home in New York for the Christmas holidays. Her aunt thought the festivities would help her to recover in full. Merry hoped they would.

Anxious to be gone from Jonathan's presence, she vowed to speak to him tonight. Both might find some peace once separated, she reasoned, unable to believe he'd be sorry to see her go.

Jonathan stirred the flaming wood with the poke he held, his heart heavy since the night she had lost their child. Twice she had ventured to speak of it, but he had felt such gut-wrenching agony that he had insisted she not speak of it. How could he have been such a fool as to believe she cared for him? Aye, she had come to his bed and brought him more delight than he had imagined possible. Judging by her cries, she had found pleasure there also, but that meant only that she was a passionate woman.

He had forced her to marry him. Fool that he was, he had believed she would one day return his love. Aye, she had told him as much, but only after he had badgered her into it. Had she even once willingly told him of her love? Nay. She had professed sorrow over the loss of the child, but how could he believe her? Nay, she had spoken too often of her hatred for the English bastards. He knew she did not want to bear his child. Her actions were proof, were they not?

Oh, God, why did he have to love her so? Every day that he spent in her presence brought him nothing but torture. Perhaps she was right after all. Perhaps he should return to England and secure a quiet divorce.

His heart twisted with pain at the thought. Nay, he could not. No matter what she did to him, said to him, he loved her beyond all reason.

Somehow, some way, he had to find a way to bring them together again. For the first time in his life, he felt helpless and ignorant. How the hell was he to go about it? It would not due for him suddenly to become loving to her. She would surely see past that and grow suspicious. How does one make another fall in love with you? What they needed was some time alone. But, what excuse could he give to get her away from here?

His thoughts were interrupted by a soft, feminine voice behind him. "Captain, I wonder if I might have a word with you?"

Forcing his emotions under control, he turned to face her. How he wanted to hold her. Why must loving someone be so painful? Would he never know the love she was capable of giving?

Merry searched his face and read no emotion in his dark eyes. She sighed wearily, giving up all hope that he could ever forgive her. "My Aunt Elizabeth has heard of the loss of the baby," she stated softly, biting her lips and lowering her gaze, as she noticed the flicker of pain that crossed his face. "She asks that I join her in New York for the holidays. I was thinking it might be a good idea."

Jonathan didn't miss her use of the word "I" rather than "we," and was struck by another twisting pain. She obviously wished to be away from here and away from him. Nay, it could not be. He'd not allow it. Gathering all his strength, he forced his voice to remain cool, belying the torment that flooded his body and mind. Finally he managed, "I see no problem with the plan, Merry. A round of parties can do you no harm, and I will be but a few hours ride from the fort should a problem arise. I see no reason why I could not take leave."

Merry looked up with surprise, but quickly covered her amazement with a genuine smile. He wanted to go with her. He had not suggested she go alone, even though she had hinted at such an idea. Her heart felt light and pounded wildly in her breast as an invisible weight seemed to lift from her. Could it be that he had forgiven her? Was he as anxious as she to see the end to this estrangement? For a long moment she studied his face, but, no matter how she tried, she could not convince herself that the cool expression in his eyes in any way resembled the warmth she longed to see. Her spirits sank. "Will you inquire about your leave on the morrow?"

"I will," he agreed. "I think it would not be unreasonable to plan on leaving early on the day after. We should be able to reach your aunt's home before the midday meal."

Merry smiled, suddenly happier than she had been for weeks. "I will be ready."

"Are you tiring?" he asked, his dark gaze searching her face.

"Nay. I fear I have rested overmuch these past weeks. My confinement stretches endlessly. I long to breathe fresh air and relieve myself of this restlessness."

"If you dress warmly, I see no reason why you should not take a walk. I will accompany you."

Merry almost jumped to her feet in her anxiousness to be outside. "I'll be back in a minute," she shot over her shoulder as she dashed from the room, her heart twisting with happiness as she heard Jonathan's soft chuckle while she sped up the stairs.

Merry breathed a sigh of relief as the rented coach pulled away from the inn at last. Tied securely to its boot and roof were three trunks filled to overflowing with all the beautiful dresses and accessories Jonathan had given her. At last, she thought, with no little excitement, she was going to be able to put them to some use.

She smiled to herself, as she visualized wearing any one of them while serving in the taproom. Not one among them could be considered serviceable. Leaning back in the comfortable leather seat, she gave thanks silently for the next few weeks. For once she could forget the inn and the constant and endless chores that were always waiting for her.

Glancing out the coach's window, she wasn't surprised to see snowflakes falling gently about the countryside, for the sky was heavy and white and the temperature the coldest she could remember. She snuggled deeper into the sable-lined velvet cloak she wore and pulled a matching fur across her knees to ward off the chill. Never before had she known such luxury. From the satin garments that lay closest to her skin, to the furs that completed her ensemble, she knew she was dressed as fashionably as any aristocrat.

She glanced at her husband who sat across from her, his attention on the passing countryside, allowing her to study his face. How was it a doctor in the King's Dragoons could afford to dress his wife in such elegance? Was he a man of independent wealth? How strange, she thought silently, to be married for all these months and still not know the man she called husband.

He had claimed to be a simple doctor, called into service for his king, and yet he was obviously more than that. She longed for the closeness they had once shared. She wished she could ask him so many things, yet his cool demeanor dared her not.

She gave a soft sigh, and the sound brought Jonathan's gaze to rest on her. "Are you experiencing some discomfort?"

She smiled at his serious expression, "Nay, Jonathan. You need not concern yourself. I am fine."

Jonathan watched her closely. The cold air had added color to her cheeks, and her eyes sparkled with the delight of a child eagerly awaiting a special treat. His chest twisted with the unspoken love he felt for her. How in God's name was he to get to her? Would the day ever come when she might return some of his feelings? How much longer was he to suffer?

Suddenly, the carriage hit a particularly deep rut, and for a long, terrifying moment skidded dangerously out of control as the wheels slid over an icy patch of road. Merry was flung against the side of the coach, striking her head sharply.

Jonathan was instantly at her side pulling her into his lap, carefully examining the red mark on her forehead. She could feel his warm breath against her face as he watched, with growing concern, the red welt darken to blue. She breathed deeply of his clean scent, overcome with desire for him. It had been weeks since they had been this close, weeks since he had touched her. She had to force herself not to raise her mouth to his. He had made it all too clear that he did not want her. And she couldn't bear it should she offer her lips only to be refused.

Jonathan gazed down to his wife's haunting loveliness. The scent of lemon that assaulted his senses was very nearly his undoing. He wanted more than anything else in life, to touch his mouth to hers. But, what purpose would it serve? He didn't doubt she would respond to him, but he wanted to awaken more than her desire. He wanted her love and he'd not take her again until he knew he possessed it.

His voice was strangely husky and deep when he spoke. "Is it giving you pain?"

"Nay, Jonathan. You fuss overmuch," she remarked, trying to keep her tone light and seemingly unaffected by his nearness, while her heart pounded wildly against her breast. "'Tis not necessary for you to hold me thus."

"It causes me no hardship, Merry. I will hold you," he returned, his tone giving her no choice but to accept his actions.

She settled herself into his arms and leaned her head to his chest, listening to the muffled sound of his heart beating beneath her ear.

"I've not often seen it snow," he remarked after some time. "It reminds me of when I was a boy and my father would take my brother and myself north to hunt."

She sat up straight, her face showing her interest as she asked, "Is your father still alive?"

"Nay," he sighed. "He died some years ago."

"And your mother?"

"By last account, she fares well."

"Do you miss her?"

"Very much."

"Will you not tell me more? I've had no one but my father since I was a baby and I hunger to hear of your childhood. Where you happy? Did you have many brothers and sisters? Where in England did you live? What did your father do? What did you do before you became a doctor?"

He laughed, "Which question shall I answer first?"

She smiled and gave a small shrug. "Till now you've told me nothing of your family, Jonathan. Do you find fault that I am inquisitive? Would you have me not ask?"

"Nay, Merry," he answered with a grin. "I will tell you. 'Tis no secret."

And for the next hour he told her of his family, relating hilarious stories of his childhood, while carefully avoiding mention of his father's title.

She was laughing at the story of how he and his brother were chasing each other around the kitchen, each holding a glass of milk and threatening the other with it. Jonathan had finally flung the contents at his brother, only to see him duck and his father catch the full glass of milk square in the face, as he chose just that moment to enter the room.

Suddenly, the carriage pulled to a stop and Merry in the midst of laughter and easy camaraderie, was loath to leave the warmth of the moment.

For a long time they simply stared at one another. The laughter had momentarily melted their reserve and each could suddenly read the longing in the other's eyes. Merry gave a soft gasp at the intensity of desire she found in his dark blue gaze. Without thinking, her face lifted as his descended. Their lips were but a hairsbreadth apart, when the door to the carriage was suddenly flung open.

Merry jumped at the unexpected intrusion, as her aunt poked her head inside. "Well? Are you going to sit there all day?" And then spying the guilty look on her niece's face, she laughed, "Merry, you needn't blush. A lady may sit upon her husband's lap." And when she only succeeded in growing redder, her aunt commented with a bit more admiration than Merry deemed necessary, "Had I a man such as this one, you'd find me no where else."

Jonathan laughed, as he exited the carriage and assisted his bride to stand beside him. "Have I the honor of addressing Aunt Elizabeth?"

"That you do, Jonathan," the spirited redheaded lady countered, "but should you dare call me aunt again, you'll see first hand what it means to rile a redhead."

Jonathan laughed again, obviously much taken with the fiery lady who was now hustling them up the stairs and into her home.

For the first time, Merry realized just how young and pretty her aunt was. Elizabeth was only ten years Merry's senior which made her a mere two years older than Jonathan and, Merry realized with no little shock, quite capable of being her rival. How was it she had never seen it before? Jonathan had certainly not missed any of her charms, and the look of delight that had yet to leave his face made Merry want to stomp on his toe, which she instantly did.

Feigning clumsiness, she smiled sweetly at his surprised expression and whispered low, "Forgive me, Jonathan. I did not see your foot."

"Indeed, Madam," he returned, his mouth lifting in a happy grin, "it appeared to me you not only saw it, but made a point of seeking it out. Perhaps I have done something of which you do not approve?"

"Certainly not."

Jonathan laughed, as he slipped his arm around her waist and held her to his side. "Are all the women in your family so fascinating?"

Merry only groaned at his question, which caused him to laugh again.

"Come out of that drafty hall, you two," Elizabeth ordered as she took their coats and handed them to the silent butler standing directly behind her. "Sit yourselves before the fire."

Merry felt herself ushered into a small, warm sitting room, and then was pretty much ignored as Elizabeth made much to do over her husband. Jonathan was offered a view of Elizabeth's ample charms, as she bent to prop his feet on a footrest and placed a glass of brandy in his hands.

Merry was amazed. Her aunt was flirting outrageously with her husband, and Jonathan was obviously enjoying every minute of it.

"You can help yourself, can't you, dear?" Elizabeth asked, as she made herself comfortable beside Jonathan on the small settee. "After all, this is like your own home."

Merry was so filled with anger, she could barely speak, and it took her some minutes before she could trust her voice. "I think I shall forgo a drink right now, Aunt Elizabeth. The ride was more tiring than I had supposed. I think I will go to my room and rest."

"That's fine, dear," Elizabeth answered, not bothering to look at her niece, so enthralled was she with the man who sat at her side.

Merry sped from the room before Jonathan could ask if she was feeling poorly and by the time she reached the top of the stairs, she could hear their murmured conversation and accompanying laughter as if they had long been the best of friends.

Discarding her dress, she lay on the bed in her chemise and gazed up at the ceiling, a headache threatening to overtake her. She groaned aloud to the empty room. Why did he have to come? How was she supposed to relax and enjoy herself while watching her aunt make eyes at her husband? *My own aunt? How could she?*

Elizabeth was her father's younger sister. Having married a particularly elderly gentleman, she had been widowed nigh on twelve years now.

Now that she was here again, she remembered quite clearly all the admirers who were constantly at her aunt's side during every visit. Why did she not think her husband might be taken with her also?

Merry moaned with disgust and turned her head to the pillow, suddenly too tired to care.

Chapter Eighteen

AN HOUR LATER, MERRY AWOKE TO FIND JONATHAN grinning as he leaned over her. "Elizabeth sent me up to see if you want to eat."

"In truth?" she snapped a bit nastily, coming fully and instantly awake. "Do you mean to say she allowed you from her side long enough to ask me?"

Jonathan chuckled above her. "Undoubtedly, she is a lovely lady. Are you jealous?"

"Jealous?! Me?" she shot him a look of utter contempt that he should find this so amusing. "Jonathan, if you prefer her company to mine, how am I to stop you?" She shrugged as if it were of little importance, "'Tis clear she has eyes only for you and ignores me as though I was not present. Perhaps I will take a stroll and visit a few shops. You may tell Elizabeth I am not hungry."

Getting up from the bed, she washed her face and adjusted a few wisps of hair that had come loose of their pins, before pulling on her dress.

Jonathan watched his wife, as the sweet ache of longing once again twisted his loins. She truly cared so little that she'd leave them alone. He felt so suddenly and desperately rejected that for one wild moment he thought he would wring her neck. "Would you leave me alone in the lady's clutches, Merry?"

"I think you are old enough, Jonathan, to decide if you want the lady's attentions or not. I certainly will not act as your duenna for the remainder of this visit."

For just an instant, she saw the pain in his eyes and spoke more gently, "Indeed, I am sorry, Jonathan, but you seemed not to mind her attentions overmuch."

"Your aunt is a beautiful and desirable young woman, Merry. Any man would feel flattered to be the recipient of her attentions."

"Apparently," she agreed with the tiniest hint of sarcasm.

"Does that bother you?"

"Not at all, Captain," she replied a bit frostily, as she picked up her reticule and made to leave the room. At the threshold she paused and then finished with an elaborate shrug, "Ask any number of women, I'm sure they would love to hear of the fine qualities of another."

With that she slammed the door behind her and fairly flew down the stairs and out the front door. "Damn them both," she muttered under her breath. Two can play this game, Captain Townsend, she vowed wildly. We shall see how well you fare should the tables turn.

What had come over him, she thought. He wanted

her to be jealous. No doubt he believed that would mean she had some feelings for him. She stopped dead in her tracks, as suddenly as if she had come up against a brick wall, as the idea took hold. Why? Why was he so disappointed when she had told him it did not bother her to see him flirt? Why should he want her to care?

Because he still loves you! Merry's heart sang with joy. He still loved her! He had invited himself to come along, had he not? Hadn't he ignored her intentions of visiting Elizabeth alone? Hadn't he treated her tenderly when she was bounced about in the carriage? If he did not care, would he have insisted that she sit in his lap for most of the journey?

She gave an evil snicker. Captain Townsend, for what you are about to go through, I could almost feel sorry for you, but I know not another man more deserving.

With a lightness to her step and a devastatingly beautiful smile playing about her lips, Merry walked the cobblestoned sidewalks of New York.

Jonathan had purchased more than enough in the way of lady's clothing, and her own quick fingers had taken care of any alterations. In truth she could think of nothing she needed. So it was that after two hours she had bought only one small bottle of perfume.

Tired of shopping, she hailed a hackney and leaned back and rested against the soft upholstery of the hired cab. It would do no harm, she reasoned, as long as she was about, to see if anything of importance could be learned, and a visit to Jimmy Rivington's tea shop would be just the place to do it.

Glancing out of the carriage's open window, she couldn't help but notice the starkness of the city. This was the first time in some months that she had visited the city in daylight, and she couldn't help but notice its half-ruined state. Totally stripped of trees, after seven years of war, it was a sorry sight indeed. British colors flew over the Battery and she gave a sharp gasp as the carriage passed the now black ruins that was once the Trinity Church.

A short time later she was sipping tea in Jimmy Rivington's small shop as serving girls ran busily from the kitchen to the tea room carrying trays laden with tea and cakes. Stopping by her table, Jimmy bid her good day and then most daringly, under the very nose of three English officers sitting no more than ten feet away, proceeded to tell her that Washington was of a need to know the strength of Carleton's troops and the exact count of men still stationed in New York.

Rivington himself had the numbers and their locations, but he needed someone to deliver this information. Brewster would await a message every night on the shore of Jamaica Bay, starting three nights hence. Rumor had it that Culper Jr. had lost heart since his lady had been taken captive and died on the prison ship Jersey and there was, at present, no other in the area that was trustworthy enough to do it. With only the slightest hesitation, Merry agreed.

"Elizabeth," Merry offered, as the three of them sat in the library sipping sherry after the evening meal, "I fear for your safety as the war winds down. It will not fare well for you to stay in New York. Word has it the Tories will suffer dearly, particularly those left in the city."

"Oh, Merry, do not worry overmuch. No one can

seriously take me for a Tory or a Rebel. I was simply smart enough to concede to the occupying forces. Besides, I have an offer or two I am pondering at present. Should I take either, I will no doubt be joining you on the voyage to England."

Merry laughed. "You are mistaken Elizabeth. I shall not be venturing from my home."

Elizabeth was clearly shocked, but a definite gleam of interest entered her eyes as she asked, "Will you not be joining your husband, then? Surely, you cannot mean to live an ocean apart?"

"Our plans are unclear at present, Elizabeth," Jonathan interrupted, lest Merry say more.

Before Elizabeth had a chance to press the matter, the butler announced the arrival of gentlemen callers. Merry was amazed to find no less than five men enter the library, each calling out to Elizabeth in the most familiar phrases.

Introductions were soon made and Merry was a bit startled to find these men more than a little interested in her attentions. She had never before been the center of all interest and found, to her surprise, she did not dislike the position in the least, unlike her husband, who seemed to grow quieter as each hour of frivolity passed. It took some time, but Elizabeth finally managed to end the evening by promising a ball at the end of the week.

As the men bade their hostess and her guests good night, each tried to outdo the others with his choice of outrageous compliments to the two ladies. By the time the last of them departed, Jonathan was livid.

Elizabeth, not ignorant of Jonathan's response to the

attention shown his wife, quickly left the couple, unwilling to witness the argument that was sure to ensue.

Silently, Jonathan paced the floor like a caged tiger and thoughtlessly downed a goodly sum of brandy in one gulp, barely tasting the fiery brew as it slid down his throat and warmed his chest and stomach, and then proceeded to curse the waste.

Feigning ignorance, Merry asked, "Is something amiss, Jonathan? You seem unusually tense on this night?"

"Madam, we've barely arrived and I already grow weary of watching my wife fawned over by a gaggle of horny toads."

Merry's eyes opened wide with astonishment, a twinkle of humor obvious in them, as she replied, "You surprise me, sir. In truth, I cannot see how you've managed to notice. Up till now, I was positive Elizabeth held your every attention." And then referring to his comment, she injected, "And I thought gaggles were used in reference to geese?"

"Save your witty answers for your admirers, Merry. You do not impress me at this moment," he raged.

"Do I not, Captain?" she smiled disarmingly, as she came to her feet and approached him. Reaching out a lone finger, she touched his chest as she continued, "Perhaps, in the future, I shall practice my wiles upon my own husband. You could then tell me if they are worth my while."

Jonathan tensed, as if he'd been slapped. Muttering a low curse, he spun away from her and slammed the door behind his departing figure, fearing the chit might goad him beyond all reason.

He couldn't imagine what had gotten into her. In a matter of hours she had changed from a shy sweet girl, to a practiced flirt, causing him no little amount of suffering. How had she managed the transformation? Good God, the way she fluttered her fan and looked at a man, one would think she had recently come from court, rather than the country.

He knew it irked her to see Elizabeth devote herself to him. Was this her way of returning the favor? Jonathan had to admit Elizabeth was titillating company. She was a vivacious beauty with golden red hair and a full voluptuous figure. At any other time in his life, he would have been more than willing to take advantage of the lady's obvious offer. As luck would have it, however, he found himself foolish enough to have fallen in love with his own wife. And try as he might to feel otherwise, he knew it would always be so. Should he succumb to Elizabeth's delicious charms, he knew the momentary satisfaction would be marred by a pair of liquid golden eyes.

Aye, he wanted no other but his wife, and he doubted there'd ever be a time when she'd want him in return.

Merry smiled as she heard the front door slam, knowing it would bring no harm for Jonathan to realize his wife was a desirable woman, particularly in the eyes of others. But her smile turned into one of delight, as she mounted the stairs to her room and spied Jonathan's bags.

Elizabeth, having no knowledge of the rift between them, had put them in the same room. Merry laughed softly at the suffering Jonathan would soon be forced to bear. He loved her, of that she had no doubt. But he knew not if his feelings were returned. She laughed again, as she envisioned many delicious ways of showing him just how he erred in his thinking.

Stripping off her clothes, she pulled a sheer pink gown over her head and, after brushing her hair, she climbed into the lonely bed, confident she'd not be lonely overlong.

Chapter Nineteen

MERRY AWAKENED ALONE THE NEXT MORNING TO THE delicious aroma of frying bacon. A quick glance to the rumpled pillow on her right confirmed her suspicions. Jonathan had returned after she had fallen asleep and was up and gone before she awoke.

In her sleep, she had felt his warm body press close to hers. She was sure now, as she remembered back. It was not a dream, but Jonathan who had held her in his arms and spoken low, tender words of love against her hair.

It would have been so easy for him to have made love to her and yet, he had resisted. Apparently, he needed to hear her declaration of love. It was obvious he believed she did not return his feelings.

He had once before waited to take her to his bed. Then he had needed her complete and total surrender. Now his feelings ran deeper. He knew she'd not deny him the act, but he wanted more, and she could only imagine the loss of their child had left him with doubts.

She smiled as she stretched, more sure of herself than of any time since she could remember, for she did love him completely. She was faced with only one problem. How was she to convince him of her love?

She pushed the covers back and came to her feet. Splashing cold water over her face and arms, she then dressed hurriedly. It was with a light step and a radiant smile that she entered the morning room, where Jonathan and Elizabeth were already in the midst of breakfast.

"Good morning," she stated cheerfully, and was not sorry to see the glow of approval in her husband's eyes, as his gaze swept her from head to toe. As he answered her greeting, he took in the lovely pale pink gown of raw silk that complemented the glow of creamy golden skin. A green velvet ribbon held her hair back and it tumbled down her back in a riot of soft, rich curls he longed to touch.

Jonathan felt a warm rush of such longing as to equal torture. She was so lovely, he knew not another to compare. And when she smiled as she did now, she took his breath away.

Last night it had been late before his anger had left him, and he had returned from a long bone-chilling walk only to find to his dismay that he had not been told in which room he was to sleep.

Entering Merry's room, he noticed his bags and reasoned Elizabeth had meant for them to stay together. With a sigh, he had undressed and slipped beneath the covers to join his wife.

In her sleep, Merry had reached out for him and

snuggled her head into his shoulder with a sleepy sigh of comfort. She was so soft and warm, the scent of her a long-dreamed-of delight. Hours passed, as he lay rigid and stiff next to her, fearing to relax, lest he lose all control and make love to her.

In the morning he had left her bed at first light, not trusting himself should he linger.

"You were up and about early this morning, Jonathan. Could you not sleep?" she teased wickedly, while forcing the laughter from her voice so she might appear consoling.

"I slept well enough," he countered a bit stiffly and then changed the subject. "I've learned a shipment of injured men are due to arrive from the south this morning. A ship will be readied soon for their journey home. In the meantime, rather than wile away the hours each day, I believe the hospital staff could use another hand." Taking a last sip of his tea, he rose from the table and made to leave the room. "You ladies will excuse me, will you not?"

"Jonathan, a moment of your time please," Merry asked, as she hurried after his departing figure.

In the hallway, he waited for her to join him as he shrugged into his heavy coat. His expression turned from inquisitiveness to pure shock, as she finally reached him and ventured to ask, "Do you think the hospital staff could use still another, if somewhat inexperienced hand?"

He gave her a tender smile. "These be British soldiers, Merry. Have you lost your aversion toward your occupiers?"

She looked up with gently pleading eyes. "Jonathan, do not tease me on this. You know I have long ago lost my hatred for the British. I hope I have found a bit of maturity over these past months."

His heart swelled with mounting hope. Was she telling him she no longer cared that he was English? Unable to refuse her anything, he touched his finger to her smooth cheek. "Twill not be a pretty sight, Merry. Many will have open, draining wounds, while others will be missing legs or arms. The moans and stench alone have caused many a brave heart to weaken."

Forcing aside her disgust, Merry countered, "Have I suddenly become a hothouse flower, Jonathan, so delicate as to crumble with the first breath of chill? I think not."

"If it be as bad as you say, will there not then be a need to bring a calming hand to those who suffer?"

His eyes glowed with pride. "I think the men will find your comforting hand more than they bargained for, Madam. Were I one of them, Merry, I could not deny the lifting of spirits your care would bring."

"Were you one of them, sir, and I waiting in England, I'd be most grateful to any lady who chose to comfort you."

Jonathan's eyes widened at his wife's tender words. "How long before you can ready yourself?"

"I am ready now. Just let me tell Elizabeth and I will join you presently."

Merry and Jonathan sat across from each other in the hired cab in amicable conversation. For the first time in weeks, she felt the distance between them growing smaller. Having gained new respect for his wife, Jonathan couldn't keep his admiration for her compassion and courage from his voice and manner.

All too soon the carriage stopped before the dreary

brownstone. Injured men were lined up outside, as carriage after carriage unloaded their human cargo. The hospital was filled to overflowing and, as there was no more room to be had, the injured had to further suffer the winter cold while waiting for a place to lay their weary bodies.

Merry was aghast that such suffering was allowed. The skimpy blankets that proved to be the men's only protection against the freezing weather were no better than dirty rags. Her dog Muffit fared better than these poor souls.

She was barely inside before an elderly matron grabbed hold of her arm and almost dragged her to a small linen closet, where she practically threw a long white apron at her. "Put this on and hurry."

And when Merry hesitated, the woman who had introduced herself as Mrs. Quigley snapped, "I've no time for the vapors, gel. These men be hurtin' somethin' fierce and need care on the double. If you've no stomach for this ye best be leavin' now. I've no one available to cater to a faintin' spell."

Merry tied the apron over her gown, swallowed hard and returned, "Where should I start, Madam."

"That's the ticket," the woman smiled appreciatively. "Follow me."

Merry did as she was told and was soon deposited in a long ward, in which beds took up every available space. Some beds held two men, some three. A tall, gaunt man, his hair thin and gray, but pulled back and tied neatly at the nape of his neck, stood beside one bed. He wore a tight grin and spectacles adorned the end of his nose. A long blood-spattered apron covered his dark suit. "Doctor Greyton, I've found ye some help," Mrs. Quigley offered, as she turned and left Merry at his side.

Merry took in the bedlam that surrounded her. There was nowhere she could look that she did not see pain and suffering. The stench of unwashed bodies and human feces was almost overpowering. In her wildest dreams she could not have imagined such horror. A hand suddenly clutched her arm, and a weak voice cried out, "Please, please make them give me something for the pain."

Merry turned to see who was holding her arm in a vicelike grip. Her free hand touched the sick man's forehead and she was amazed to feel how hot he was. She had never known a fever to rage so and still allow its sufferer to live.

Merry took a clean cloth from a cart that sat at the foot of the bed, fetched a bucket of water from another attendant, and bathed the man as best she could, trying to relieve his discomfort with the cold cloths. Barely had she started, when the man in the next bed cried out from the pain he suffered in his foot. Hurrying, Merry turned to help him and found he too suffered a fever. Lifting the stained sheet to see if she could ease the suffering in his foot, she swayed weakly as she found only a bloody, blackened stump where his leg had been taken at the knee.

Another called her, asking for water, while still another begged for relief from the pain he suffered. She worked faster than she had ever thought possible, bringing comfort where she could and cursing her ineptness where she could not.

Doctor Greyton called her to his side. Two burly men

were holding another to the bed. The prone man's eyes were wild with fright, as he cursed the doctor soundly and begged all around him for help in avoiding the doctor's knife.

Merry looked in amazement at the scene and marveled that the doctor should take no notice of the man's rantings. Rather, he simply ordered her to stand by his side and wipe the blood, so he might be about his job.

"I'd rather die, you Goddamned butcher," the man screamed. "Keep your bloody hands off me."

"Come on, mate," one of the men that was holding him tried to soothe. "Be a good lad. The doc says the leg must come off. You'd not be wantin' to die."

"I'd as soon be dead. What good am I without all me parts?"

Understanding full well that he thought himself only half a man without both his legs, Merry felt her heart swell with pity. Somehow she knew pity would not suffice here. Forcing herself, she somehow gathered the strength to give him a long meaningful and obvious leer. She placed her hands on her hips and taunted, "'Tis been my experience, soldier, the true measure of a man lay in his pants, not the length of his legs."

How she kept her face from turning scarlet with her daring words, she had no idea. Still, her eyes did not waver as she silently dared him to call her a liar. She breathed a long silent sigh of relief when at last she saw a glimmer of humor flash in the man's eyes while a grin teased his lips.

"Were you my man," she continued, "I'd want you home, alive and well, no matter the shortening of one leg."

The operation began immediately and Merry, although horrified to see more blood than she had ever before imagined, kept her face emotion-free as she wiped at the oozing cut. When the doctor took the saw and cut as easily as if he were severing a branch from a tree, it was nearly her undoing. Her sight blurred and a lightness crept into her brain, but she forced the faintness from her. She wanted not to look, but it was impossible, as she had to wipe away the continuous flow of blood.

The man bit down hard on a piece of folded cloth. A cry of torment was unwittingly torn from his throat. His eyes bulged, sweat formed and soaked his entire body. He jerked, he shook, he roared in agony and then, thankfully, there was only blessed silence as he fainted.

Tears blurred her vision, and she hastily wiped them away with the back of her hand as she continued to assist the doctor. Merry was amazed that it had been accomplished so quickly. A few minutes later, the severed artery was secured and almost all the bleeding had stopped. Once the stump was bandaged, the realization of the horror set in and she began to tremble uncontrollably.

Doctor Greyton offered her a brisk thank you as he went on to the next patient.

The two men who had held their friend were not ignorant of the lady's suffering and respect for her courage showed in their sweaty faces.

She gave them a quivering smile as both thanked her and one remarked, "You be a gutsy one, Miss. Not many would have stood that sight."

She smiled shakily again. "I'm not at all sure I did

stand it, Seargent." When one of the men brushed his scratchy face against hers and deposited a kiss on her cheek, the tears came tumbling forth. Her hands shook, as she tried to staunch the flow.

Realizing the lady was close to the end of her endurance, one of them suggested, "Mayhaps you should step outside for a breath of air, Miss. The cold night might revive your spirits."

"Perhaps I will," she agreed and, after a quick glance at the unconscious soldier, she left.

Merry walked outside and was more than a little surprised to see it was dark. She had worked the entire day and never realized the long hours till now. The crowd was gone. Apparently, room had been found for all, she knew not where. She never noticed the cold, as her mind returned to the suffering of those inside. She sat for a long moment on the top step, taking in huge gulps of cleansing air.

She couldn't remember when she had been so tired. How could these people do this day after day? Where did they get the stamina? She felt a wave of disgust at her own weakness. How dare she complain of tiredness, while these poor men suffered so horribly? She leaned her head against the stone railing. I'll go back in a minute, she promised herself. But the next thing she knew, Jonathan was there wrapping her in her fur cape.

"Merry, I've been looking for you everywhere. Whatever possessed you to sit out here without your cloak?"

Sleepily, she murmured, "I needed a breath of air. I didn't mean to fall asleep."

"Come on, Rebel," he whispered tenderly against

her cheek as he took her in his arms. "It's time for bed."

Hailing a cab, he held her against him and she slept soundly during the ride back.

"I feel much better, Jonathan. There's no need for you to carry me about," she insisted, as the hackney pulled to a stop at Elizabeth's door and he made to lift her into his arms again.

"Indulge your husband, Merry. It costs me no great effort to carry you. Did you manage to eat anything today?"

"I had not a chance," she replied, only now beginning to feel hunger, while remembering the hundreds of bowls of soup she had handed out and the dozens of men she had spoon fed.

"As I thought. After I put you to bed, you will eat. Elizabeth!" he called out the moment he stepped inside and Merry's aunt came running. He calmed her worries, "She is tired, is all. Send some soup and tea to her room, right away, will you?"

He was already at the top of the stairs before Elizabeth managed to overcome her surprise and hurried to the kitchen to do as he bade her.

"Jonathan, I cannot go to bed without bathing first. The stench of the ward is on me."

"You can take off your clothes, Merry, and wash the worst of it in the basin."

"Nay, I need hours of soaking."

"That will have to wait till the morrow, Merry. For tonight you will do as I say," he stated simply. Gently, he sat her on the bed and removed her boots and stockings. Discarding the stained apron she wore, his nimble fingers undid the buttons of her dress and slid the garment from her. Her petticoats soon followed the rest of her clothing that now lay in a pile on the floor.

While he searched for a warm gown, Merry washed what she could of the sickening scent of blood and feces from her arms and face.

"The odor will pass in time, Merry. Worry of it no more."

"I can still smell it, Jonathan. It clings to my skin."

"Nay, it does not. 'Tis only in your mind. It happens to all of us the first time."

Gently, he removed her chemise and drawers and slid the gown over her head. Fluffing the pillows, he bade her to lay down and covered her with a heavy quilt.

"I am not an invalid, Jonathan. You needn't fuss so."

"I know you are only tired, Merry, but if you do not take care, you will become ill." He breathed a long sigh as he allowed his finger to trace the delicate line of her jaw. "I did not realize the hours had passed so quickly. You should have come to find me."

She smiled. "I didn't realize how much time had passed, either."

She was tired, but felt pleased with herself. For too long she had hated. Today, as never before, she had come to realize that the men she had known as a hated enemy, were in fact, simply men. Men who were frightened and injured. Men who would bleed when cut and who cried when they spoke of their loved ones waiting at home.

"Thank you, Jonathan," she whispered as her eyes glowed with undeniable appreciation.

"You've no need to thank me, Madam. 'Tis I who would thank you. There are not many who would have done her job half so well."

She smiled and then covered her mouth as she yawned, just as a knock sounded on the door. Elizabeth entered carrying a tray of soup and sandwiches, while a servant followed her holding tea and cakes.

"For goodness sakes, Jonathan, did you have to work the poor child so hard? Just look at her! She's exhausted."

Coming quickly to his defense, Merry answered, "Elizabeth, 'tis not Jonathan's fault. I forgot the time, is all. Every one there worked as hard or harder." She sighed wearily. "I cannot begin to tell you of the suffering I've seen this day. It makes the skin crawl. Thank God, they will be on their way home tomorrow. I can only hope the ship is not so crowded as the wards, for I can't see how they will survive if it is."

"You must stay in bed tomorrow, lest you fall to some illness."

"Nay," she sighed, "I must go back. They will need many hands. I will rest in the afternoon."

Jonathan sat for a long time, watching his wife sleep. As each day passed, he discovered more about her to admire and love. And God, how he loved her. She had shown today such strength and compassion in caring for what she had once thought to be her enemy. At last she had come to realize these men were neither English nor Rebel, but simply injured men.

Perhaps she saw that he, too, was a man rather than the representative of a government she hated. He could only hope and pray.

With a sigh, Jonathan stripped away his clothes and joined his wife, too weary to ponder his problem any longer.

The sun was barely over the horizon when Merry saw Jonathan leaving the room and pulled herself from the warmth of her bed. After splashing cold water over her face, she dressed quickly, secured her hair beneath her mobcap, and grabbed her cape.

"Were you not going to wait for me?" she asked, stopping him just as he was about to exit the front door.

Jonathan sighed as he reached out a finger to stroke her cheek. "You were sleeping so soundly, I had not the heart to disturb you."

"Will you wait?"

"I'd see you eat something, before we go," he insisted, as he shrugged out of his coat and, with his arm around her shoulder, led her to the morning room and breakfast.

Merry spent the morning much like the day before, seeing to the comfort of the wounded. She wrote letters for two of the men, one who had lost his eyes in a cannon blast and another who had lost his hand.

Before she knew it, the injured men were being moved out. Those that could walk left first, while the others were soon carried, all to the wagons that would take them to the ships and then home.

Jonathan found her standing in the doorway to the main ward, staring blindly into the large, eerily empty room. Smiling, he came up behind her. "Are you sorry they've gone?"

Merry lifted her head and smiled at her husband. "I'm sorry for the whole of it." She sighed softly. "'Tis a terrible sight to see these proud young men torn and ravaged. It should never be allowed to happen."

"Aye, Merry," he agreed, as his arm circled her waist and drew her back to rest against him. "On that you are right. Too many believed war to be the answer. In truth, it brings only destruction, pain, and death."

"Come, you need to rest," he said, as he guided her toward the front door. "Elizabeth is giving a dinner party tonight and I'm sure you will want to meet her guest of honor."

"Will I? Who is it?"

"Benedict Arnold."

Merry stopped short, looking at first amazed, then shocked, and finally incredulous. "You cannot be serious?"

"Indeed, I am, Merry."

"I'd as soon meet the devil himself, Jonathan. I've no wish to be in that traitor's company. I will give Elizabeth my apologies, for I will no doubt be suffering a most abominable headache on this night."

Jonathan chuckled as he pulled her to him. "Surely, Madam, you are not showing a weak heart at this late date. I would have thought you'd be most anxious to meet our newest hero."

"Is it heroic in your eyes to accept the sword of defeat and then to slay seventy-three men *after* the colors were struck? Nay, Jonathan, do not tell me such, for I was only now beginning to grant you and your countrymen a measure of respect.

"'Tis a wonder to me how your government can stand the fool. Not only has he brought dishonor to your name, but being the glory seeker he is, he inadvertantly helped Washington by tying up Clinton's warships. He is accountable as much as any other for Cornwallis's defeat at Yorktown."

Jonathan nodded his agreement for he too had little use for a man who could so easily be swayed to change sides. To run like a thief in the night, to leave his wife unattended and her safety unknown. Also, he wasn't ignorant of the dishonor the man had brought upon himself with the slaying of Colonel William Ledyard at Fort Griswald, but Jonathan was, in fact, only a Captain in the King's forces, and had no say of the politics that could make a turncoat a hero.

When he remained silent, Merry asked, "Would you have me revert to my old hatreds?"

"Nay, Merry, never that." He chuckled. "I don't know if I have the strength to combat your hatred again. If you would calm down long enough to listen to me, I think meeting the man would bring you little harm. Is it not wise to know your enemy?"

"Perhaps you are right," she reasoned, after some thought. "As you say, the meeting can bring me no harm and perhaps much could be gained."

"Whatever you're thinking, stop it this instant!"

"Never fear, Jonathan," she smiled up at his worried frown, as her quick mind sought a plan to bring this man to justice. "I will do naught to bring danger to myself."

"Don't be a fool, Merry. The man is guarded day and night. No one can reach him."

"Jonathan," she remarked with mock surprise, "do

you think me so valiant as to do the man in while he is surrounded by his guards?"

"Merry," he groaned warily, "you think nothing is beyond your capabilities. I believe you are brave enough to do nearly anything and, revenge being as sweet as it is, Arnold poses a mighty strong temptation for this feisty Rebel."

Chapter Twenty

MERRY EASED HER TIRED BODY INTO THE STEAMING, scented bath with a grateful sigh. Indeed, she was weaker than she had thought, for a day and a half of strenuous work had left her drained of energy. Perhaps, as Jonathan insisted, she was not recovered as yet from the miscarriage. She felt a stab of annoyance as she realized she hadn't half the stamina she could once boast.

She sighed again as she leaned back and allowed the hot water to soothe her aching muscles. In truth, she felt stronger daily and she had no doubt she would soon be her old self again.

Still, her weakness was not the most pressing problem at hand, and she wondered for the hundredth time if she could bridge this gulf of emptiness between her husband and herself. Jonathan seemed to grow more relaxed in her company, but there were moments when he still hid his innermost thoughts and feelings behind a facade of cool smiles.

Was she breaking down the barrier? She knew not, for he had yet to touch her, even though he had twice slept in her bed. She knew he had been hurt by her careless act. Perhaps he was afraid still to allow her close to him, fearing more pain. That's it, she reasoned. Had he not insisted on marrying her? Had he not sworn his love? Had he not treated her tenderly and gazed upon her with adoration? Surely he was not so shallow as to lose his love over one mistake. Nay, she knew him to be of sterner stuff. 'Twas fear of further hurt that kept him from her.

Merry knew Jonathan was due to return momentarily from the docks, where he had gone to see to the further comfort of the men before their departure. She waited until she heard the front door slam and his brisk footsteps on the stairs before she pushed herself from the now tepid water. He was whistling a jaunty tune as he swung open the bedroom door and froze in his tracks.

Merry had to bite her lips lest he see the glee she felt at his response to her nakedness. She clutched a small linen towel to her in feigned surprise, knowing full well it offered nothing in the way of cover.

"I'm sorry," she managed at last, "I did not realize the time. I seemed to have dallied overlong in my bath." .

Jonathan had yet to speak. Suddenly, he seemed to . realize he held the door open and she was visible to any and all eyes that might pass. He quickly slammed it shut.

"Would you hand me my dressing gown?" she asked

innocently, as she rubbed the towel with enticing slowness over her glistening skin. Forcing her gaze from his, she lowered her face, lest she burst out laughing at the stunned look that had yet to leave her husband's face.

Without taking his eyes from her, he walked to the bed in an almost trancelike state, retrieved her gown and handed it to her. Discarding her towel, she slid her arms into the garment and tied it at her waist.

Merry sat before the large mirror at the dressing table and removed the pins that had held her hair high on her head.

Jonathan, still in his coat, stood silently where she had left him. With some effort, he managed to tear his eyes from the beauty who sat so indifferently, brushing her golden hair into smooth, liquid waves of silk.

Finally, he pulled off his heavy coat, as he berated himself for having shown such shock at seeing his wife in her bath. How many times had he seen that luscious body? Why should it effect him so drastically? He knew the reason, no matter how he might wish to deny it. He loved her. He loved her beyond all else in life and wanted nothing more than to possess her again.

He could take her now, but to what avail? In truth, he wanted, nay needed her body, but he had to have more than that. He wanted all of her. He wanted her forever.

He was shaking as he sat on the bed, his back to her, as he pulled off his boots. His body was suddenly drenched in sweat. Sweet Jesus, how was he to bear this? He forced himself to think of other things; his hands shaking as he unbuttoned his jacket and shirt. His voice held a trace of the trembling he couldn't control. "Would you mind if I call for fresh water, Merry. I've a need to bathe off this grime."

"Of course," she replied politely. "T'would bother me not at all."

Busy with her rouge pots and curling irons, Merry tried not to watch her husband in his bath, lest she simply join him. She wondered what his response would be if she did just that. No doubt he would not refuse her advances, but she wanted more than that from him, she wanted what they'd once had.

Traitorously, her attention refused to remain on the elaborate coiffure she was trying to attain. She gave a mumbled oath as a heavy lock fell again.

Jonathan chuckled tenderly. "I cannot think why you should bother, Merry. In truth, your hair looks its loveliest when tousled about in some disarray, particularly when rising in the morning."

She smiled into the mirror at his reflection. "Would you have others see me thus? Nay, I think it would cause no little amount of scandal should the wife of an English officer show herself less than perfectly attired."

Turning to face him, she allowed her robe to part and watched as his eyes hungrily sought the length of her bare leg. "Would you care for a glass of port? Elizabeth thought you might be in need of it and sent it only moments before you arrived."

"If you would join me."

Merry nodded and poured two glasses of the rich red brew and handed one to her husband.

Jonathan rested his back against the tub, and took a long swallow of the soothing liquid and sighed. "Bless Elizabeth."

Merry laughed throatily. "Perhaps, if you ask her nicely, she might be persuaded to come and scrub your back." Hearing his tender chuckle, she continued, "In truth, I believe she'd offer little resistance should you not ask nicely."

He laughed again and Merry's spirits soared that at long last she was able to bring a smile to his lips.

"Should I find the need, Madam, I shall keep your remarks in mind. Although I doubt I should seek out another, when I have a wife that could as easily do this chore."

Seated at the dressing table once again, Merry smiled at this remark. Again she permitted her robe to part, watching as his gaze left her face and slid to her exposed leg. After taking a sip of her wine, she returned, "Umph, I believe I was conscious of that fact the moment she set eyes on you."

"Do you believe she has singled me out above all her admirers?"

"Do you believe she has not?"

"She is your aunt, Merry. She is merely being kind."

Merry muttered a word she had no business knowing and ignored his answering laughter. "She is a beautiful woman," she countered truthfully, "and if you believe she is merely being kind, then I was right from the first as to the intelligence of the English."

She smiled, as he obviously caught his next thought before he put it into words. So, he was not ready as yet to speak of his feelings. She smiled again. Well, neither was she. It was enough, she reasoned, to gain this camaraderie, to be able to laugh, to tease, and, most importantly, to relax in each other's company. If they were to make a new beginning it had to be based on more than lust. If they were to make it at all, they had to grow to trust.

Merry put a touch of perfume behind each ear and on her wrists. Satisfied, she gave a nod of approval at her reflection in the mirror. The dark golden velvet gown matched her eyes exactly. While barely covering her shoulders, it fell to wide sleeves caught at each elbow with satin ribbon and then went wide again to her wrists. The neckline was deep and showed more than she was used to baring in public; still she smiled at the graceful swells of smooth skin that would surely tease the senses.

She couldn't wait for Jonathan to see her. Her hair was piled high in a halo of riotous curls, while many had already escaped their pins and fell in soft tendrils of curls about her face and neck.

The only jewelry she wore was her wedding ring. The elegant cut of her gown sought no added adornment, for it parted just below her waist and revealed a slip covered with gold embroidered threading and matching velvet bows. Gold slippers peaked from beneath the hem.

Jonathan almost groaned as he spied the petite form of his wife descending the wide stairway. Good God, did she know the spectacular sight she made? He couldn't remember seeing anything lovelier in his life. He grimaced as he watched a group of at least half a dozen young bucks make their way toward her, each seeking her attention. He'd have a time of it tonight, he mused with no little annoyance. This was something he was going to have to get used to, he supposed. With a wife as lovely as she, he couldn't hope others would not notice. Still, it did not sit well with him to watch those men fawning over her. The officer he was standing with spoke, but Jonathan heard nothing as he strained to listen to the outrageous compliments paid his wife.

Captain Hall laughed at Jonathan's expression of aggravation. "Not many here can claim a lady half so lovely, Jonathan. You can consider yourself lucky indeed."

Jonathan, only half hearing his fellow officer, grunted. "In truth, Richard, I'd not be averse to see her suddenly grow warts and perhaps gain thirty pounds."

Richard laughed at his friend's obvious jealousy. "'Tis no need man," he grinned conspiratorially. "There be a simpler and more effective way to keep the wolves at bay."

"And that being?"

"Keep her belly filled with your seed man," he laughed, as he slapped Jonathan on his back.

Jonathan nodded his agreement, while wishing he was about that chore at this exact moment. "Until that time," he grinned wickedly, "I believe the lady might be in need of rescuing. If you would excuse me, Richard?" He nodded slightly and moved to join the group that surrounded his wife.

Merry watched from the corner of her eye as her husband advanced toward her. Knowing it would do no harm for Jonathan to rage a bit more, she smiled toward one of the men who stood nearest her and asked sweetly, "Would you care to escort me to dinner, sir?"

"I . . . I'd be delighted, Madam," the startled man stuttered, while turning beet red.

Jonathan came upon the small group almost as if he

dreaded it, his chest instantly twisting with frustration at the sound of Merry's lilting laughter. It took some effort not to show his annoyance. What the hell did she find so funny? When would she laugh for him again? God, how he missed it. How he missed her gentle smile, her whispered words in the dark of night, the touch of her warm body beside him.

Shaking himself, he forced away the thoughts that plagued him at their every encounter and gave his wife a heart-stopping smile. "Good evening, Merry."

Jonathan stood before her, blocking out the others in her mind. He had taken to wearing his uniform since coming to New York and, although she had often raged at her hatred for the red and white garments, she couldn't deny he was magnificent.

A gentle smile curved her full lips as his eyes slowly swept the whole of her tiny form. His blue-eyed gaze grew almost black, as his eyes rested for a long, breathless moment on the gentle swell of her breasts, and she knew without a doubt that he longed to reach out and touch her.

"Would you care to meet the guest of honor, Merry?" Jonathan's eyes twinkled with humor, knowing full well the mere mention of the traitor caused her blood to boil.

Merry flashed him a grin that promised retaliation at some future date, while belying the raging emotions that flashed in her eyes with a sweet smile. "Of course, Jonathan. In truth, I'm anxious indeed to meet such an honorable officer of the King." Placing her hand on his arm, she allowed him to lead her to the object of their discussion.

Merry was surprised to find Arnold to be quite personable. She had imagined him to look as villainous as she knew him to be, but she had to admit he seemed amicable enough.

Oddly, she found herself feeling deep sympathy for his young wife. The woman acted gay and carefree, as she twittered about greeting guests, but the telltale signs of desperation and terror clouded her eyes the moment there was a lull in the conversation.

Later, Merry found herself alone with her husband for a moment.

"Jonathan, he is a monster. I cannot remember feeling such disgust. Had I half the courage I'd wish for, I'd run him through and the devil take the consequences."

Jonathan sighed and shook his head wearily. "Had you any more courage, Merry, I'm not sure I could live with it."

"I pity his poor wife. Imagine being married to that turncoat? Have you noticed her actions? I fear she is close to the end of her rope. She acts as if she expects Washington to come marching through the front door at any moment. I've never seen anyone so nervous."

Jonathan smiled at his wife's comments. "Dissuade yourself of the thought that she is an innocent, my love. She was a dominant factor in the changed loyalties of her husband. Her only fear is that the brute might yet leave her behind as he did in West Point."

Merry shook her head. "I've not the heart for such intrigue, Jonathan. 'Tis simpler, I think, to follow your heart."

"Unless of course, it happens that the side you

choose is not the same as your husband's," he grinned, his eyes softening at her answering smile.

Merry shrugged, "As long as each knows the other's beliefs."

"If that is the case, do you think that merely knowing will allow them to live together in some degree of harmony?"

Merry knew he was referring to their own marriage and she didn't hesitate in her answer. "Have we not done as much, sir? We've both known from the onset that we believe in different causes, yet we've managed to overcome that obstacle."

Jonathan chuckled, "Aye, Madam, we overcome it when I let you be about your business."

"Exactly," she reasoned. "Do I not let you be about yours?"

"Aye, but mine does not involve espionage. No danger lurks at my every turn."

She gave a small shrug, "Still, each of us must do what our conscience dictates."

"Thank God, this conflict is nearly at its end. I've a need to see you in a more placid environment."

"Would you prefer your wife dull and dreary?"

Jonathan laughed, "'Tis no need to worry on that score, Madam. No matter the circumstances, I can never imagine you to be dull and dreary. After this cause is completed, I've no doubt you'll find another."

Merry's eyes glittered with devilry and she made to answer his statement, but was interrupted by the announcement that dinner was being served.

Jonathan gave an obvious scowl, as he was stopped in his attempt to escort his wife into dinner. A young officer suddenly appeared at his side. Stuttering and turning red again, the officer asked, "I believe I have the honor of escorting you to dinner, Madam."

Smiling sweetly at her husband, Merry placed her hand on the young man's arm.

Elizabeth sat at the head of the table, flanked on her right by Benedict Arnold. Jonathan, to Merry's annoyance, was asked to sit opposite Elizabeth, while Merry found herself at Arnold's right. She gave a silent groan upon seeing her name scrawled upon the small place card. How was she to eat sitting next to this vile creature, she mused silently, as she sent her husband a glance that clearly spoke of her dislike.

Elizabeth played well her role as hostess. Tonight she wore a daringly cut gown of emerald green silk that brought out the highlights of her flaming tresses and caused her ivory skin to glow. For once, thanks to Jonathan, Merry did not feel like the country mouse in comparison to this lady of astonishing beauty.

Merry watched as Elizabeth smiled down the table at Jonathan. It was obvious that Elizabeth felt a tenderness for the man, and Merry wondered if her aunt would have hesitated should he return her interest. Even though she knew Jonathan thought Elizabeth beautiful, she also knew he had never shown her more interest than any hostess might deserve.

Of course, she had known her aunt to take lovers, but until this particular visit, she had never felt herself the rival. Still, Merry could not muster any resentment toward the woman. She knew the attractiveness of her husband. Hadn't she suffered endless sleepless nights because of it? She felt mildly sorry for Elizabeth as she flitted from one man to another, always searching, but never finding the special one that would hold her heart forever.

Bringing her thoughts back to the pressing problem at hand and finding she had no choice, Merry took her seat and acknowledged the gallant nod of her dinner partner.

During dinner, Merry was amazed to find she could relax, and even more surprised to realize that she was enjoying herself.

"Tell me, sir, are you planning to leave us soon?" Merry asked Arnold animately.

"Aye, Madam." He smiled with undisguised interest at the lovely young woman at his side. "I expect to receive orders to travel within a fortnight."

Merry gave an obvious and in Jonathan's opinion, overlong, sigh of disappointment. "Indeed, sir, I am sorry to see you go so soon, for I had hoped to become better acquainted with you and your lovely wife. No doubt you are aware of the high esteem in which you are held."

No doubt, Jonathan raged in silent sarcasm from the end of the table, wondering just what was going on in that devious mind of hers, while nearly choking, as he heard her tell Arnold that she planned to ride in the park during the next afternoon.

Was she trying to get him alone? What was she up to? As far as he knew, she had no ability to contact any of the Rebels at this late date. Surely, she wasn't planning anything outrageous. He almost laughed at the wild thoughts that assailed him. Did she expect to make him her prisoner and deliver him, like she had so many others, to Washington?

He knew her well enough to believe she contemplated just that. All at once he wanted to laugh at her unbelievable gall and then strangle her for her foolishness. It was obvious she thought herself invincible, and smart enough to outwit the most brilliant opponents. Vowing he'd not let her from his sight, Jonathan called a halt to his thoughts and soon joined the amicable dinner conversation.

Chapter Twenty-one

MERRY AWOKE THE NEXT MORNING TO THE MUFFLED sounds of an awakening house. She stretched languidly, her lips curving into a delighted smile, as vivid pictures of last night came flooding into her consciousness.

When the men had finished their port and joined the ladies, someone had suggested a game of cards. Tables had been set up and for the next few hours, the guests had entertained themselves with games. Jonathan, for the most part, had done no more than stand across the room watching his lady.

Merry smiled again, as she remembered the countless times she had lifted her eyes to find him watching her with a tenderness that had caused her breathing to grow short and quick, and her cheeks to flush warm and pink. Once he had realized her response, and had gazed at her with such intense and obvious hunger that his eyes had darkened from blue to almost black.

As the evening had progressed, Merry had grown bold in her glances and almost giddy in her happiness. She felt beautiful and desirable, and her eyes flashed with daring laughter at the easy conversation and lavish attention she received from the men who constantly surrounded her.

Later, feeling the beginnings of a headache, she excused herself to take a break from the overheated room and stepped outside into the chill night for a breath of air. The night was balmy for mid-December and she breathed a sigh, as her fingers brushed against the heavy railing that bordered the stone terrace. Suddenly, she sensed a presense behind her and then she heard the deep sound of her husband's voice. "You shouldn't be out here without a wrap. You will get a chill."

Merry smiled as she felt him slip his jacket over her shoulders. "Now *you* will get a chill," she said and then, a moment later, gave a low, throaty laugh. "Should any of my compatriots see me thus, they'd believe I've gone over to the other side."

Jonathan grinned and gave a short nod. "Perhaps we can have a uniform fitted for you. I know your liking for male garb."

Merry laughed softly at his teasing. "Would you prefer I dress as a boy?"

"Madam, I prefer you dressed as I found you this afternoon. I know not a lovelier sight."

She gave a slight shrug. "You said naught of it then," she remarked in a voice that barely restrained her laughter, as her thoughts went back to his startled expression that afternoon.

Jonathan looked closely into her upturned face. She was altogether too cheerful about his obvious suffering and an idea flashed in his mind. "I begin to wonder, Madam, if you planned it."

Gazing up at him with supposed innocence, she laughed softly as she hit his arm with her fan, "Shame on you, Jonathan. How would I know the time of your return?"

He nodded again as he realized the sense of her comment. Surely, she could not know. Take hold of yourself, man, he berated himself. Before long your desire will have you babbling like an idiot.

"You look lovely tonight, Merry. I'd not be sorry to see you somewhat less comely, for, with all your conquests, I had little chance to be near you all night."

"You have a chance now," she answered boldly, her lips parted, and she trembled slightly as she waited breathlessly for his answer. Would he accept her blatant offer or would he once again hide behind a cool smile and a witty response?

Somewhat taken aback, Jonathan gave a sharp gasp and stared down at her beautiful face. Obviously, he seemed to make some decision, for he smiled brilliantly. "I have, haven't I?" he chuckled tenderly, just before his descending lips found the warmth of her mouth.

Slowly, his arms reached around her slim waist and drew her closer, as a deep, rumbling sound of sheer hunger escaped his throat and he pressed her tighter to his lean, hard form.

God, how she had wanted him. Had it not been for the fact that they had been interrupted by an urgent plea sent by Mrs. Remington, who had finally gone into labor, she had no doubt they would have found their way to the bedroom.

The rumpled sheets showed that he had joined her after she had gone to sleep, yet, once again, he was up and gone before she had awakened.

As she slipped into a dressing gown of pale green satin and pushed a brush through her long hair, she thought about him sleeping with her. Why had he not awakened her? She knew he wanted her. What was he waiting for? Did he think her unwilling to breach this gulf between them? She laughed softly, as she tied her hair back with a dark green velvet ribbon and surveyed the sparkle in her eyes and the soft flush that tinged her cheeks pink. She nodded her approval of her reflection. Jonathan had done well with the clothing he had ordered, for she knew they suited her to perfection.

With a happy smile, she left her room intent on seeing the one man who was always on her mind as of late.

She never knew just how lovely and appealing a picture she made as she entered the breakfast room, to the man who ached to claim her as wife again. Jonathan's hand, bringing a cup of tea to his lips froze in midair, as he watched her smile sweetly and heard her bid Elizabeth and himself good day.

My God, she is so lovely as to take your breath away. How much longer was he to bear the torture of not having her. He smiled in appreciation of her slender form, as she filled a plate with eggs and toast at the sideboard, his eyes following her until she sat at the table.

The conversation at the table soon turned to the plans for the day. Margaret Manchester, a friend of Elizabeth's, was giving a ball that night and they were all invited.

Merry didn't miss the look of surprise in Jonathan's eyes, as she casually mentioned her appointment with the Arnolds to ride that afternoon. "If you are free, Jonathan, I'd enjoy your company on this outing."

Jonathan smiled, as his tender gaze rested upon his wife's face. "I am always free for you, my love."

Merry's eyes glowed as she listened to his gentle words, and a feeling of pure rapture came over her, nearly stopping her breathing. She answered his smile with one of her own, positive she'd never love him more than at this moment.

Taking his eyes from hers, he finished his tea as he came to his feet. "I want to check on Mrs. Remington this morning. She had a boy at three o'clock. I'll be back before you're ready," he promised as he dropped a quick kiss on her lips and bade Elizabeth good-bye.

Elizabeth grinned as the front door slammed behind him. "Had I a man like that one, I'd not let him out of bed until he begged for mercy, much less allow him to check on a woman, ailing or not."

Merry laughed at her aunt's coarse statement. "He is a doctor, Elizabeth."

"Still . . ." Elizabeth responded, leaving words unsaid, but her meaning loud and clear.

For just a moment, they were no longer aunt and niece, but two women.

"Were I you, I'd go find one of my own. This one is mine," Merry stated, her laughter softening the sharp warning in her words.

For the remainder of the morning, Merry and Elizabeth lounged about, chatting and planning a shopping spree for the following day.

After a light luncheon, Merry returned to her room and dressed in a velvet riding outfit of midnight blue. Securing her hair beneath a matching bowler hat, she pulled the attached veiling across her face and tied it on the top of her head, allowing the excess veiling to fall in graceful blue waves down her back. Polished black leather boots peeked from beneath the full skirts.

Jonathan entered as she was pressing her fingers into the black kid gloves that finished her ensemble. "You are ready, I see. Elizabeth left word that our horses are waiting for us."

"Isn't she joining us?"

"I think not. She has another gentleman caller secluded in the library."

Merry smiled seductively. "You mean I have you all to myself for the entire afternoon? I had visions of vying for your every attention, with Elizabeth hanging on to your every word."

"Mayhaps we might forgo our ride and spend the afternoon here. Then you could hang on to my every word and anything else you might fancy," he teased as he ogled her outrageously.

Merry laughed happily. "I have promised Mrs. Arnold to meet with her in the park."

Eyeing her warily, Jonathan escorted her down the long flight of stairs to the foyer. "One begins to wonder why a lady like yourself should find such interest in the Arnolds. You wouldn't be thinking of doing anything foolish, now would you?"

"Foolish?" She glanced sharply at him and asked in a tone of total innocence. "Me?!"

Merry pulled her dark cloak over her ball gown and covered her bright golden hair with the hood, as she slid silently out the side door of the Manchester home. Confident she had not been seen, she hailed a hansom cab. With some luck she should be back before anyone noticed her disappearance.

Obviously, the driver would think she was keeping some sort of midnight rendezvous. She cared not. It was imperative Caleb be told of Arnold's intentions to leave the colonies within a fortnight. What a feather in her cap should she be able to lead Arnold to Washington. She would know in a day or two if Washington approved of the plan.

She silently went over the figures Jimmy Rivington had passed on to her. Carleton had his forces stationed from Brookline to Increase Carpenter's House, some two miles east of Jamaica. Once Washington was in possession of this information, he would then be able to make a true assessment of his enemy.

She leaned back and tried to relax, as the carriage bounced her about while it fled along the cobblestone streets to Jamaica Bay. She hoped Caleb was already waiting. She cared not if she had to explain to Jonathan what she had been about, but should she be delayed overlong, he would have just cause to worry about her absence.

The cab finally pulled to a halt. Anxious to be about her business, Merry opened the door herself and jumped down, bidding the driver to remain where he was and await her return.

Positive now that the lady was meeting her paramour, he grunted and sighed, knowing from past experience that he might have to wait some time before she returned. At least his pockets would feel the weight of this long night, he mused.

Merry moved quietly between the trees. The night was pitch black because clouds hung low in the sky, blotting out the moon's rays. Twice she walked into trees. When her hand scraped against the frozen bark of yet another, she cursed softly.

"I see marriage has not curbed that tongue of yours, lassie," sounded a deep and merry voice behind her.

Merry spun about and was instantly caught in a bone crushing hug, as Caleb's thick arms circled her tiny form. "You'd best be puttin' some meat on those bones, if you want to keep that Britisher you call husband."

Merry laughed softly. "He has not as yet complained."

"I dare not linger, lest my boat be spotted. The blasted English search these waters nightly. Have you brought the information?" Caleb asked, as his arm circled her shoulder in a brotherly fashion.

Merry quickly imparted her news, then repeated it as Caleb nodded slowly and memorized it in silence. Then she spoke of Arnold and her hopes to see the traitor in Washington's clutches.

"Aye," Caleb responded. "I'd do much to see the coward swing. Have you gained his confidence?"

"I believe, from the short time I've spent in his company, that he confides in no one. He knows that the colonists eagerly await a chance to show him their hospitality. Therefore, he is wary and cunning. It will take much to bring this wily fox to heel."

Caleb shrugged. "We'll see. I'll send your idea along with the rest. In a day or two we should know if the General thinks the turncoat worth the risk.

"Word has it the Prince of Wales is soon to visit. Mayhaps that will bring us some excitement."

A moment later, and with a quick kiss to her cheek, he had disappeared among the trees.

Merry's confidence at not having been seen leaving the Manchester's party was a bit premature, for Jonathan, of late, noticed everything his wife was about. He did not miss her excuse to leave the dancing and followed, as she retrieved her cloak and headed for the side door that would lead to the mansion's long, winding drive.

He was some distance from her, as he helplessly watched her hail a cab and drive away. He cursed. He knew she was once again involved with her work and he raged silently that she should put herself in such danger. Luckily, within a few seconds, he managed to wave down another cab and ordered the driver to follow her.

The twit might keep her assignment, he groaned in silent anger, but she'd have him to answer to once he caught up with her. T'was best, he reasoned, that he did not have her before him at that moment, for he was not sure if he could resist the desire to take out his fury on that little piece of baggage.

Before long the driver pulled his vehicle to a stop along the roadside that bordered Jamaica Bay. All about was thick-wooded land. He could smell the clean scent of seawater, as it brushed up against the shore some short yards beyond the trees.

As he paid off her driver and sent him on his way, he turned to survey the area. The night was as black as pitch, and he cursed again as he strained his eyes, hoping to find her amid the trees.

Fearful of missing her in the black of night, he waited some yards from the cab for her return. He had not long to wait. A mere ten minutes passed before he saw the darker form of her cloak move among the trees.

Merry was making her way back to the cab when a band of steel grasped her from behind and snaked around her waist, while a huge hand clamped itself securely over her mouth. Like a sack of potatoes, she was slung beneath a massive arm and held as if weightless. Trying to squirm free of the vicelike hold brought her nothing but pain, as his arm tightened at her every movement. Her kicks proved useless, as her legs only swung at empty air.

In her terror, she managed to notice her cab was gone and in its stead stood another. The door to the coach was open and waiting as she was flung, none too gently, inside. She landed with a hard bounce and banged her back against the seat. A low grunt of pain escaped her and before she could come to her feet, a giant form was entering the cab, obviously prepared to pounce on her.

"No!" she cried out, still unable to see her attacker.

His hand was once again over her mouth, preventing all but muffled, vague sounds of her screams, as she bombarded his chest and shoulders with a flurry of punches. For all the good it did, she might as well have been hitting a tree. He sat above her and lifted her so that she faced him on her knees, his legs on each side of her pinned her to him and easily prevented any movement.

Clouds must have drifted overhead for suddenly a shaft of light from the uncurtained window caught her attacker's face. Jonathan! She gasped silently and nearly choked on her indrawn breath. It was Jonathan! Somehow he had followed her and had purposely scared her. Her terror vanished instantly to be replaced by a rage that knew no bounds. She felt a moment's pleasure, as she swung her opened hand and contacted smartly with the side of his face.

He gave a muttered curse and ordered the driver to move on, as he instantly pinned her hands behind her. With his free hand, he grasped a handful of hair and forced her head back.

She was fearless in her rage as she snarled, "You bloody bastard! Do you find pleasure in terrorizing women?"

He was so close she could feel his warm breath brush against her face as he spoke. "Only one woman," he whispered, his voice growing suddenly husky and strained. "God help me, there'll always be only one woman." His face contorted as if in pain. Suddenly consumed in a flame of surging desire, he took her mouth with such force and savagery, that she was helpless to do more than moan against his vicious assualt.

Still the violence of his kiss did not instill revulsion in her. Having so long wanted his touch, she found herself sagging weakly against him, instantly caught up in her own white-hot flames of longing.

Her lips parted willingly, nay eagerly, and his tongue greedily sought out once again the pleasure of her sweet mouth in a kiss that demanded no further waiting.

He was wild for her. He couldn't remember ever wanting her so desperately. The anger and fear for her safety he had suffered this night served only to inflame his need until he was consumed, blind and deaf to everything but the thought of possessing her. Now that he held her safe at last, he'd never let her go. He crushed her to him. His mouth left hers only to gasp for air and then would instantly return, sucking and licking at her sweetness, leaving her without a doubt as to how starved he was for her.

He released her hands and she clung to him, crying out her own need, pulling him closer to the edge of the seat, closer to her. She felt him jerk, as her hand slid up the hard length of his thighs and easily opened his pants. His long, low growl of desire filled her ears and she gasped as the sound seemed to propel her recklessly forward. Throwing the last of her caution and restraint aside, her fingers reached beneath his shirt and caressed his chest. With a soft moan she touched him everywhere.

His buttons came undone and her mouth tore from the ecstasy of his lips with a gasping cry and began to cover his chest and stomach with desperate, aching tastings. She slid lower, his moans encouraging her to taste the flesh of this man who had for so long held himself from her.

Jonathan groaned each time her hot, moist mouth touched his body. Leaning back, he was helpless to do anything. Flames of sweet agony licked through him, as she ran her hands over his burning flesh with an urgency he had only known in his wildest fantasies.

All too soon her fingers slid to his neck and spread through the thickness of his long dark hair, pulling his mouth to meet her own again. Her lips ached with the pressure of his hungry mouth, the sweetest aching she'd ever known.

Her cape had fallen open and the low décolletage of her ball gown proved to be no obstacle, as Jonathan suddenly tugged it lower still and released the heavy golden mounds to his view.

He lifted her easily into his lap and his mouth soon rediscovered the silkiness of her flesh. Merry, in her intense need to be touched, felt her body quiver beneath his lips. "Oh, God," she moaned softly. She had wanted his touch for so long.

Jonathan's control was gone. The intensity of the blinding love he felt for her swept over him and left him with nothing but driving need. Her response to his kisses had pushed him past the point of no return. She was his. She would always be his. She was telling him so with every movement of her body, every softly murmured sigh.

His breathing was harsh and ragged, as his fingers reached beneath her skirt and pulled off her frilly drawers. Turning her so she faced him with her knees on each side of his hips, he lowered her upon his throbbing, aching desire.

When he entered her Merry thought that her mind had exploded, and she arched her back sharply as she breathed in a gasp of air through clenched teeth. She would have fallen if his arms had not held her to him. She cried out with the almost unbearable pleasure, the sound sure to reach the driver's ears, but for the pressure of Jonathan's mouth muffling her cries.

"Jonathan," she gasped low and throatily into his warm neck. "Jonathan, love me. Never stop loving me."

"I'll never stop, Merry. Never, never," his voice aching and raw as he choked out the love he had hidden for so long.

Merry was overcome with sensation as he rolled his hips beneath her. She forgot the outside world passing in the dark of night. She did not hear the driver urging his horse on. She knew nothing but the scent and feel of this man who held her so desperately, ached to feel him fill her again, deeper, stronger, again and again.

Choking out disjointed, meaningless words, she let him know of her need. Her arms were around his neck and she clung to him, desperate to see an end to this suddenly unbearable torture.

He held her so tight her ribs ached and still it wasn't enough. His mouth claimed hers one final time, as he drove against her warm flesh with unleashed power, groaning out his ecstasy while absorbing her cry of love.

For a long time Merry rested her face against his shoulder. Her fingertips touched his cheek as she whispered his name. Jonathan's large hand cupped her head, as he planted tender kisses on her hair and temple. "Oh, Merry, I've wanted to do that for so long. I cannot think why I've waited."

"Nor can I," she sighed, as she kissed his neck. She never wanted to leave the warmth of his arms.

"'Tis finished this, Merry. 'Tis done! I'll worry no longer that you may be found out. You will not again repeat these nocturnal assignments."

These were not the tender words of love she longed to hear and she pulled back sharply. Searching his face for a glimmer of the love he had just shown her, and finding it not, she snapped, "Do not presume to order me about, Captain. I will do as I deem necessary."

"Will you indeed?" he asked sardonically. "Perhaps I shall see to it that you have no further opportunities then."

Disengaging herself from his hold, she retreated to the opposite seat and adjusted her clothing before she faced him. "And how do you propose to do that? Will you keep watch like a guard dog?"

He shrugged a massive shoulder and replied nonchalantly, as he too worked at repairing the damage their loving encounter had done to his uniform. "If I must. The day will come, Madam, when you will concede me the master. Until then, I will do as *I* deem necessary to ensure your obedience."

She laughed humorlessly, "Do you think I would permit anyone that much control over me?"

Jonathan chuckled, "'Tis obvious, Madam, that your humor has not improved with the last few eventful moments. Perhaps another sampling is in order to curb the sharpness of your tongue."

"Unlike some I do not believe a quick toss to be the answer to every question and problem."

"Still, it will do till something better comes along," he commented dryly, one brow lifting.

"Rogue!" she snapped, her eyes flashing with anger. "Everything must be your way. I'm to desist in my work and allow you to have total say over my life. Nay, Jonathan, it cannot be. I shall never submit. I will do as I must."

"Do you love me?"

"Indeed, sir, you pick the most inopportune moments to ask."

"If you loved me as you've professed, you would accede to my request and desist in these nocturnal escapades."

"That is total nonsense. No one but a blockheaded Englisher could think so ridiculous a notion to be true. What matter is it to you if I do what I believe is my duty? How does that take anything from you? Do you love me less because you are loyal to George?"

"I do not put myself in danger, Madam. Therefore, I give you no cause to fear for my safety. When you love someone, you are conscious of their suffering and do much to see that it does not come about."

"I am in no danger," she snapped and cursed silently, for she knew her voice held a childish whine.

"Madam, I have only your word that you are not and it is not enough. You've said much the same before and still managed to acquire a bullet."

She sighed, knowing the truth of that statement and the horrible emptiness the resulting trauma had caused between them.

"Very well, Jonathan, I will concede you this point. If it causes you distress, I shall not again repeat these nightly assignments. But do not ask more of me, for I shall continue my work as I see fit. Does that satisfy you?"

Jonathan grinned as he watched her stuff her frilly drawers in the cape's pocket. "As long as it poses no threat to you, Merry, I am satisfied."

Chapter Twenty-two

HAVING RETURNED FROM A SHOPPING-EXPEDITION ELIZabeth and Merry were sitting in the day parlor admiring the beautiful feathers on the elaborate hat Elizabeth had been unable to resist, when the butler entered bearing a white envelope on a small silver tray.

Elizabeth was quite beside herself as she watched Merry take the envelope. Thinking it a note from one of her niece's many admirers, she bade her to hurry. Quickly, Merry opened it and read the note her father had written.

"It's from Father, inquiring as to my health. He says all goes well in my absence," Merry stated, hoping to relieve her aunt's inquisitiveness as she pocketed the letter.

A servant entered then with a tray of tea and small sandwiches, preventing her escape. Merry had difficulty containing her excitement as she forced herself to sit through the meal and make idle conversation.

Under the pretense of needing to rest, she soon left Elizabeth and fairly flew up the steps to her room. In an instant she had the letter free of its envelope again. Rummaging through her drawers, she found the bottle of developer. As fast as she could, she spread the clear liquid over the spaces between the lines and then gasped, as the writing became clear and legible.

They were going to do it! They were actually going to kidnap the Prince of Wales. She laughed softly. This would show these arrogant English who they were up against.

What a coup! She grinned and began to laugh aloud. Suddenly, she realized a large form was standing directly behind her. Merry spun around, the note clutched behind her in her hand, her eyes widening with surprise to find Jonathan barely inches from her.

"You startled me!" she accused.

"Did I?" he grinned quite wickedly. "I seem to be doing that quite a lot lately. What were you reading that instilled such humor?"

"Nothing important." She shrugged, as she turned away. "Just a note from Father."

"What did he say?"

She shrugged again, while her mind raced for an answer. "He was relating Muffit's antics. It seems he tried to attack Samuel Hanes. He apparently thought the man was trying to abuse Rebecca."

Jonathan knew, by the nervous laughter and twitch of her lip, she was lying. Never before had it appeared so obvious, for he had known Merry to remain calm in even the most disturbing circumstances. This must be something of dire importance.

"Read it to me."

She stiffened. "I doubt you'll find the humor in it, sir."

"Let me be the judge."

"Perhaps later. Right now I have an appointment to meet Elizabeth. We have plans to go shopping."

"The shopping can wait a few minutes, can it not?"

"I am sorry, Jonathan. She is waiting, and you know how impatient she can be."

"Merry, let me have the note."

"Jonathan," she tried to laugh, but it came out a strangled croak. "Why is my correspondence suddenly so important? Have you so little to occupy your thoughts? Perhaps you might care to join me in my outing, if that be the case."

He smiled at her attempt to lead him to other areas of thought. "I'll see that note, Merry. Now!"

"Jonathan," she returned, feeling anger at his insistence, "you forget yourself. Being my husband does not give you the right to invade my privacy."

"On the contrary, Madam. Being your husband gives me every right."

He reached around to grasp the hand that held the now crumpled note, but she moved to the right and evaded his fingers.

She laughed softly, trying to bring a teasing quality to their encounter. A quick glance at the fire told her she had only ten feet or so to cover and the note would be gone forever.

Jonathan didn't miss the longing look Merry gave the

flames and knew beyond a doubt that the note was of the utmost importance. "Merry," he warned, as he stalked her, "do not try it. I have no wish to take it by force."

"Oh, Jonathan," she laughed softly, as her hand reached out to stay his coming form. "Surely, you would not bring harm to your wife."

"Merry, I would do much to see you unharmed."

Again she backed away. Still he continued his stalking. "I will have the note, Merry," he insisted as he closed the short distance between them.

This was getting her nowhere, she reasoned as her mind worked quickly to remedy the situation. What she needed to do was take his mind from the letter. But how? Suddenly an idea formed and she shot him a look that she hoped contained pure sexual promise. She knew it was an obvious ploy, but what alternative did she have? She had to stall him until she could dispose of the note.

Jonathan was somewhat taken aback by the sudden change in his wife, but, being a man who had long sought her attention, he did not refuse the look of pure lust that clouded her eyes.

He pulled her to him and covered her parted lips with his own as he felt one of her hands reach out and begin to unbutton his white shirt.

Merry felt his arm reach around her, his hand sliding down the length of her arm, finally closing over the hand that held the note. For a long moment his warm mouth worked against hers. Prying her lips further apart, his tongue touched first the sensitive flesh of her inner lips and then ran along the smooth surface of her teeth, causing her to forget all else for a moment. She felt herself softening against him, her knees weakening. Valiantly, she forced aside her desire for him. Pretending to stumble, she moved them closer again to the fire. Jonathan was forcing her fingers open, his mouth working feverishly, so she might relax and allow him to gain the paper.

Merry groaned silently. This was not working. She had to get his mind off that note. With a soft grunt, her hand opened at last and Jonathan took the crumbled paper. Having a more delightful objective in mind, he ignored its message and put it in his jacket pocket.

Merry pulled away, intent on throwing every abuse she knew upon him, when she was suddenly struck with still another idea. He was not anxious to read it or he would have done so immediately. Nay, he wanted her. She could feel it in his kisses and now, as she gazed down the length of him, she could see his obvious response and awakening desire.

Breathless from his hungry kisses, she smiled tauntingly and began to remove her clothing. Jonathan did nothing but stand and watch in amazement, as his wife seductively slid each garment from her body, until she stood before him naked, her skin glowing smooth and golden in the flickering light of the fire.

Jonathan's eyes widened with appreciation as they moved down the length of her small frame. His voice was husky with need as he asked, "What of Elizabeth and your shopping?"

She smiled wantonly from beneath thick lashes and answered with his own words, "The shopping can wait, can it not?"

It wasn't until some time later that Merry leaned her head against his shoulder and gave a soft, contented sigh. Her fingers traced a pattern in the damp hairs of his chest, idly following the dark, thick mat to the thin line it formed at his stomach.

"Jonathan?" she asked.

"Mmm," he returned, as he pulled her closer, loving the feel of her softness beside him and unwilling as yet to leave the world of splendor they had just visited.

"How is it we can find such delight in this act, yet still believe in different causes?"

Jonathan chuckled softly, as he pulled her to lie along the length of him. "It matters not, Rebel, what our beliefs might be. One fact remains above all else. There is a love between us that has not been matched."

She smiled down at him, her golden eyes glowing with warmth and tenderness. "You do not believe others to feel as we do?"

His fingers touched a long, golden curl and held it to his face. "I believe others can only dream of it. In truth, there's not been a love to compare to ours."

She laughed, as her fingertip traced the sculptured line of his lips. "Always arrogant, English. Don't you think others might have said the same?"

He shrugged. "Perhaps, but they were mistaken."

She shook her head and laughed again. Her eyes glowed with the love she felt for him. "What am I to do with one as stubborn as you, sir?"

He grinned in return. "Madam, I am not the only one in this room with that trait."

She giggled and then agreed, "Aye, 'tis the truth you speak, but at least I can often see another's point of view, whether or not I agree. If it were not so, I should still hate you for simply being English."

"And I do not?"

"Not if you insist no others can love as we."

He grinned, "Very well, perhaps one or two are as blessed."

She laughed as she spread dozens of kisses over his closed eyes, his cheeks, his nose and his chin, carefully avoiding his tempting, smiling mouth, while murmuring, "Obnoxious, arrogant, thickheaded, closed-minded, and English to boot. What, may I ask, do I find to love in you?"

He gave a tender chuckle as he turned over and held her pinned beneath him. "Be assured, Madam, I find myself asking much the same about you."

"Tell me sir, what have you found?"

His blue eyes darkened as he gazed at her loveliness. 'Besides your beauty?"

"In later years, sir, I shall not look as I do now. What will you love then?"

"Madam, you will always be beautiful to me," he said and sighed wearily, "and to others, I fear. Richard told me I should keep your belly filled with my seed in order to turn the young bucks away."

Merry laughed and gave his shoulder a gentle punch, "Is that how men talk when alone?"

He grinned and ignored her question. "Where was I?"

"What do you find to love in me?" she prompted.

"Oh, yes. Well, let's see. I love your smile, the way your eyes flash when you're angered . . ."

"Stop! Something besides how I look, remember?"

He nodded and began again. He took such a long time before he began that he gave Merry some cause to wonder if there were anything to mention. Finally, he began, "I love your sense of humor, your gentleness, your compassion. Shall I go on?"

"Oh, please do," she grinned and then covered her mouth and pretended to yawn in boredom. "One never tires of hearing the truth."

He chuckled tenderly. "Your loyalty, even if it is misplaced, is still commendable." She stiffened and he laughed as he went on. "Your temper, your rages, your laughter. More?"

She nodded.

"Your stubbornness, your jealousy, the way you kiss, the way you love."

"I am not jealous!" she interrupted.

He laughed, as he caught her to him and rolled on his back again. "Elizabeth's attentions toward me bother you not in the least. Am I right?"

"Right!"

"Then you don't mind that she wants me to be her lover?"

"What!?" She stiffened and sat up, her legs straddling his flat stomach. "Did she actually say that?"

He shrugged noncommitedly.

"What did she say?!" she raged. "My own aunt! I knew she had designs on you. Did I not say it before? I'd like to wring her neck. Just yesterday I warned her off and still she . . ."

Jonathan laughed at her ravings. "All right, all right," he conceded wickedly, while shooting her a knowing grin, "perhaps you are not jealous."

Merry caught the teasing look in his eyes and his accompanying, happy smile and couldn't contain the delighted laughter as she swatted his chest. "You beast! Jonathan, I believe that was quite the most wretched thing you've ever done to me."

"Did you really warn her off?" he asked, his heart swelling with such happiness, he was not quite sure he could bear the joy of it.

She shrugged, suddenly refusing to look at him, while worrying her bottom lip with her teeth.

"Did you?" he insisted, as he rolled her beneath him again.

"In a manner of speaking."

"What manner was that?"

"I told her to find her own man. This one was mine."

Jonathan laughed. "Did you now? And what did the lady say to that?"

Merry smiled up at his look of pure adoration. After a moment she gave a slight shrug, "She accepted it. What choice had she? Would you see us fight for you?"

"Would you fight for me?" he grinned.

She laughed. "From the look in your eyes, I believe you would enjoy that, sir."

"You did not answer me. Would you?"

"Take heed, English," she warned, as her nails pressed none too gently into his shoulders. "Never give me cause, for after I've finished with the lady, it will be you who must face my wrath."

Jonathan chuckled, as he buried his face against her neck. "Madam wife, there is much upon which we do not agree, yet this is a fact I cannot deny. I love you more than anything I hold sacred in life. 'Tis you alone

I wish at my side, till God chooses to call me home. I want to grow old with you. I want our children and our children's children to fill our home with love and laughter. And, as the years bring us closer to the end, I want to look back on a long life and say, "I've no regret, Merry, that I've held to you and to you alone, for there could never be another quite like you."

It was some time before either of them thought to leave the loving contentment they found in each other's arms. Merry watched, as Jonathan finally swung his long legs over the side of the bed and sat up.

Spying his jacket and knowing full well the exact position of the note, she remarked innocently, "I seem to have lost my slipper. Could it be on your side of the bed?"

From the corner of her eye, she watched as he bent to look for it. In a flash she was up, his jacket in her hands, the note secure in her fist.

She made a dash for the fire, but Jonathan interrupted her before she could throw the note. Catching her hand in midair, he held it tightly within his own. Steely dark blue eyes bore into defiant golden, until she finally shrugged, conceding him the superior in strength and knowing she had lost her chance, she gave it up.

While his eyes scanned its contents, she slid her chemise over her head and began to pull on her stockings.

The note read:

Dear Merry,

Been advised of your plan, but must reject it. The inn runs smoothly. I hope you are taking

WHISPERS IN THE WIND

Word has it he is leaving us shortly in any case.
this chance to regain your strength.
Another more interesting subject is soon to sail
Am looking forward to seeing you soon.
upon these shores. Perhaps we might use the plan
All here are well.
for this one. Would do much, I think for morale.

Father
G. W.

Jonathan looked up at her, puzzled. Returning his gaze to the paper, he studied the confusing note until it began to make sense.

Every other line was written in a different hand. The first, third, fifth, and seventh lines were in ink that seemed somewhat blurred.

Slowly, he read the first line and then the third. It made sense. Next he read the second and then the fourth.

Throwing the note into the flames, lest it be found by others less prone to protect his wife. He stepped into his pants and faced her.

"Who is it you are planning to kidnap?"

She didn't answer him, her stockings seemingly taking all her concentration.

"Who is it, Merry?"

She shot him a blank look and he knew nothing less than torture would convince her to speak the words. Nevertheless, he continued, "Is it Arnold? Is that why you've been attempting to form a friendship with him?"

With a stony expression she left the bed and sat before the mirror at the dressing table, ignoring his presence as she brushed her hair. There was nothing concrete in the note. Nothing that would give away the plan, she reasoned. It did not matter what he guessed at or thought. She would never tell him, no matter how he might badger her.

"The note mentioned another. What did it mean?" When she didn't respond, he finally raged, "Merry, answer me!"

"Jonathan," she remarked sweetly, smiling at his reflection in the mirror. "I forgot to ask. How is Mrs. Remington?"

Jonathan spat a curse. Never before had he been so tempted to throttle her. His hands clenched at his sides as he fought a battle of control. Feeling more frustration than he'd ever known, he raged on, "Sweet Jesus, do you know what they'd do to you if you were discovered to be a member of the Culper Spy Ring? You delude yourself, Madam, if you think being married to me would save you."

Merry gave a short gasp. "How do you know the Culper name?"

He sighed wearily. "Merry, all the English bastards are not simpletons." And when she still offered no information, he finally managed, "Very well, if you will not tell me, we are leaving."

"What!?"

"You heard me well enough. I cannot trust you to stay out of trouble, so I will make sure trouble stays away from you. We will be returning to Huntington within the hour."

"I will not go!"

"Madam," he spun her about and lifted her to stand before his menacing form, "you will pack your things or I will have Elizabeth send them on. In any case, you and I will leave here immediately and I care not if I carry you kicking and screaming all the way."

Chapter Twenty-three

TRUE TO HIS WORD, NOT AN HOUR LATER AND AMID MUCH hugging and teary good-byes, Merry sat across from Jonathan in a hired coach fuming at the high-handed manner of the man she called husband. How dare he whisk her away from New York and her aunt's home, regardless of her expressed wish to stay? What right did he have to bully and threaten her? Who did he think he was, her lord and master? Aye, that was exactly what he thought and, by law, he was right.

On one hand she enjoyed the feeling of being cared for, but she raged that he should not allow her the freedom to be about her business. Surely, she'd think less of him were she able to control him. She admired his strength, but did he have to be this strong?

What good did it do to fight for the cause of freedom, only to attain it and have your freedom checked by an arrogant husband?

Jonathan chuckled at the daggers of hatred she sent across the coach. "It will do you little good, Rebel, to glare at me so fiercely. I would not see harm come to you and I will do much to see my ends accomplished." —

"And that includes dragging me from my aunt's home, no matter my objections?"

"It does, when I know you are up to no good."

"No good to you means quite the opposite to me."

"Merry," he began, trying to reason with her, "do you believe I love you?"

"No sir, I do not! For if you loved me, you'd have some consideration for my feelings."

"On the contrary, I do consider your feelings. But more than that, I consider your safety. Can't you understand I only want to know you are not in danger?"

"What is it you want of me, Jonathan? Shall I become some simpering miss, fainting with the vapors at the slightest happenings?"

"Nay, Merry. I love you because of what you are. I've no wish to change you, only to see to it that no harm comes to you."

Merry sighed with disgust. "Jonathan, for pity's sake, how am I to rage at you when all you will say is that you love me?"

She punched the seat, her whole being filled with frustration. Surely her plan would have brought the biggest boast of morale possible to these hungry, cold and bedraggled colonists. Suddenly, a thought struck. She need not be at the center of the action. T'was pride and arrogance alone that persuaded her another could not do as well as she. A word to Caleb and another would surely be found. She smiled smugly. The Prince of Wales might yet become an honored guest of the Rebels.

Jonathan didn't miss the satisfied look of victory that filled her eyes and groaned aloud. "Now what has entered that devious mind of yours?"

"Why, nothing," she answered in her sweetest tone. "Why do you ask?"

"Madam, I've yet to see a more beautiful face, nor one that has a harder time of hiding the truth."

"Jonathan, you are being absurd. What could I be thinking? I've merely come to see your point of view. Would you fault me for that?"

"I'd give much to know what plans are festering."

Merry laughed softly. "And have you so much? Do you realize we've married for some months and I've still no idea as to your worth? You shower me with the most beautiful clothes, yet I know a soldier's pay cannot possibly afford them."

He laughed. "At least I cannot accuse you of marrying me for my money, since you have no knowledge of it."

"Have you money, then?"

He shrugged. "I manage."

"Do you have your own home in England?"

"Aye. My mother lives there and watches over it while I'm gone. Would you like to see it?"

"Perhaps someday."

"Merry, I'm afraid 'tis past the time for you to realize I will not be returning home alone."

"Must you return at all?"

"Aye, I must. I have responsibilities that cannot be ignored."

"What do you mean when you say you will not return alone?" she asked warily.

"You, as my wife, will accompany me."

"Out of the question! Never will I live in a country that is ruled by a king. What do you think I've been doing these past years, playing a game? I mean what I say, sir. I will not leave this land, particularly since we've found our freedom at last."

"What do you propose? Shall I leave and you remain? Perhaps there is a place somewhere in between where we can meet occasionally. Is that what you want for a marriage?"

"Nay, I want you to stay here."

"And I would if it were at all possible. As I've said, I have responsibilities that cannot be ignored."

"And what of my responsibilities? What of my father? Suppose he should become ill? Who would care for him? What of my friends? Shall I leave everything without a backward glance?"

"I know it will not be easy, Merry. If it is your wish we can return quite often. Perhaps your father could sell the inn and join us."

"Never! The day will not come when either of us will stand on English soil. You cannot know what it's like to long to be free of the tyrants and now you are asking me to become one of them. I will not!"

Jonathan's eyes glowed with the love he felt for this spirited lady. "We will see," he grinned as he moved to sit beside her and gathered her small form into his lap, his strong arms holding her close to him.

She rested her head on his shoulder as she gave a long sigh. "Jonathan, do you realize the embarrassment I will no doubt cause you?"

"I care not."

"I cannot abide the ruling class and I will be as outspoken as any, of their mistreatment of those they consider less important."

"I'd expect nothing else from you, my love," he answered as his hand reached inside her heavy cloak and began to undo the buttons of her bodice.

"Perhaps they will throw me in prison. Would that not bring you mortification?"

Jonathan smiled as he realized she was no longer arguing that she would not go, but warning him of her actions once they got there. He nuzzled her neck with his warm mouth as his thumb brushed tantalizingly against her nipple, bringing it to a hard throbbing bud. "I care not what you say and do, as long as you are at my side," he whispered.

"Are you telling me I may rant and rave, because no one will listen in any case?"

"Oh, Rebel, I've no doubt you'll find many who will listen and still more who will join your causes. If they are just, I would be the first to do so."

"There is much injustice at home, Merry. No doubt you, as a newcomer, will see it before I."

Merry smiled, suddenly more than anxious to see to the remedy of these injustices, never realizing she was no longer fighting against leaving her home.

"Jonathan," she sighed softly, "I love it here and would miss it sorely. Would you promise to return every year?"

"We would spend most of our lives aboard ship, if that were the case. Would not every third year suffice?"

"Second?"

Jonathan laughed, as his lips ran across the delicate line of her jaw. "If it is your wish, Merry, for the first few years at least. I'd not see you unhappy and it will pose no hardship."

After a few minutes of nuzzling the sensitive spot beneath her ear, he whispered, "When will you tell me who you were planning to kidnap?"

She laughed, "After it is done."

"So the plan remains, only the participants change."

His mouth claimed hers in a long, searching kiss that left the two of them gasping and hungry for the privacy of their bedchamber.

His hot lips were searing the side of her neck, when he suddenly gasped and pulled away. His dark blue eyes were filled with shock and admiration at her audacity. "The Prince of Wales is soon to visit these shores. Merry, you cannot be so arrogant as to believe he could be kidnapped?"

"And why not . . ." she stopped suddenly and then continued in her sweetest tone. "Jonathan, I haven't the least idea as to your ramblings."

"Why, you little wretch! Thank God, I got you away from there before you had time to put your idea into a plan of action." After a moment of hesitation, he asked, "You did not have the time, did you?"

Merry laughed, "Truly, sir, I've no idea as to your meaning."

"Dammit, Merry, not the King's own son! Have you totally lost your mind? Do you wish to instill the final degradation?"

"I look not to degrade, sir. Merely to ensure an end to this war."

"Merry, you have the power to infuriate me past the point of reason, while, at the same time, I love you beyond all else. I know not whether to kiss you or strangle you."

She smiled seductively, as she lifted her hands to circle his neck, "Shall I show you which one I prefer?"

Chapter Twenty-four

NETTIE WAS GETTING MARRIED. NOW THAT THE WAR WAS officially over, Jeremiah reasoned he'd be able to care for his new wife, and the long awaited plans were at last put into effect.

The small town was a beehive of activity. The English soldiers had been ordered home, but Jonathan had been more than willing to stay until their friend's wedding day. The townsfolk's first order of business was to demolish the fort and rebuild the rectory and church.

This was done with no little amount of happy celebration and Jonathan, with all the others who had mustered out of service and decided to stay on, gave long, hard hours toward seeing to its reconstruction.

The endless winter had passed at long last and, in general, life was good. Hope for the future bloomed again and people went about their chores with a lighter heart.

Only one flaw marred the otherwise peaceful existence of the community. Bands of privateers were raiding the North Shore, now that the English frigates were no longer there to patrol the coast.

From Southold to Jamaica, they plundered the towns, savagely destroying what they could not carry back to their ships.

Merry, returning from Nettie's home, where she had been helping the future bride sew her wedding dress, was laughing, as she raced Muffit back to the inn. The puppy had almost doubled in size and he barked with excitement, as his mistress sped along by his side.

Muffit made a momentary detour into the brush, hot on the trail of a squirrel, until the smaller animal sought refuge in a tree and the happy puppy came bounding back to his mistress.

It was growing dark, and Jonathan would be worried for her if she did not hurry home. Bending down, she picked up her dog and moved along at a fast, steady pace.

Her thoughts returned to her husband as she walked the deserted patch of dirt road. She knew he was responsible for word being passed discreetly to Clinton that the guarding of the Prince of Wales should not be relaxed. The plan to kidnap the King's son had never come to pass. In her heart, she could not rage at his interference. Would she not have done the same?

In the end his capture was not needed and the peace had been signed this past April.

Suddenly, the distant sounds of male laughter and

heavy footsteps broke into her reverie. They were between herself and the inn. Merry hesitated only an instant before she scrambled into the woods, her heart pounding, as she watched eight ragged and bearded men come out of the brush that bordered the coast and turn toward the inn.

Muffit uttered a low, menacing growl and Merry held her hand over the puppy's jaws to prevent his barking.

She watched until the heavily armed men were out of sight and then sped in the opposite direction to Samuel Hanes, praying every step of the way he was still at the mill. Not twenty agonizing minutes passed before six of Merry's cohorts were gathered about her.

Instantly, she related her sighting and, ten minutes later, the seven shadowy, armed forms made their way across the open yard. In deadly silence, they entered the dark kitchen of the inn.

Jonathan almost groaned out loud, as the moon silhouetted the petite form of his wife sliding silently through the inn's back door, followed instantly by six larger forms. For a moment, they blended into the shadows of the dark room, while waiting for a sound of the intruders.

"Hurry, mates," came a voice from the taproom, as barrels of rum were heaved from the cellar. "I'd not face another like the wild man we downed in the kitchen. Bring the rum up and be quick about it."

Merry gave a soft gasp. Who was it they had slain? Were they all dead? Why was there no sound save the small whimperings of a girl? Where were Jonathan and her father?

Straining her eyes, Merry searched the kitchen.

Beyond the wooden table lay an inert form and, try as she would, she could not make out who it was.

She moved silently along the walls, inching her way toward it. She was behind the table now, down on her hands and knees. Jonathan's hand came quickly over her mouth. "It is I."

She nodded, as a wave of relief washed over her, so intense as to bring tears to her eyes. Bending close to his ear, she whispered, "Where is my father?"

Soundlessly, he pointed in the direction of the tap-room.

Merry nodded again and whispered once more, "Are you injured?"

Silently, he shook his head.

An instant later, she left him to move back to her comrades. A soundless, whispered command and four of them left the kitchen to await the men who must pass to bring the rum aboard ship.

The bulky form of one man, staggering under the weight of a huge barrel appeared at the doorway. His leg hit into the table; his sword clanged, as it brushed against the stove. He finally walked through the kitchen and out the back. He never returned.

Merry waited in silence, her heart pounding with dread, hoping beyond reason her father was alive. Rebecca's soft sounds of terror were still coming from down the hall. Muffled as they were, Merry reasoned they had either gagged her or locked her in the linen closet. Perhaps both.

"Come on, mates. Get a move on," a voice ordered. "I've a need to put some distance between us and this town."

Another man came into the kitchen, muttering a round of curses, as he strained to balance the rounded keg. He too passed through the room, never to return. One more moved through the kitchen and followed his comrades into the fiery depths of hell, to claim his just reward.

Merry waited, every nerve on end, her mind screaming against the caution she must demonstrate. The strain of not knowing what she'd find once she entered the taproom nearly pushed all reason aside. She longed to burst into the room and lay low these intruders.

The four men returned and stood crowded together in the kitchen. Samuel argued they should storm the taproom, reasoning the privateers would be too engrossed in their work to offer any resistance.

Merry longed to take his advice, but hesitated, unwilling to jeopardize her father's welfare, for, although she feared he was already dead, she clung to the slim hope he was not.

One of the men scuffed his boot on the floor, bringing an instant response from the privateer's leader. "Who's there?"

He received only silence for an answer.

"Show yourself, man," the voice ordered fiercely, and Merry knew she had lost her chance of surprising the brute.

Jonathan, at Merry's side, tensed, ready to spring into the next room, eager to give these bastards their just desserts. But, before he realized what was happening, Merry moved away from him. Helpless to do more than watch her, he gave a round of silent curses, as she walked into the taproom.

"It's only a wench," one of the men commented.

"And a comely one at that," another remarked, as she came further into the room.

"What's happening here?" she asked, as if she had just come upon them.

The five remaining men laughed at her surprise. One held a sword leveled to her chest, while the other four brought still more barrels from the cellar.

"Move over there, wench," the one ordered with a wave of his sword, indicating she should stand near the tables.

Merry gave a silent sigh of relief to see her father sitting at one of the tables, holding his palm over a lump on his forehead. Their eyes met and held for one long moment, before Merry nodded imperceptibly.

"What are you doing?" she asked the one man who appeared to be the leader of the group, since he only stood and watched the others work.

"My men and myself found ourselves possessed of a powerful thirst, gel." After eyeing her thoroughly, he continued, "After we see to it, I think we would enjoy a toss or two. You and the one down the hall should serve our purposes."

Suddenly, an almost deafening pistol shot rang out, followed by countless others. Merry threw herself to the floor, as one barrel was dropped and splintered. Huge amounts of rum ran over the floor to mingle with the blood of four of the remaining privateers. One man fell head first into the cellar and, by the time the shooting stopped, Noah Gates was clutched to the leader's chest, her father's form providing a most effective shield.

As Merry came to her feet, seven men walked into the taproom.

"Back off, mates, or this one will see the last of his days," the privateer warned, while bringing the edge of his sword dangerously close to Noah's throat.

With deadly calm, Merry stated softly, "Sir, if you treasure your life, you will release him. At this distance, I cannot miss."

The man began to laugh, as his eyes registered the tiny female form who stood so bravely before him, but was brought up short, as she raised the barrel of her gun to his view. Having previously held it unnoticed in the folds of her skirt, he was amazed to see her point it at him.

"Step no closer, wench, or I'll run him through."

"You may, of course, do just that, but the moment you do, you will die; and I promise you, sir, you shall die slowly and most cruelly."

For a long moment no one spoke or moved. The privateer had no intention of releasing his only chance of escape, while Merry insisted he not be allowed to leave with her father. Without a doubt, once outside, the man would kill him.

"It appears we are at an impasse sir," she reasoned calmly. "What say you if I give my word my men will allow you safe passage to your ship?"

He laughed and asked in a condescending tone, "Your men?"

Merry ignored his jeering remark and asked again, "What say you?"

"What of my men?"

Merry looked pointedly at the lifeless bodies that

littered the floor. "I'm sorry, but it appears your men will have no further need of your solicitude."

Jonathan's eyes registered surprise that his wife could so calmly talk of the death that surrounded her.

"Still, sir, you do have more than a good chance to survive this night. What say you?"

"What would you have me do, bitch? Would that I was fool enough to release him, I'd like as not have the pack of you on me before I could blink twice."

"Before you could blink once, sir," she corrected easily, "but not if I say nay."

"Not good enough. How can I trust you?"

"Jamie," she spoke softly, her eyes never leaving her adversary's face, "load your gun."

The man did as he was told.

Merry nodded as he came to stand at her side. "Now take it and put it on the table and then back away." Addressing her opponent once again, she nodded toward the gun. "Release him and take the gun. No one will fire on you without knowing you could return the favor. No one, that is, unless you fire first."

The privateer looked from one hard face to another, trying to understand how a tiny wisp of a girl could order these burly men to do her bidding. Finally, he gave a silent shrug. As of this moment the only thing of importance was to get out with all his parts intact.

He nodded slowly, as he pulled Noah with him toward the table and the gun that awaited him. "'Tis you missy, who'll take the first shot if your men fire on me."

"I'd expect no less," she returned, not a flicker of emotion showing on her face.

The man's eyes widened with admiration and, for

one instant, he wondered how he could get her aboard his ship. This was one woman he'd not soon forget. Bringing his mind back to the problem at hand, he took another step toward the table. His left arm reached for the gun, and Noah was pushed to the floor as he stepped back.

Still Merry registered no emotion as she watched the man, sword in one hand and a loaded pistol in another, back toward the door. There were five guns pointed at his belly, as the door swung open behind him and he disappeared into the night.

Two of the men made to give chase, but Merry's voice stopped them. "Nay, let the beggar go," she ordered. "I'd see no others die on this night. As like as not he's halfway to his ship by now."

"Jamie, would you help my father to his room, so Jonathan might look him over? Not a word from you, Father," she ordered as she watched him begin to object. "It will only take a few moments and it will soothe my worries." She gave him a tight hug, before she watched him move slowly up the stairs to his room. "Samuel," she spoke somewhat shakily, "would you see to Rebecca and ask her to stop that infernal noise?" And then, quite unbelievably, she found herself trembling, as tears rolled slowly down her cheeks.

Jonathan lifted her quickly into his arms and she surprised herself further still by sobbing into his neck, as he mounted the steps two at a time.

"I was so scared," she whispered softly, as he sat on her bed and held her close to him.

"Merry," he whispered softly. "Do not cry so. All is well now. You are the bravest person, man or woman, I've ever known."

"Nay." She laughed tearfully, as he pulled her tighter to him. "I was terrified. I thought they had killed you and my father. When I saw you on the floor, t'was nearly my undoing."

"T'would be a foolish show of courage to fight eight armed men overlong," he reasoned. "One of them hit me and once I awoke, I thought I might as well wait for more even odds before I returned the favor. And then, like an avenging angel, you walked through the door." After a moment's hesitation, he continued, "Woman, should you ever endanger yourself again, I will wring your neck."

Merry laughed, as she clung tighter to him, "Indeed, sir, if you wring my neck I shall have no further opportunities."

Chapter Twenty-five

MERRY SMILED AS SHE WATCHED A SAILOR CLIMB THE MAIN mast and run along the yardarm to untangle a corner of the sail that had twisted on one of the hundreds of yards of cordage that was strung from mast to deck.

The ship rocked and swayed, as the wind hit the sails full blast and pushed it through the salty, dark blue water. Spreading her feet for balance, she gazed out over the endless sea of blue, her eyes resting on the horizon where blue water met the lighter blue of sky. A smile, never far from her lips these days, came more fully to life as her husband moved to join her at the railing.

"You've never been aboard a ship before, yet you take to it like a sailor," he remarked, his admiration obvious in his words and the long look he bestowed on her.

"I love it," she answered truthfully. "Especially when the wind blows this lustily."

A blast of spray covered them, as the ship pushed into a large wave. "The sea is rising, Merry, come below before you get soaked."

"In a moment, Jonathan. I care not if I get wet. This is too wonderful to leave as yet."

Another gust of wind dislodged the pins that held her hair and the long golden tresses whipped wildly about her head.

"We dine with the Captain tonight. Perhaps you would care to rest this afternoon."

Merry laughed, her eyes flashing with delight. "You seem to have an intense need to see me below deck, sir. Could it be you have thoughts other than resting on your mind?"

"It could indeed, Madam," Jonathan grinned as his arm came around her waist and he escorted her to their cabin.

Captain York was an astonishingly attractive man. He sported the most brilliant red hair and beard, which accentuated the darkest skin Merry had ever seen. His blue eyes were the most vivid possible and held the good humor of a man well satisfied with his choice in life.

Many times Merry had to force aside her surprise, as this great bear of a man proved himself no stranger to the ways of gentility. They had been at sea for more than a week and she had heard the man and his mate often scream out the most vile obscenities. Still, in the presence of ladies, he was polished and soft-spoken as the finest gentleman.

"Are you enjoying the voyage, Countess?" he asked, as they stood away from the other guests and sipped at the sherry he had served after dinner. "I've noticed you often at the bow, unmindful of the damaging winds that whip at your hair and clothes."

Merry laughed. "Aye, Captain York. Indeed, I am enjoying this voyage. I find the sea most invigorating and I envy you your choice of work. But, why is it, sir, you address me as Countess? You said it three times on this night alone?"

Captain York was obviously taken aback. "Excuse me, Madam. Did you not wish anyone to know your rank? I confess I have been privy to it since we have set sail, having known your husband and his family. In truth, the Earl served under me when he was but a lad. If you prefer, I will address you as Mrs. Townsend."

"Oh no, Captain," Merry managed with a weak smile, as her mind worked feverishly to sort out this information. "Do not concern yourself. I . . . I . . . It was simply that I knew not your understanding of my circumstances." After a moment's hesitation, she continued, "It seems I am suffering the most vile of headaches. I beg you to excuse me, sir, for I have an immediate need to seek the privacy of my chamber."

"Of course, Countess. Forgive me for keeping you overlong. Shall I inform your husband of your distress?"

"Nay, do not!" she snapped, as her furious gaze swept across the small salon to rest for a long moment on the object of her anger. "Thank you, sir, but I can make my way to our cabin alone."

Merry was hardly conscious of her words, as she bade the amicable Captain good night, so filled was she with icy rage. The door to the small cabin slammed with no little force behind her small figure, and she longed to scream out her rage. Instead, she held herself in stiff control, as she paced the tiny space of her quarters, her mind racing, as she tried to digest the information so suddenly thrust upon her.

She was a Countess! Her husband an Earl! The cowardly brute had said nothing of his title, she raged silently. How could he do this to her? He knew of her hatred for the ruling class. My God, she couldn't bear to speak of them without a note of disgust in her voice.

She paced more quickly now. No wonder he could not leave his beloved England. He was an Earl, after all. A Lord of the realm. I'd like to throttle him for this deception.

A cold chill shivered down her spine, as she wondered what other surprises he had in store for her. Would she be expected to show herself at court? "Oh no, I cannot," she groaned aloud. "I will not!"

The wretch. The bloody, wretched beast.

"I've a good mind to divorce him the moment this ship docks," she murmured aloud.

The door to their cabin closed silently behind her. "I'm afraid that will not do, Madam. There will be no divorce. We are married and, whether you want it or not, we will remain husband and wife until one of us dies."

Merry spun about, surprised at first at his silent entrance, and then raged all the more that he should once again impose his will on her. Picking up her brush, she flung it at him. "Then perhaps I should take pains to see that that circumstance comes about."

"Merry, I know you are angry, but, if you will do me the courtesy of listening to my explanation, I'm sure I shall put your anger to rest."

She said nothing as she turned her back to him.

"Will you listen?"

Still she said nothing.

"Merry!" he raged as he picked her up and flung her to the bed. An instant later, he knocked the breath from her as he landed on top of her.

She struggled beneath him, but his weight held her immobile.

"Listen to me! I couldn't tell you. I loved you too much to let you go. You'd never have married me, had you known.

"I wasn't born to the title. My brother was the heir. He died while I was in the colonies and the title came to me. I knew your hatred for the ruling class. How the hell was I to tell you I was one of them?"

He watched her for a long moment, her face a stony mask showing nothing. "Merry, for God's sake, rage at me. Do something. Say something."

Icily, she responded, "What does a Countess say, sir? I fear I've not the slightest notion."

"Oh, God," he groaned. "What would you have me do? Shall I give up the title and all the lands and wealth that go with it? Would you take from our children what is rightfully theirs?"

"Would you give it up for me?" she asked, her eyes growing wide that he might sacrifice so much for her.

He sighed as he looked down into her face, "I would, Merry. If you hate it so, I would. But think, Merry, think of what you could do, think of the power you could wield as the Countess of Hampshire. Think of the good you could accomplish."

For a long moment Merry did just that. Finally, she gave him a wary look. "Would I be expected to appear at court?"

A smile teased the corners of his mouth. "Not unless you desired it."

Again she thought for a long moment, knowing in her heart the words he spoke to be truth. Indeed, she would not have married him had she known. Perhaps he was right; perhaps more good could be gained by using the title to its best advantage than to abandon it.

Her voice was soft, low and slightly breathless with the enormity of what she was about to say. "I find myself most willing to be your Countess, Jonathan, for no matter what you are, I find I love you above all else in life."

Shocked at her tender words, he seemed able to do no more than just stare at her.

"Jonathan, I wonder if you love me enough. I'm afraid the future will test it sorely."

He closed his eyes and groaned with relief, imagining no pain to equal the fear he had just known. Finally, he answered shakily, "Never fear, Merry. It matters not what the future brings. I love you more than my life. That will never change."

Her small hand reached up and began to unbutton his shirt. Her mouth at his shoulder, her tongue running across the hard line of his collarbone to his throat, she whispered, "Will you show me how much, Jonathan? Will you show me through this night?"

The palms of his hands on her cheeks held her head still, as his thumbs caressed the softness of her lips and he groaned, "I will Merry, through this night and the next and the next."

About the Author

Patricia Pellicane lives in Long Island, New York, with her husband and their six children. She loves to read, particularly about America's Revolutionary War. *Whispers in the Wind* is her third novel. Readers can write to her at Post Office Box 2250, North Babylon, NY 11703.

Tapestry

HISTORICAL ROMANCES

POCKET BOOKS.